HARMON'S GALAXY

HARMON'S GALAXY

JIM HARMON

COSMOS BOOKS

CONTENTS

IN ANOTHER GALAXY

Richard A. Lupoff

Robert A. W. Lowndes was known as "Doc." He wasn't a medical man; as far as I know he did not hold any kind of doctorate. But he had a scholarly air about him and was, indeed, a deeply thoughtful person. He spent a lifetime editing books and magazines, generally with microscopic budgets and nonexistent staff support, yet he always managed to produce remarkably good publications.

I once asked him what he would do if he ever had a decent bank account to work with, and he admitted that he would probably be lost. "I'm so used to making bricks without straw," was the way he put it, "I don't think I'd know what to do with real money."

One of Doc's great virtues was his terrific sensitivity as a "slushpile" reader. He could look at a stack of manuscripts, almost all of them by hopeless amateurs, and pick out the one or two or three that had real merit, and whose authors had real talent. If you have any doubt of that, think *Roger Zelazny*. Think *Stephen King*. If that doesn't convince you, think *Philip K. Dick*. And if you still need convincing, think *Jim Harmon*.

Jim Harmon?

James Judson Harmon, a twenty-one year old sometime science fiction fan and would-be author, made his professional debut in the November 1954 issue of *Science Fiction Quarterly*, with a story he'd written two years earlier, at the age of nineteen. *SFQ* was one of the last of the classic-style science fiction pulps. Jim Harmon's story was called "Voting Machine."

Lowndes was the magazine's editor, the pay rates were as usual tiny, but young Jim Harmon, eager to join the hallowed ranks of Heinlein, Bradbury, Asimov, and Clarke, had made it. He had surmounted the barrier that separates the masses of wanna-be "writers" from the real professionals.

It was almost two years before Jim Harmon's next story appeared. This was a little gem called "Name Your Symptom." Most of the science fiction magazines were now in the smaller digest size, and Jim moved up to one of the top periodicals in the field, *Galaxy Science Fiction*, the superb monthly created by the difficult, cranky, brilliant Horace L. Gold and continued, after Gold's retirement, by the highly talented Frederik Pohl.

"Name Your Symptom" was a perfect *Galaxy* story, an extrapolation of social trends carried almost to the point of *reductio ad absurdum* and injected into the reader's bloodstream with a sharply pointed needle and a healthy dose of sardonic humor.

From his home in Mt. Carmel, Illinois, Jim produced slowly and carefully, but steadily: two stories in 1957, one in 1958, then five in his breakthrough year of 1959. Thereafter he continued to appear in the science fiction magazines until 1967. His favorite market was *Galaxy*, a magazine that specialized in psychological and sociological stories, with occasional forays into *Galaxy's* sometime companion magazine, *Worlds of If*, and into the highly-literate *Magazine of Fantasy and Science Fiction* when that periodical was under the brief tutelage of the erudite and sometimes acerbic Avram Davidson, and *F&SF's* companion, *Venture Science Fiction*.

Jim's stories were marked by wit and concern. His most successful story was probably "The Place Where Chicago Was," a much-reprinted examination of the implications of enforced pacifism. This story, first purchased by editor Frederik Pohl, has been anthologized over and over. Other stories in Jim's career are marked by a nostalgic fondness for the mass culture icons of his boyhood, and by questions of identity and reality comparable to some of the best stories of his near-contemporary, the late Philip K. Dick.

The years of Jim Harmon's science fiction career were some of science fiction's finest, with an amazing array of authors producing a steady stream of brilliant stories. But in this same era, paradoxically, the science fiction magazines were dying off. Jim's favorite market, *Galaxy*, was among the casualties. From the capable hands of Horace Gold and then Frederik Pohl it passed to a series of increasingly cynical publishers and decreasingly competent editors. It disappeared, reappeared in a new format, then disappeared once more.

After a lengthy hiatus, *Galaxy* returned still again, this time under the aegis of Eugene Gold, the son of *Galaxy's* founding editor. But, alas, the magazine's time had passed. It still exists today, after a fashion, as a Website—an electronic simulacrum of its once robust ink-and-paper self. It's the kind of thing that might have happened, once upon a time, in a story in *Galaxy*.

From a peak population of more than forty titles in the early 1950's, the science fiction magazines dwindled to the handful that survive, just barely, to the present day.

What killed the rest?

A combination of factors, including the collapse of the traditional system of distributing periodicals, and the competition of the new medium that science fiction had so long predicted, television. But mainly, I think, it was a matter of size. Just as the pulps had given way to the smaller and more convenient digests, the latter were replaced by the still smaller and more convenient paperback book. Two major paperback science fiction lines made their appearance in the early '50s—Ace Books, edited by pulp veteran Donald A. Wollheim, and Ballantine Books, guided by canny publishing mogul Ian Ballantine.

Most of the leading science fiction writers switched from short stories, which the magazines had gobbled up in huge numbers, to novels, which the paperback houses preferred. Those who were unwilling or unable to make the switch soon faded to minor status in the field, or else disappeared entirely.

But Jim Harmon did neither. Instead, he moved into several very different realms. He did write a number of novels, but rather than science fiction they were of a more esoteric nature. Now out of print, they are eagerly sought by avid collectors who stand in line at collectors' shows to get Jim's autograph and to meet the man who wrote such treasured volumes as *Vixen Hollow, The Celluloid Scandal,* and . . . *and Sudden Lust!*

Jim edited several magazines dealing with motion picture history, then found his true *metier,* popular culture. In this latter realm he is the author of several highly-regarded works including *The Great Radio Heroes, The Great Radio Comedians, The Great Movie Serials,* and *Radio Mystery and Adventure.* He present his scholarship with the same entertaining and witty flair that marked the best of his stories.

As for myself, I first had the pleasure of meeting Jim Harmon in 1960, at the World Science Fiction Convention in Pittsburgh, Pennsylvania. Jim was one of the bright young stars in the field; my wife, Patricia, and I were a couple of excited young fans. To our delight, shortly after returning to our home in New York, Pat and I received a visit from Jim Harmon.

Not only did he visit us at our apartment, he actually stayed there, sleeping on our living room couch, while he was in New York. We couldn't have been more thrilled and flattered if President Eisenhower had arrived and asked permission to pitch his pup-tent in our parlor.

In retrospect, Jim was probably just saving the price of a hotel room—but we didn't see it that way in 1960, and I still treasure my memories of that generous visit by the famous professional writer to the home of two admiring fans.

In the years that followed, Jim and I maintained a sporadic relationship, entirely by correspondence. He commissioned me to write an article for one of his film magazines, and I was happy to earn the few dollars that the magazine paid. In return Pat and I commissioned Jim to write an article for our fanzine, *Xero*, and when a collection of articles from *Xero* was published later Jim received some return for his efforts.

He even talked me at one point into trying my hand at the literary agent business. Jim was my first and, it turned out, my only client. I earned a fat zero dollars for him, and dutifully took my commission, ten per cent of zero. It was a profession in which I was not cut out to shine.

We didn't see each other for nearly forty years. Then our paths crossed once more in the late 1990's at a mystery convention in Monterey, California. By now we were both living on the West Coast, and have managed to get together from time to time ever since even though our homes are several hundred miles apart.

At one of these meetings we were joined by Sean Wallace of Cosmos Books. I urged Jim to assemble a collection of his science fiction stories, urged Sean to consider taking on the book for Cosmos, and, to my inexpressible delight, both agreed.

The result is the book you are holding now.

Maybe I should have hung on in the literary agent business after all.

Most of the stories in this book are from Jim's era working for the science fiction magazines—*Galaxy, If, F&SF, Venture*—but others come for rather different and perhaps unexpected sources. There's one from Jim's magazine, *Fantastic Monsters,* one from Jim's book, *Radio and TV Premiums,* and one, a reconstruction of a "lost" collaboration with the great Robert Bloch, from *Scientifiction*, the journal of an organization of veteran science fiction fans.

A special treat is "Pyramid of the Visitors," newly written for the present book but actually a skillful and deliberate throwback to the days of radio adventure shows, a subject on which Jim Harmon is a world-class authority.

Somewhere in another universe there may be a planet almost identical to our Earth, where the only difference is this: the "paperback revolution" of the 1950's never quite got off the ground. As a result, *fictionmags* galore elbow one another for display space on the sales racks. The forty science fiction magazines that existed in 1953 are still going, along with several dozen more.

The science fiction short story, instead of being a minor companion piece to the novel, is still the chief focus for writers, editors, publishers and readers.

Galaxy Science Fiction is the world's most popular magazine, with planet-wide circulation of some fifty million copies every month. Maybe every week, who's counting? The magazine's pay rate starts at ten dollars per word, and its most popular author is Jim Harmon, who of course receives a huge bonus rate over the standard ten bucks a pop.

I like to think of that universe as *Harmon's Galaxy*.

Richard A. Lupoff
2004

PYRAMID OF THE VISITORS

The digital clock on his desk showed 1:00, the time for his future clients to arrive. Paul Thorson leaned back in his swivel chair and waited. The voice on the phone sounded likely enough for him to shave and put on a clean white sports shirt. In his opinion the only people in Hollywood who wore a tie and suit coat were doctors and lawyers.

Not quite on the stroke of the hour, but at 1:02 there was a rap on the frosted glass of his office door.

"Come in," Thorson said.

There were two of them, a tall, businesslike woman, fair complexion, and a man, not so tall, dark, with thinning black curly hair.

Thorson stood up and extended a hand to the two of them. The woman shook first, firm, no nonsense, then the man, strong but moist.

The dark man said "I am Barney Stein and this is my partner, Susan Phelps. We represent joint interests in hiring your services for the trip to Yucatan."

"Well, I'm certainly available for hire," Thorson said. "I think I have the experience and equipment for anything you require for the trip."

Susan Phelps smiled. "I doubt if your experience will equip you for this venture, Mr. Thorson."

Thorson waved them to a couple of leather padded steel chairs. They sat down.

He came from around his desk and sat on the front edge, to be closer and more intimate with these two.

"*Adventure Cams* has shot 35mm film to 8mm video. We can record SOF or tape it on a Uher. I've got my passport, had my shots, and I and my crew are ready to go where you need us."

Stein held up a hand. "We've investigated your credits. You know we are headed for Yucatan but you don't know exactly what we intend to do there."

Thorson shrugged. "Some sort of outdoor film, I suppose."

"Those have been done to death on Yucatan," Susan said.

"There are a lot of cable channels," Thorson said.

"This is not an outdoor film, "Stein said. "As a matter of fact, it will be shot mostly inside one of the old temples—pyramid might be a better term."

Thorson immediately began calculating the lighting involved.

"I take it this is an old structure of particular interest," the filmmaker ventured.

"We believe so," Susan said. "Mr. Stein and I have allied interests, but competing ones. We want to investigate the Pyramid of the Feathered Crocodile, located between Valladolid and Chichen Itza."

She seemed to wait for a response from Thorson.

"I take it you have never heard of it," she continued. "There have been some newspaper and magazine accounts of it, even a few shots of it in TV documentaries about that sort of thing."

"What sort of thing?" Thorson asked.

"You know, strange goings on," Stein offered. "The paranormal . . . "

"Or the supernatural, "Susan added.

"You mean a place with a strange reputation," Thorson said. "Sort of like the mysterious Winchester House up near San Francisco."

The two visitors exchanged a glance. Stein offered an unconvincing smile. "Yes, something like that. You see, my organization is 'Paranormal Trust' and we believe the many reported irregularities around the Feathered Crocodile constitute strange but logically explainable events—events empowered by science, even if it is a science we do not yet understand."

"On the other hand, my group, 'Belief Beyond,' believes these events are truly supernatural, the work of God or the devil, or creatures somewhere between."

"Are you sure you're really not saying the same thing?" Thorson ventured. "It might be just a difference in semantics."

Stein laughed. "Mr. Thorson, you are getting into religion here. The difference between one religion and another may seem trivial to a person who subscribes to neither but they make a world of difference to the members of the two faiths."

"I suppose so. In any case, my job would be to get good clear imaging of everything and leave it to you two to interpret it."

"Exactly," the young woman said. "You don't need to take sides. But we needed to tell you what we were interested in getting from this expedition."

"I'm beginning to understand," Thorson said." but I need to know what you expect to photograph—ghostly apparitions, strange distortions of the atmosphere . . . What?"

Stein stood up. "Here. Let me show you something."

He extracted a small leather case from his inner coat pocket and removed a coin. It looked like tarnished copper. Perhaps gold. He held it between thumb and forefinger in front of Thorson's eyes.

"Very old," Thorson said. "Ancient. Is it Mayan?"

"Older than that," Stein said. "Watch this."

Stein held the coin over Thorson's desk and released it.

The coin stayed where it was, not falling, suspended in the air.

Thorson passed a hand over it, under it, all around it.

"I've seen stage magicians do that," the filmmaker ventured.

Stein nodded. "They can do something like that, but it requires powerful magnets. We have not installed such equipment above or below your desk."

There was a tanning salon below Thorson's, and the roof above him. It seemed unlikely they could have put in big motors in those places.

"I could take this coin out on the street corner and it would float just as it does in my office?"

"Take it to your favorite bar," Stein said. "Collect some bets with it." He paused. "Not really. Some of this information is proprietary."

Thorson reached out and moved the coin over a couple of inches. It stayed in its new location.

"Okay, what is it?"

"We believe this coin contains the secret of anti-gravity," Stein offered.

"Uncle Sam should be interested in that," Thorson said.

"And Uncle Abdulah and everybody else's uncle," Stein said. "For the moment, we are keeping it ourselves."

"Whatever it is, it must operate on scientific principles." Thorson turned to Susan. "You don't claim a ghost is holding that up in the air, do you, Miss Phelps?"

She smiled. "We do not know what is holding the coin in the air. To us, it might as well be magic as science."

"Okay, we'll use hand held cameras if objects are liable to change positions suddenly. It's none of my business, but could I ask you where you got that hunk of metal?"

"That *is* proprietary, Mr. Thorson," Stein said. "We will tell you it came from the area in or near the pyramid."

Thorson looked at the small tarnished disc floating in the air.

"I think you are telling me that this will not be the most unusual sight I see on this junket?"

"Are you willing to go, expecting that?" Susan asked softly.

"So long as you pay my rates, that's why I'm in business."

* * *

The made-made cavern was huge. Thorson could hear the retreating footsteps of the tourist group, taking their own circle of light with them. All of them carried a lit battery-powered lantern clipped to their belts.

Thorson and his group included Susan Phelps, Barney Stein, and Thorson's assistant Manny Romero, who was carrying a light bar whose handle fitted into a harness at his waist. He also held a light-weight camcorder loaded with digital tape, while the rest each carried some miniaturized electronic instruments on shoulder or waist straps.

"So now we explore a tourist site," Thorson said.

Stein nodded. "As we are paying you to do."

"Sure. Far be it from me to argue with the golden goose."

Susan came farther into the light. She was wearing khaki shorts and top, still crisp despite some time in the outdoor humidity. "I assure you, Paul, with our equipment and special skills we will find things not discovered by thousands of tourists in this pyramid."

"Manny!" Thorson motioned to Romero. "Ready to get all those discoveries in the box?"

Romero patted his camcorder. "If we can see it, I can shoot it."

"And we won't be relying on what we can only see," Stein added. "My instruments can detect electromagnetic fields, record barely audible sounds."

"Lead the way," Thorson said.

Susan gestured ahead. "Further into the structure."

Their booted feet sounded like an army moving in the echoing dark. "Anything?" Susan asked Stein.

He waited. "No."

"Get our light crawling along the wall, over those pictographs or whatever."

"Got it covered," Romero said.

More of the echoing army.

"Hold on," Stein said. "Here's something."

"You have a reading?" Susan asked.

"Electromagnetic activity." Stein stared at the dials of what Thorson had taken to be a Geiger counter.

"Where is it, Mr. Stein?" Romero asked. "Is it distorting the atmosphere, something I can get a shot of?"

"There would be no disturbance of that sort," Susan explained.

Manny suppressed a shudder. "Sometimes I wonder why I came down here. I may have been born Mexican but I spent most of my life in Hollywood."

Stein wasn't paying any attention to the remarks. "The electromagnetism seems to come and go. As if it swoops down on us, glides over, and then returns."

"Like a big bird," Thorson ventured.

"Or a bat," Romero said. "There might be bats in the big, old dark tomb."

Stein's mouth became a thin line. "This is not a tomb, and the disturbance is not a bat or a bird or anything alive. It doesn't give off heat as living things do, just magnetic force. Here it comes again."

Thorson concentrated on trying to feel it, to see if it made the hair on his neck stand up. But there was nothing. "Is there anyway we could photograph it? We aren't using old photographic film. Could it disturb iron filings for instance?"

"It might, if we had any with us," Susan said.

"Had you thought about how Manny and I can do our work? You didn't seem to want to talk much about things like this before we left."

"Record the activity of the dials on the instrument," Stein said.

"Oh, I've been doing that," Romero said. "Shooting over your shoulder."

Thorson suddenly needed oxygen. "Can't breathe!"

"Allergic reaction?" Susan ventured.

Thorson clawed at his throat. "Something is grabbing me—choking me."

Romero was active with the camcorder. "Get your hands away, pard, so I can get a shot of it."

All of them were looking but there was nothing to see except Thorson getting red in the face, and pawing at his neck.

"This can only be evil," Susan said, as she fumbled in her belly pack. She drew out a small bottle, uncapped it and splashed it over Thorson's face and neck. "Let Evil be washed away by the tears of Christ!"

Suddenly Thorson could breathe. The choking was gone. He looked at the others through flashing rings of red from the oxygen deprivation.

"What was that stuff?" Thorson asked.

"Nothing scientific," Susan said. "Holy water, blessed by a priest."

"Effective," Stein admitted. "But perhaps its effectiveness lay not in the 'holiness' but in the water. Perhaps the force that held Thorson was disturbed by H-two-O. Perhaps the water shorted out some electrical connection."

"Say, how many tourists get strangled in this Temple of the Feathered Crocodile anyway?" Romero inquired.

"This is not a usual occurrence," the woman managed.

Stein thought for a moment. "It was nothing. Thorson only had an anxiety attack."

Thorson passed his hand through the air, as if to wipe away the idea. "I'm used to filming charging elephants. I wouldn't react like that to a dismal atmosphere like this."

Everyone turned, their senses alert, to a scuffling beyond their lights.

"Something out there, coming this way," Romero said.

"We all know that, Manny," Thorson said. "Be quiet and be ready."

A few more scuffling sounds, and into their circle of light came a very thin, very old man in a tattered outfit that looked like the costume for a Mexican peon in an old movie—battered straw sombrero, cotton shirt and pants washed a few thousand times. His lined face sported a drooping mustache.

"Seventy pardons for this intrusion, but you seek something, *señores*? Pedro is good at helping visitors find things."

"It has to be Pedro," Thorson commented.

"Oh, sure. Pedro, he is much better than Jose or Manuel."

"I am Manuel, or Manny to you," Romero said. "And how are you better than me?"

"Oh, *señores*, I am not better using your motion picture Kodak than you, but I think after forty years I am a better guide to this temple."

Susan brightened. "'Temple.' Then you regard this place as a sacred or religious site?"

Pedro removed his sombrero. "If you like. If you say this is a religious place, Pedro he say so too."

Stein stepped forward. "What if I say this is just an archeological site, with no religious significance?"

"Oh, *señor*, I am more than anxious to agree with you."

Romero snorted. "Wait a minute, *compadre*, you don't have two heads. You can't agree with both ideas."

"Oh, for the right number of Yankee dollars I can agree to anything."

"Look here, Pedro," Thorson put in, "we need more than a yes man. Do you really know your way around this place?"

"*Sí*, lot more than those fancy pants uniforms you wisely did not hire."

"Yeah, our party wanted to go off on our own," Thorson said. "But now I'm beginning to think somebody who knew their way around here could help. What do you two say?"

Thorson looked to Stein and Susan. "Let's give him a chance," Stein said.

"Yes, I think he knows what this place really is," Susan said.

Thorson took out his wallet. In the glare of the light bar he started to pull out a twenty, then selected two fives and stuffed them in the old man's hand. "There's more where they came from if you do a good job, Pedro. My handle's Thorson. Manny introduced himself. This is Mr. Stein and Miss Susan."

"I do a good job," the old fellow said. "I do such a good job you may even save your neck." He laughed.

Thorson grabbed the old man by the arm. "What do you know about my neck?"

"You think you are the first person to be choked into submission in this place, *señor*? The long time residents do not like, how you say, the skeptical."

Thorson tightened his grip. "Pedro, all of a sudden you are talking a lot more educated than you were before you got my money."

Romero was having trouble balancing the light bar and the camcorder. "Smart or not, what does he mean by 'long time residents'?"

Pedro laughed again, showing surprisingly good white teeth. "I think maybe that is what you are here to find out, what kind 'long time residents' we got down here."

"Ease up on him, Thorson," Stein said. "Let go of his arm. Now, Pedro, what sort of 'residents' do you think we will run into down here?"

"Oh, I no have to tell you, *Señor Stein*. They will show you."

Romero's shoulders shook. "Anybody notice how cold it can get in these old stone chambers?"

There was a darkness deeper than the other darkness near the ceiling of the chamber. After a long time, there came the concept that the darkness was "I" to that which was capable of making a concept. This which recognized it had a self had been there a long time. Forever was comfortable. The mobile bits of heat that came across the floor in furtive waves irritated that which conceptualized only faintly. To dive and weave among them sometimes was fun. Other times there was chasing and hiding from others of its like. That was fun too.

Occasionally, as the years flowed like water, one of the heat units would irritate this one. At this time, it was the tall unit who seemed to command the others. This unit could not harm the one who thought. It was safe forever in the flow of time. But just as hiding and chasing was fun, this one thought it would be fun to destroy this one who told others what to do where all should be only as the thinker willed.

This one had cut off the oxygen supply to the tall one. Without oxygenation, the heat would go out. But something had interrupted that experiment. What was it? What was it?

Below, the tall one and the other units continued to interrupt the darkness with their light. Another irritation. Light interrupted the flow of eternity.

Romero was complaining again.

"Paul, you got to get a light man on our next gig. The harness for this light bar gets in the way of my operating the camera."

Thorson nodded. "I can see that. But we didn't have the biggest budget in the world for this trip. Maybe I should hold the light bar for you."

"Hey, you're the director. Who said you knew how to handle lights?"

Thorson shrugged. "You do what you have to do. I wasn't paid extra for sewing up your pants in Burma."

"I thought we weren't going to talk about that ever again."

"Oh, yeah, sorry."

Susan Phelps and Stein had been conferring in low voices only a few feet away. The two researchers approached the film crew members.

Stein spoke. "I think we have seen enough for one day. We could go back to the hotel for dinner and the night."

"Did you get enough for your money today?" Thorson asked.

"It was a remarkable day," Susan said.

Romero looked around sharply, and patted his backpack. "Say, where did that old fellow, Pedro, go? And did he take anything with him?"

Susan laughed. "Pedro's sleeping over there in the corner."

"Sleeping on the cold stone floor?" Romero asked.

"That seems to be just what he is doing."

"He probably had a lot of experience doing that," Thorson said. "He must have been hanging around this old pile of stone for years, trying to cadge a few bucks off tourists."

Stein smiled. "He adds a bit of color to this dismal place. I suppose we should wake him up. He will probably want to walk out with us. We can't just leave him in the dark. I don't think he even has a flashlight."

"How did he get down here in the first place without a light?" Romero asked.

Stein shrugged. "He probably drifted in with a guide and a bunch of tourists. Probably gives the guide a few dollars from time to time to tolerate him."

Thorson put his clipboard under his arm. "Well, let's round up Pedro and get on our way."

That which was aware of the messaging of the heat units made its descent on them.

Thorson had expected Romero to wake up the old man, but the photographer was still struggling to get all his equipment ready to go. The filmmaker went over to the sleeping Mexican himself. As he bent over the old fellow, he became aware of something. He couldn't put a name to it, but he knew he had experienced something like this before—before when something cut off his air.

It hadn't liked the holy water Susan had tossed on it. Maybe it didn't like water in general. He unhooked the canteen from his belt and slung it all around him, forming a wet circle around himself on the worn stone floor.

Abruptly the old guide was awake, and on his feet surprisingly fast for a man of his years. He was holding a small crucifix. Pedro stood beside Thorson, and turned the crucifix to face the various points of the water circle.

"*Sí, sí,* you did the correct thing, senor. The circle will keep out the thing that wills us not well."

"I can't live in this ring forever," Thorson said. 'The water is drying up fast, anyway."

"Ah, but you have stopped him for the moment. These things do not have much energy. They must rest before they try something more."

"You are an expert on these arcane forces, just as you are on everything else down here?" Thorson said.

"I should be most expert, Senior Thorson. These things they have killed my son."

"Your son?"

"*Sí,* a little boy."

"You—a man of your years—has a small boy for a son?"

"I did—thirty years ago. That was when these somethings kill him."

The rest of the crew had been preoccupied with their own things and had not paid attention to what Thorson and Pedro had been doing and saying. But first Stein, then Susan and Romero began to take notice.

"Has Pedro been telling you something useful, Thorson?" the scientist asked.

"He says his son was killed thirty years ago—by something that seems to be taking an interest in me right now."

Susan took in air sharply. "You were attacked again?

The filmmaker lowered his head and rubbed the back of his neck. "No, not attacked. But I felt something was coming near me, maybe to examine me. Maybe getting ready to strike."

Romero chuckled. "Pard, you got to have some imagination to make films. But you shouldn't let it have the run of the house completely."

"It's more than imagination, Manny. Do you think I imagined that attack on me, or that I faked it?"

"No, no, I wouldn't say that," the camera man said.

Stein cleared his throat. "We knew there would be strange happenings here. Susan and I aren't the ones to doubt Mr. Thorson."

Thorson turned sharply to Stein. "Look here, something choked me, and Pedro here says something killed his son. Why is this place open to the public if it is so dangerous?

"These events are very rare," Stein said. "Over the years a number of people have committed suicide by leaping from the observation deck of the Empire State Building. But the site has not been closed to the public permanently—at least before the events of 9-11."

"I think they put up some kind of fencing so people couldn't jump," Romero said.

Stein nodded. "Yes. Perhaps some sort of precautions should be made in this pyramid. But the threat is not so real, not so immediate, and the government is slow to act."

Old Pedro stepped forward. "If I may be permitted to speak."

Thorson nodded. "Go ahead. You probably know more about what is going on than any of us."

"Mr. Thorson!" Susan spoke sharply. "I resent that. I am a recognized authority in my field."

"You may be paying my salary, but I'll take Pedro's thirty years of experience at the moment. What do you have to say, Pedro?"

"You say the menace is unreal. I say it plenty real. It kill my son. It hurt you. It move slow, but it rests and get stronger. I think maybe it don't like you, *Señor* Thorson."

"You could be right, Pedro. Maybe we better make tracks out of here."

The old man shook his head. "No, no, it do no good. It follow you. It followed my son. There are haunts here, but they not really haunt this pile of stone. They haunt people."

"You know, he has a good point," Susan said. "In my research, I have often found ghosts follow certain people from one house to another. It often does no good to simply leave one structure to go to another."

"I am not admitting the force here is a supernatural ghost," Stein said.

"But we have seen some kind of being can take action here. I know the theory of aliens from another star system visiting here in prehistory is an old one, but perhaps one that need not be dismissed out of hand."

"Aliens visited here thousands of years ago?" Thorson said. "And they are still hanging around here as invisible entities? Why?"

"I can tell you," Pedro said anxiously. "My people have tales of visitors from the sky. They come a long time ago, and they still here because they died."

"Died and still here?" Thorson said.

"*Sí*, the alien visitors died but their ghosts are still here."

"Ghosts of outer space visitors," Romero said. "Say, the *National Inquirer* would run that story."

The filmmaker put his hand on the old Mexican's shoulder. "Pedro, if we are in danger, and we can't ease the danger by leaving, what do you think we should do?"

"Only one thing," Pedro said breathlessly. "We got to kill the ghosts!"

"Kill the ghosts," Thorson repeated.

"*Sí*, I want to kill them. I want to pay them back for killing my son. I wait thirty years and now I want to kill them damned ghosts!"

A murmur of laughter went around the group.

Stein became serious first. "I suppose one could say a ghost could be sent to another plane, Heaven or Hell, and thus be dead in this world. Or as a scientist I would prefer to say the energy or matter of any being could be so dispersed it would cease to exist."

"An exorcism has been traditionally said to end the existence of a ghost," Susan supplied.

"The one thing this thing does not seem to like is water," Thorson said. "I've had equipment shorted out by water—a spilled drink, or rain water—to know that water is not good for things electrical. This thing must be electrical."

"Until more complex theories came along," Stein said, "everything in the universe was considered to be in the final essence electricity."

Susan's face flushed. "Are you seriously thinking of destroying that which dwells here with water? Do you take the ravings of this poor old fellow seriously? Water can't destroy a spiritual being. And if it could what right would we have to end the existence of something that has been here for countless generations?"

"The right of survival as far as I personally am concerned," Thorson said. "I believe it has developed a bad attitude towards me."

"Yeah," Romero said, "and I been with you on too many of these trips. Sometimes I get splattered by some of the crap that gets thrown on you."

Thorson turned on his two employers. "You two haven't told me everything. What is the recorded number of people who have died under mysterious circumstances in this pyramid?"

Stein appeared shocked. "We . . . we know of no attributed deaths to paranormal influences. This place has been open for years. A certain number of heart attacks, falls, strokes, have taken place."

"They just weren't attributed to the source you sent us looking for," the filmmaker said.

Romero nodded. "We went looking, and we found it too fast for me."

Thorson searched the darkness but saw nothing. "We found it with the light. This thing has been here in the dark for eons. There have been little flickers from the guide's lights for tourist parties, but this thing has never seen anything like our light bar—bright, intense lighting. That's why it doesn't like us—particularly me, since I am directing the lights!"

Thorson took Romero aside to give him directions. The two spoke in a quiet whisper for a few moments, then turned back to the rest of the group.

Susan was obviously disturbed by what was going on.

"What is this?" she demanded. "What are you planning?"

"On a need to know basis; you don't need to know," Thorson answered.

Thorson, Romero and Stein had put material from their back packs in one heap, and were standing around it.

Susan's lips moved silently. Thorson realized she was praying.

"NO!" she screamed. She lifted her face to the darkened roof of the cavern. "You-who-are-so-much-older-and-wiser . . . " she ranted in a continuous stream "My-life-is-yours-but-do-not-let-yourself-be-harmed . . . "

Thorson grabbed the ranting woman and pulled her to the floor, covering her body with his own, surprised at his own protective instincts.

"It's getting closer. I can feel it." Thorson could not repress a shudder.

That which was there approached the nest of heat units. In them, it sensed the usual energy but near them, nearly on top of them, there was more energy, delicious energy it had to absorb. Now it was absorbing that energy in a dizzying rush, absorbing, absorbing, and not being able to absorb more but doing so.

The group members observed a wavering of reality, as summer heat rising from a country road, wavering above their pile of photographic equipment batteries.

"Now I kill you, you damned ghost!" old Pedro shouted. He had strapped a sharp blade to the longer shaft of the crucifix he carried. Pedro flung himself into the shimmering waves, striking again and again at them with his weapon.

More energy was making itself available to that which belonged there and it was absorbing it, but it was having an irritating problem containing it, and then it could not contain it.

A blinding flash, a rush of force, and then blackness.

The forms that had been thrown to the cavern floor began to stir, and call to one another. Finally there came mumbling from the woman.

"I guess we're all alive," Thorson managed.

"By my sainted Madre, what happened?" Romero asked.

"Stein is the scientist," Thorson said. "Maybe he can explain."

The scientist cleared his throat. "There was something here that had been starved for energy for a very long time. We made very concentrated energy available to it and it took it. It took more than it could hold."

Gushes of light began to dimly light their surroundings.

Thorson had the source of light in his grasp. "Everything with a battery is as used up as old Pedro, but this little squeeze-grip generator will give up enough light to get us out of here. I always carry one for emergencies."

Susan was on her feet now, not quite steady, but very sober. "Pedro's faith was greater than mine."

Romero hefted his equipment into carrying position. "That thing—it waited hundreds of years, but when it got it off, it really got it off!"

The three men were seated abreast in the tourist section of the jet liner headed back to Hollywood. Susan Phelps preferred to sit alone in the back of the plane.

"The tape is all blank," Romero said.

"What did you expect after a burst of energy like that?" Thorson asked.

"The experience provided enough information to make the trip worthwhile to me," Stein said.

"One thing, Stein," Thorson said. "How did that little device that defied gravity, the thing you showed me in Hollywood, how did it fit into this?"

Stein looked down. He might have been blushing. "It didn't. Susan and I thought we had to show you something remarkable to whet your interest. That artifact was actually one from a site in Venezuela where we plan to do our next dig. Perhaps we could interest you two in joining us?"

"Is Saint Susan coming along?" Romero asked irreverently.

"No, another member of her group is scheduled for this one—Dr. Beverly O'Connor. A brilliant academician, and a lovely red-haired woman, although I must say, in the common tongue, a real ice princess."

"Sometimes they thaw," Thorson said. "What is this site called?"

"The Shrine of the Million Year Old Virgin," Stein said.

Romero smiled broadly. "A million year old virgin. Boy, by this time, she must be *really* ready for me."

AFTERWORD

I wrote science fiction short stories and novelets for many magazines, primarily *Galaxy*, from 1954 to 1967, some of which were anthologized. After moving to Los Angeles in 1960 from the small town of Mount Carmel, Illinois I also wrote a number of sexy paperback thriller novels, some of which contained SF elements, such as *Vixen Hollow* and *The Man Who Made Maniacs*.

But when my book *The Great Radio Heroes* became a "modest best seller" in the 1960s I devoted myself to documenting the history of popular radio in a series of books. I also did some new radio dramas, including writing and directing a version of my F&SF story, 'The Depths" for the public radio series, *Thirty Minutes to Curtain*, writing, producing, directing and playing second lead in a Fiftieth Anniversary revival series of Tom Mix inspired by the classic cowboy movie star, but actually more concerned with mystery and detection than Western elements, and producing, directing, and slightly revising the scripts of the great Canton E. Morse for a new recording of an *I Love a Mystery* story, "The Fear that Creeps like a Cat," twenty episodes, five hours, for an audio book album, the longest professional reconstruction of an Old Time Radio series yet attempted.

After living in this world for decades, it should be no surprise that my first long science fiction story in some time should retain echoes of it. This story might bring to mind Latitude Zero, Peter Quill, Escape. But I hope the reader does find it a satisfactory science fiction or fantasy story. That is the question—Is it SF or fantasy, science or the supernatural?

NAME YOUR SYMPTOM

Henry Infield placed the insulated circlet on his head gently. The gleaming rod extended above his head about a foot, the wires from it leading down into his collar, along his spine and finally out his pants leg to a short metallic strap that dragged on the floor.

Clyde Morgan regarded his partner. "Suppose—just suppose—you *were* serious about this, why not just the shoes?"

Infield turned his soft blue eyes to the black and tan oxfords with the very thick rubber soles. "They might get soaked through."

Morgan took his foot off the chair behind the desk and sat down. "Suppose they were soaked through and you were standing on a metal plate—steps or a manhole cover—what good would your lightning rod do you then?"

Infield shrugged slightly. "I suppose a man must take some chances."

Morgan said, "You can't do it, Henry. You're crossing the line. The people we treat are on one side of the line and we're on the other. If you cross that line, you won't be able to treat people again."

The small man looked out the large window, blinking myopically at the brassy sunlight. "That's just it, Clyde. There is a line between us, a wall. How can we really understand the people who come to us, if we hide on our side of the wall?"

Morgan shook his thick head, ruffling his thinning red hair. "I dunno, Henry, but staying on our side is a pretty good way to keep sane and that's quite an accomplishment these days."

Infield whirled and stalked to the desk. "That's the answer! The whole world is going mad and we are just sitting back watching it hike along. Do you know that what we are doing is really the most primitive medicine in the world? We are treating the symptoms and not the disease. One cannibal walking another with sleeping sickness doesn't cure anything. Eventually the savage dies—just as all those sick savages out in the street will die unless we can cure the disease, not only the indications."

Morgan shifted his ponderous weight uneasily. "Now, Henry, it's no good to talk like that. We psychiatrists can't turn back the clock. There just aren't enough of us or enough time to give that old-fashioned *therapy* to all the sick people."

Infield leaned on the desk and glared. "I called myself a psychiatrist once. But now I know we're semi-mechanics, semi-engineers, semi-inventors, semi lots of other things, but certainly not even semi-psychiatrists. A psychiatrist wouldn't give a foetic gyro to a man with claustrophobia."

His mind went back to the first gyro ball he had ever issued; the remembrance of his pride in the thing sickened him. Floating before him in memory was the vertical hoop and the horizontal hoop, both of shining steel-impervium alloy. Transfixed in the twin circles was the face of the patient, slack with smiles and sweat. But his memory was exaggerating the human element. The gyro actually passed over a man's shoulder, through his legs, under his arms. Any time he felt the walls creeping in to crush him, he could withdraw his head and limbs into the circle and feel safe. Steel-impervium alloy could resist even a nuclear explosion. The foetic gyro ball was worn day and night, for life.

The sickness overcame him. He sat down on Morgan's desk. "That's just one thing, the gyro ball. There are so many others, so many."

Morgan smiled. "You know, Henry, not all of our Cures are so—so—not all are like that. Those Cures for mother complexes aren't even obvious. If anybody does see that button in a patient's ear, it looks like a hearing aid. Yet for a nominal sum, the patient is equipped to hear the soothing recorded voice of his mother saying, 'It's all right, everything's all right, Mommy loves you, it's all right . . . "

"But *is* everything all right?" Infield asked intensely. "Suppose the patient is driving over one hundred on an icy road. He thinks about slowing down, but there's the voice in his ear. Or suppose he's walking down a railroad track and hears a train whistle—if he can hear anything over that verbal Pablum gushing in his ear."

Morgan's face stiffened. "You know as well as I do that those voices are nearly subsonic. They don't cut a sense efficiency more than 23 per cent."

"At first, Clyde—only at first. But what about the severe case where we have to burn a three-dimensional smiling mother image on the eyes of the patient with radiation? With that image over everything he sees and with that insidious voice drumming in his head night and day, do you mean to say that man's senses will only be impaired 23 per cent? Why, he'll turn violently schizophrenic sooner or later—and you know it. The only cure we have for that is still a strait jacket, a padded cell or one of those inhuman lobotomies."

Morgan shrugged helplessly. "You're an idealist."

"You're damned right!" Infield slammed the door behind him.

The cool air of the street was a relief. Infield stepped into the main stream of human traffic and tried to adjust to the second change in the air. People didn't bathe very often these days.

He walked along, buffeted by the crowd, carried along in this direction, shoved back in that direction. Most people in the crowd seemed to be Normals, but you couldn't tell. Many "Cures" were not readily apparent.

A young man with black glasses and a radar headset (a photophobe) was unable to keep from being pushed against Infield. He sounded out the lightning rod, his face changing when he realized it must be some kind of Cure. "Pardon me," he said warmly.

"Quite all right."

It was the first time in years that anyone had apologized to Infield for anything. He had been one of those condemned Normals, more to be scorned than pitied. Perhaps he could really get to understand these people, now that he had taken down the wall.

Suddenly something else was pushing against Infield, forcing the air from his lungs. He stared down at the magnetic suction dart clinging leechlike to his chest. Model Acrophobe 101-X, he catalogued immediately. Description: safety belt. But his emotions didn't behave so well. He was thoroughly terrified, heart racing, sweat glands pumping. The impervium cable undulated vulgarly. *Some primitive fear of snake symbols?* his mind wondered while panic crushed him.

"Uncouple that cable!" the shout rang out. It was not his own.

A clean-cut young man with mouse-colored hair was moving toward the stubble-chinned, heavy-shouldered man quivering in the center of a web of impervium cables stuck secure to the walls and windows of buildings facing the street, the sidewalk, a mailbox, the lamppost and Infield.

Mouse-hair yelled hoarsely, "Uncouple it, Davies! Can't you see the guy's got a lightning rod? You're grounding him!"

"I can't," Davies groaned. "I'm scared!"

Halfway down the twenty feet of cable, Mouse-hair grabbed on. "I'm holding it. Release it, you hear?"

Davies fumbled for the broad belt around his thickening middle. He jabbed the button that sent a negative current through the cable. The magnetic suction dart dropped away from Infield like a thing that had been alive and now was killed. He felt an overwhelming sense of relief.

After breathing deeply for a few moments, he looked up to see Davies releasing and drawing all his darts into his belt, making it resemble a Hydra-sized spiked dog collar. Mouse-hair stood by tensely as the crowd disassembled.

"This isn't the first time you've pulled something like this, Davies," he said. "You weren't too scared to release that cable. You just don't care about other people's feelings. This is *official*."

Mouse-hair drove a fast, hard right into the soft blue flesh of Davies' chin. The big man fell silently.

The other turned to Infield. "He was unconscious on his feet," he explained. "He never knew he fell."

"What did you mean by that punch being official?" Infield asked, while trying to arrange his feelings into the comfortable, familiar patterns.

The young man's eyes almost seemed to narrow, although his face didn't move; he merely radiated narrowed eyes. "How long have you been Cured?"

"Not—not long," Infield evaded.

The other glanced around the street. He moistened his lips and spoke slowly. "Do you think you might be interested in joining a fraternal organization of the Cured?"

Infield's pulse raced, trying to get ahead of his thoughts, and losing out. A chance to study a pseudo-culture of the "Cured" developed in isolation! "Yes, I think I might. I owe you a drink for helping me out. How about it?"

The man's face paled so fast, Infield thought for an instant that he was going to faint. "All right. I'll risk it." He touched the side of his face away from the psychiatrist.

Infield shifted around, trying to see that side of his benefactor, but couldn't manage it in good grace. He wondered if the fellow was sporting a Mom-voice hearing aid and was afraid of raising her ire. He cleared his throat, noticing the affectation of it. "My name's Infield."

"Price," the other answered absently. "George Price. I suppose they have liquor at the Club. We can have a *drink* there, I guess."

Price set the direction and Infield fell in at his side. "Look, if you don't drink, I'll buy you a cup of coffee. It was just a suggestion."

Under the mousy hair, Price's strong features were beginning to gleam moistly. "You are lucky in one way, Mr. Infield. People take one look at your Cure and don't ask you to go walking in the rain. But even after seeing *this*, some people still ask me to have a drink." *This* was revealed, as he turned his head, to be a small metal cube above his left ear.

Infield supposed it was a Cure, although he had never issued one like it. He didn't know if it would be good form to inquire what kind it was.

"It's a Cure for alcoholism," Price told him. "It runs a constant blood check to see that the alcohol level doesn't go over the sobriety limit."

"What happens if you take one too many?"

Price looked off as if at something not particularly interesting, but more interesting than what he was saying. "It drives a needle into my temple and kills me."

The psychiatrist felt cold fury rising in him. The Cures were supposed to save lives, not endanger them.

"What kind of irresponsible idiot could have issued such a device?" he demanded angrily.

"I did," Price said. "I used to be a psychiatrist. I was always good in shop. This is a pretty effective mechanism, if I say so myself. It can't be removed without causing my death and it's indestructible. Impervium-shielded, you see."

Price probably would never get crazed enough for liquor to kill himself, Infield knew. The threat of death would keep him constantly shocked sane. Men hide in the comforts of insanity, but when faced with death, they are often forced back to reality. A man can't move his legs; in a fire, though, he may run. His legs were definitely paralyzed before and may be again, but for one moment he would forget the moral defeat of his life and his withdrawal from life and live an enforced sanity. But sometimes the withdrawal was—or could become—too complete.

"We're here."

Infield looked up self-consciously and noticed that they had crossed two streets from his building and were standing in front of what appeared to be a small, dingy café. He followed Price through the screeching screen door.

They seated themselves at a small table with a red-checked cloth. Infield wondered why cheap bars and restaurants always used red-checked cloths. Then he looked closer and discovered the reason. They did a remarkably good job of camouflaging the spots of grease and alcohol.

A fat man who smelled of the grease and alcohol of the tablecloths shuffled up to them with a towel on his arm, staring ahead of him at some point in time rather than space.

Price lit a cigarette with unsteady hands. "Reggie is studying biblical text. Cute gadget. His contact lenses are made up of a lot of layers of polarized glass. Every time he blinks, the amount of polarization changes and a new page appears. His father once told him that if he didn't study his Bible and pray for him, his old dad would die."

The psychiatrist knew the threat on the father's part couldn't create such a fixation by itself. His eyebrows faintly inquired.

Price nodded jerkily. "Twenty years ago, at least."

"What'll you have, Georgie?" Reggie asked.

The young man snubbed out his cigarette viciously. "Bourbon. Straight."

Reggie smiled—a toothy, vacant, comedy-relief smile. "Fine. The Good Book says a little wine is good for a man, or something like that. I don't remember exactly."

Of course he didn't, Infield knew. Why should he? It was useless to learn his Bible lessons to save his father, because it was obvious his father was dead. He would never succeed because there was no reason to succeed. But he had to try, didn't he, for his father's sake? He didn't hate his father for making him study. He didn't want him to die. He had to prove that.

Infield sighed. At least this device kept the man on his feet, doing some kind of useful work instead of rotting in a padded cell with a probably imaginary Bible. A man could cut his wrists with the edge of a sheet of paper if he tried long enough, so of course the Bible would be imaginary.

"But, Georgie," the waiter complained, "you know you won't drink it. You ask me to bring you drinks and then you just look at them. Boy, do you look funny when you're looking at drinks. Honest, Georgie, I want to laugh when I think of the way you look at a glass with a drink in it." He did laugh.

Price fumbled with the cigarette stub in the black iron ash tray, examining it with the skill of scientific observation. "Mr. Infield is buying me the drink and that makes it different."

Reggie went away. Price kept dissecting the tobacco and paper. Infield cleared his throat and again reminded himself against such obvious affectations. "You were telling me about some organization of the Cured," he said.

Price looked up, no longer interested in the relic of a cigarette. He was suddenly intensely interested and intensely observant of the rest of the café. "Was I? I was? Well, suppose you tell me something. What do you really think of the Incompletes?"

The psychiatrist felt his face frown. "'Who?"

"I forgot. You haven't been one of us long. The Incompletes is a truer name for the so-called Normals. Have you ever thought of just how dangerous these people are, Mr. Infield?"

"Frankly, no," Infield said, realizing it was not the right thing to say but tiring of constant pretense.

"You don't understand. Everyone has some little phobia or fixation. Maybe everyone didn't have one once, but after being told they did have them for generations, everyone who didn't have one developed a defense mechanism and an aberration so they would be normal. If that phobia isn't brought to the surface and Cured, it may arise any time and endanger other people. The only safe, good sound citizens are Cured. Those lacking Cures—the Incompletes—*must be dealt with.*"

Infield's throat went dry. "And you're the one to deal with them?"

"It's my destiny." Price quickly added, "And yours, too, of course."

Infield nodded. Price was a demagogue, young, handsome, dynamic, likable, impassioned with his cause, and convinced that it was his divine destiny. He was a psychopathic egotist and a dangerous man. Doubly dangerous to Infield because, even though he was one of the few people who still read enough books from the old days of therapy to recognize Price for what he was, he nevertheless still liked the young man for the intelligence behind the egotism and the courage behind the fanaticism.

"How are we going to deal with the Incompletes?" Infield asked.

Price started to glance around the café, then half shrugged, almost visibly thinking that he shouldn't run that routine into the ground. "We'll Cure them whether they want to be Cured or not—for their own good."

Infield felt cold inside. After a time, he found that the roaring was not just in his head. It was thundering outside. He was getting sick. Price was the type of man who could spread his ideas throughout the ranks of the

Cured—if indeed the plot was not already universal, imposed upon many ill minds.

He could picture an entirely Cured world and he didn't like the view. Every Cure cut down on the mental and physical abilities of the patient as it was, whether Morgan and the others admitted it or not. But if everyone had a crutch to lean on for one phobia, he would develop secondary Symptoms.

People would start needing two Cures—perhaps a foetic gyro and a safety belt—then another and another. There would always be a crutch to lean on for one thing and then room enough to develop something else—until everyone would be loaded down with too many Cures to operate.

A Cure was a last resort, dope for a malignancy case, euthanasia for the hopeless. Enforced Cures would be a curse for the individual and the race.

But Infield let himself relax. How could anyone force a mechanical relief for neurotic or psychopathic symptoms on someone who didn't want or need it?

"Perhaps you don't see how it could be done," Price said. "I'll explain."

Reggie's heavy hand set a straight bourbon down before Price and another before Infield. Price stared at the drink almost without comprehension of how it came to be. He started to sweat.

"George, drink it."

The voice belonged to a young woman, a blond girl with pink skin and suave, draped clothes. In this den of the Cured, Infield thought half humorously, it was surprising to see a Normal—an "Incomplete." But then he noticed something about the baby she carried. The Cure had been very simple. It wasn't even a mechanized half-human robot, just a rag doll. She sat down at the table.

"George," she said, "drink it. One drink won't raise your alcohol index to the danger point. You've got to get over this fear of even the sight or smell of liquor."

The girl turned to Infield. "You're one of us, but you're new, so you don't know about George. Maybe you can help if you do. It's all silly. He's not an alcoholic. He didn't need to put that Cure on his head. It's just an excuse for not drinking. All of this is just because a while back something happened to the baby here"—she adjusted the doll's blanket—"when he was drinking. Just drinking, not drunk.

"I don't remember what happened to the baby—it wasn't important. But George has been brooding about it ever since. I guess he thinks something else bad will happen because of liquor. That's silly. Why don't you tell him it's silly?"

"Maybe it is," Infield said softly. "You could take the shock if he downed that drink and the shock might do you good."

Price laughed shortly. "I feel like doing something very melodramatic, like throwing my drink—and yours—across the room, but I haven't got the guts to touch those glasses. Do it for me, will you? Cauterizing the bite might do me good if I'd been bitten by a rabid dog, but I don't have the nerve to do it."

Before Infield could move, Reggie came and set both drinks on a little circular tray. He moved away. "I knew it. That's all he did, just look at the drink. Makes me laugh."

Price wiped the sweat off his palms. Infield sat and thought. Mrs. Price cooed to the rag doll, unmindful of either of them now.

"You were explaining," the psychiatrist said. "You were going to tell me how you were going to Cure the Incompletes."

"I said *we* were going to do it. Actually *you* will play a greater part than I, *Doctor* Infield."

The psychiatrist sat rigidly.

"You didn't think you could give me your right name in front of your own office building and that I wouldn't recognize you? I know some psychiatrists are sensitive about wearing Cures themselves, but it is a mark of honor of the completely sane man. You should be proud of your Cure and eager to Cure others. *Very* eager."

"Just what do you mean?" He already suspected Price's meaning.

Price leaned forward. "There is one phobia that is so widespread, a Cure is not even thought of—hypochondria. Hundreds of people come to your office for a Cure and you turn them away. Suppose you and the other Cured psychiatrists give *everybody* who comes to you a Cure?"

Infield gestured vaguely. "A psychiatrist wouldn't hand out Cures unless they were absolutely necessary."

"You'll feel differently after you've been Cured for a while yourself. Other psychiatrists have."

Before Infield could speak, a stubble-faced, barrel-chested man moved past their table. He wore a safety belt. It was the man Price had called Davies, the one who had fastened one of his safety lines to Infield in the street.

Davies went to the bar in the back. "Gimme a bottle," he demanded of a vacant-eyed Reggie. He came back toward them, carrying the bottle in one band, brushing off raindrops with the other. He stopped beside Price and glared. Price leaned back. The chair creaked. Mrs. Price kept cooing to the doll.

"You made me fall," Davies accused.

Price shrugged. "You were unconscious. You never knew it."

Sweat broke out on Davies' forehead. "You broke the Code. Don't you think I can imagine how it was to fall? You louse!"

Suddenly Davies triggered his safety belt. At close range, before the lines could fan out in a radius, all the lines in front attached themselves to Price, the ones at each side clung to their table and the floor, and all the others to the table behind Infield. Davies released all lines except those on Price, and then threw himself backward, dragging Price out of his chair and onto the floor. Davies didn't mind making others fall. They were always trying to make *him* fall just so they could laugh at him or pounce on him; why shouldn't he like to make them fall first?

Expertly, Davies moved forward and looped the loose lines around Price's head and shoulders and then around his feet. He crouched beside Price and shoved the bottle into the gasping mouth and poured.

Price twisted against the binding lines in blind terror, gagging and spouting whisky. Davies laughed and tilted the bottle more.

Mrs. Price screamed. "The Cure! If you get that much liquor in his system, it will kill him!" She rocked the rag doll in her arms, trying to soothe it, and stared in horror.

Infield hit the big man behind the ear. He dropped the bottle and fell over sideways on the floor. Fear and hate mingled in his eyes as he looked up at Infield.

Nonsense, Infield told himself. Eyes can't register emotion.

Davies released his lines and drew them in. He got up precariously. "I'm going to kill you," he said, glaring at Infield. "You made me fall worse than Georgie did. I'm really going to kill you."

Infield wasn't a large man, but he had pressed two hundred and fifty many times in gym. He grabbed Davies' belt with both hands and lifted him about six inches off the floor.

"I could drop you," the psychiatrist said.

"No!" Davies begged weakly. "Please!"

"I'll do it if you cause more trouble." Infield sat down and rubbed his aching forearms.

Davies backed off in terror, right into the arms of Reggie. The waiter closed his huge hands on the acrophobe's shoulders.

"*You* broke the Code all the way," Reggie said. "The Good Book says 'Thou shouldn't kill' or something like that, and so does the Code."

"Let him go, Reggie," Price choked out, getting to his feet. "I'm not dead." He wiped his hand across his mouth.

"No. No, you aren't." Infield felt an excitement pounding through him, same as when he had diagnosed his first case. No, better than that.

"That taste of liquor didn't kill you, Price. Nothing terrible happened. You could find some way to get rid of that Cure."

Price stared at him as if he were a padded-cell case. "That's different. I'd be a hopeless drunk without the Cure. Besides, no one ever gets rid of a Cure."

They were all looking at Infield. Somehow he felt this represented a critical point in history. It was up to him which turn the world took, the world as represented by these four Cured people. "I'm afraid I'm for *less* Cures instead of more, Price. Look, if I can show you that someone can discard a Cure, would you get rid of that—if I may use the word—*monstrous* thing on your head?"

Price grinned. Infield didn't recognize its smugness at the time.

"I'll show you." He took off the circlet with the lightning rod and yanked at the wire running down into his collar. The new-old excitement within was running high. He felt the wire snap and come up easily. He threw the Cure on the floor.

"Now," he said, "I am going out in that rainstorm. There's thunder and lightning out there. I'm afraid, but I can get along without a Cure and so can you."

"You can't! Nobody can!" Price screamed after him. He turned to the others. "If he reveals us, the Cause is lost. We've got to stop him *for good*. We've got to go after him."

"It's slippery," Davies whimpered. "I might fall."

Mrs. Price cuddled her rag doll. "I can't leave the baby and she mustn't get wet."

"Well, there's no liquor out there and you can study your text in the lightning flashes, Reggie. Come on."

Running down the streets that were tunnels of shining tar, running into the knifing ice bristles of the rain, Henry Infield realized that he was very frightened of the lightning.

There is no action without a reason, he knew from the old neglected books. He had had a latent fear of lightning when he chose the lightning-rod Cure. He could have picked a safety belt or foetic gyro just as well.

He sneezed. He was soaked through, but he kept on running. He didn't know what Price and Reggie planned to do when they caught him. He slipped and fell. He would soon find out what they wanted. The excitement was all gone now and it left an empty space into which fear rushed.

Reggie said, "We shall make a sacrifice."

Infield looked up and saw the lightning reflected on the blade of a thin knife. Infield reached toward it more in fascination than fear. He managed to get all his fingers around two of Reggie's. He jerked and the knife fell into Infield's palm. The psychiatrist pulled himself erect by holding to Reggie's arm. Staggering to his feet, he remembered what he must do and slashed at the waiter's head. A gash streaked across the man's brow and blood poured into his eyes. He screamed, "I can't see the words!"

It was his problem. Infield usually solved other people's problems, but now he ran away—he couldn't even solve his own.

Infield realized that he had gone mad as he held the thin blade high overhead, but he did need some kind of lightning rod. Price (who was just behind him, gaining) had been right. No one could discard a Cure. He watched the lightning play its light on the blade of his Cure and he knew that Price was going to kill him in the next moment.

The lightning hit him first.

Reggie squinted under the bandage at the lettering on the door that said INFIELD & MORGAN and opened the door. He ran across the room to the man sitting at the desk, reading by the swivel light.

"Mr. Morgan, your partner, Mr. Infield, he—"

"Just a moment." Morgan switched on the room lights. "What were you saying?"

"Mr. Infield went out without his Cure in a storm and was struck by lightning. We took him to the morgue. He must have been crazy to go out without his Cure."

Morgan stared into his bright desk light without blinking. "This is quite a shock to me. Would you mind leaving? I'll come over to your place and you can tell me about it later."

Reggie went out. "Yes, sir. He was struck by lightning, struck dead. He must have been crazy to leave his Cure." The door closed.

Morgan exhaled. Poor Infield. But it wasn't the lightning that killed him, of course. Morgan adjusted the soundproofing plugs in his ears, thinking that you did have to have quite a bit of light to read lips. The thunder, naturally, was what had killed Infield. Loud noise—any noise—that would do it every time. Too bad Infield had never really stopped being one of the Incompletes. Dangerous people. Morgan would have to deal with them.

AFTERWORD

This was the first story I sold to a major SF magazine, *Galaxy*. Earlier, I had published a story in Bill Crawford's *Spaceway*, but Bill was never able to pay his contributors, and whether anything published here was a professional appearance is open to debate. I also did have a sale to Robert W. Lowndes' *Science Fiction Quarterly*, my only appearance in a genuine pulp-size pulp (about 7.5 x 10 in.) That classic format was going out as I was coming in, and soon all SF and mystery magazines (and a very few Westerns) would be digest-size. But the pay from *SF Quarterly* was low (forty dollars, I believe) and I got $150 from *Galaxy*. That pay doesn't sound too bad today, but in 1956 that figure was worth about $750 in 2002 dollars. It was enough to inspire a young man in his twenties to work hard at being a science-fiction writer.

I had already done my homework to write this story. I had made lists, graphs, and analysis of what kind of stories editor H.L. Gold was using, and constructed this story to match. Obviously, my analysis was correct. The story ran not only in *Galaxy Magazine*, but in two later *Galaxy* anthologies.

A BIT FOR MRS. HALLORAN

Yes, Mrs. Halloran, I can tell you one reason a man shouldn't love horses.

How much do you know about them? Owner and fancier? Very well, that gives you quite a bit of knowledge about horses, which is more than I have.

No, I wouldn't say it was just a prejudice on my part. I have a logical reason for not wanting to go to your horse show.

I could make an exception and go with you to a Western movie, where I *might* be able to agree with you objectively about equine beauty. I could admire Currier and Ives prints or paintings by Remington and value the symmetry of the animal. But I would never—damnably well never—go with you to a horse show.

Nothing personal, you understand.

Yes of course, it's only right that I explain, Mrs. Halloran.

It's nice to walk in this bar and have a drink when I really want to and I was glad to see you come in too. But you are asking for this.

I'm going to tell you the whole story of the vacation Elizabeth and I took on Mars a few years ago.

Yes, I said Mars. You hadn't thought about Mars, had you?

* * *

It was like staring at a demanding sheet of stationery until you went snow blind.

"There just isn't anything to see," I said, frowning, blinking my eyes and looking out once again, hopefully, across the off-white desert tracked with the sweep of our tire trail.

"I like it." Elizabeth sat steering our runabout effortlessly. At the—inn?—she had grabbed the half-circle of the steering wheel. Her hands were competent. Perspiration illuminated the clean lines of her face. Above her mouth, the salty beads collected quickly, accentuating her sensuous pink lips.

"It's picturesque," she said, looking determinedly for something to point out to me, at the same time tracing the biting line of a bra strap under her terrycloth shirt. "It's lovely. Better than South America."

"*Sure*," I drawled. I lifted myself from the seat where it was getting hot and sticky, and hitched my knickers down to cross my legs. "Best vacation we e had," I grumbled.

(We always tried to go somewhere different every year. We ran into you, Mrs. Halloran, several times—London, Rome, mostly on the continent, wasn't it? Elizabeth and I took in a lot of other places—Rio, the Islands, Africa. You should go to Kenya State Park and watch the animals. No cages. You can run around in Fords and see them right on the game trails and in their lairs. We had to stop once and let a pride of lions cross the road. No, it isn't completely out of a Professor of Ethnology's line; seeing how the beasts lived showed me a lot about how the natives *had* to live . . . On Mars there didn't seem to be anything to see or learn no matter how far you drove.)

"Want me to take the wheel?" I said, wearily. "You must be tired."

"Not a bit," Elizabeth assured me.

"You sure?"

Elizabeth shook her head. I thought that was rather odd. She was a pretty lazy girl, which I had thought was cute and sexy the first time I met her, and she had never been too sloppy about it since so I had never been completely disillusioned.

"The air on Mars must have vitamins in it," I suggested.

She smiled and expanded her lungs. "Lots. I feel like I could lick the world. And Mars, too!"

"Just let me know if you suddenly feel like pickles and ice cream, honey," I muttered.

There was something out on the desert. I blinked my eyes to make sure. I had been staring so hard at the white sands I could see the germs floating across my retina clearly. But this was no germ.

They were horses.

I put my arm around Elizabeth and pointed them out to her. "Just like in a field back in Ohio or Illinois, baby. A black one and a brown one."

"Sorrel."

I had been looking at the bright sunlight on the desert too long. A wave of vertigo flowed over me and passed. I found myself thinking about what had happened to the horses we had seen at a bullfight in Madrid and my lips were curled back over my teeth in a wide, wide smile. I wanted that to happen to these horses.

I rubbed my hand over my eyes briskly. That was silly. It had made me sick at the time and it would take more than latent sadism to make me want to see it again. It would require a secret masochism.

For no obvious reason, I suddenly thought of something. "Elizabeth, this is our *first* vacation on Mars, isn't it?"

She smiled briefly. "You know it is, Doug."

"Sure," I said. "Sure, only where did we go last year, Mrs. Marley?"

Elizabeth stretched her neck and looked out of the bottoms of her eyes. "Station up ahead. I think we need a fresh charge."

I looked around. I hadn't seen the station before. It was squat and ugly, blazing red.

"These electric cars are damn inefficient," I told her. "Give me a Model A any day. There's a real classic. People will be driving them fifty years from now.

Elizabeth slid the runabout in neatly between the totem spirals.

"Not on Mars," she said.

The attendant stirred himself out of the deep shadows of the roof's overhang.

"I don't know," I grunted. "If they could get them here, they would be a lot better than these mobile sardine cans. There must be transportation technicalities—Damn, I'm taking the ancestor of all headaches. Any aspirin in the glove compartment?"

She glanced at me with a flick of her gold eyes.

"No glove compartment," Elizabeth said, half in humor, half gently.

I cussed under my breath and watched the attendant fasten our car's cable to the induction coil. He was dressed in clean coveralls, his face oddly flat and expressionless. Like all of them, he was a complete nonentity.

I shook my head. "All of these Martians look alike to me. Exactly alike. I don't see how anyone could tell them apart."

Elizabeth ran her carmine-tipped fingers through her hair. It fell into its natural waves instantly, as usual.

"I don't even try telling one from the other."

I boosted her out of the driver's seat unceremoniously.

"Neither do I," I admitted.

She waited to answer that until I scooted under the steering wheel and got out on her side, away from the attendant, and said "That isn't like—like you."

I groped for the cobalt sky with cramped arms and stuck that way. It sure as an early Christian Hell *wasn't* like me. I was interested in all peoples. Why shouldn't I be interested in the Martian race? Here I had a gold-plated opportunity to study them close at hand and I was ignoring it. It would be a valuable pioneer work. Or at least I was sure the subject hadn't been exhausted. In any case, personal reports are always of some value.

Without realizing it, I had moved away from the silent attendant.

I don't fear or hate people I don't understand—only people I don't *want* to understand.

"Want to stretch your legs?" I asked my wife.

She told me no.

It had been a long drive but I realized that there wasn't anything more I wanted at the station either.

"Let's go back to the inn and have dinner," I suggested.

I didn't pay the attendant—this, like the rest of it, had been taken care of. I helped Elizabeth in and took the wheel myself.

"I *like* this car," she offered after we had left the station half a mile behind. "Maybe we could take it back with us."

The horses were off to the side of our route across the trackless sand again.

"You like this whole vacation, don't you?" I said, knowing the answer as I thought of the question.

Horses up ahead.

"Yes," she whispered. "I can relax. Think. This time there isn't the constant worry about having to go back to the old grind. The same old grind, Doug. I'm sick as hell of that old grind, Doug."

Then—the horses.

After it was over and I was rocking back and forth behind the steering column half-suffocated, gasping for air, holding myself in my seat with hands slippery with moist fear on the wheel, I couldn't believe I had really done it.

It was so blasted *silly*.

I had tried to run down one of the horses with the car.

"Darling, darling," Elizabeth was crooning. I became aware. "Is it your heart? Your heart?"

That always made me blind mad. Years before, I had had a little trouble and ever since whenever I caught my breath sharply Elizabeth asked about my heart. It made me feel so *weak*. And I wasn't.

Sometimes when I was feeling mean I used to tell Elizabeth she wasn't always so considerate of my heart at night.

This time I stroked her hair. "I just dozed off at the wheel," I lied. "Psychosomatic relief for the headache, maybe. Startled myself when I jerked up awake." I looked around over the desert. It was absolutely barren.

"I didn't hit the horse," I stated.

"No," Elizabeth said.

I was sorry, with a sorrow deep as death, dark as ecstasy . . .

Elizabeth gasped and I leaned forward in the seat. I looked at my watch and cursed silently. It said five-thirty. We were hungry.

"Let's get back to the inn for dinner," I said.

"Yes." Elizabeth nodded quickly.

We were very hungry.

I drove fast.

We always got hungry at five.

* * *

Elizabeth was at the white clothed table when I entered the empty dining room. I had changed my clothes to be formal, not out of necessity. They weren't dirty. Not after traveling around all day. Mars was sanitary.

"Have you ordered?" I asked as I reached the table.

Elizabeth nodded shortly. "For both of us." She smiled.

I sat down, produced a cigarette and sucked it alight. "You're getting—pretty aggressive these days," I said.

"*Damn*. I ordered dinner. Don't tell me that wounds your masculine vanity?"

I made a smile for her inside the smoke. "You drove the car today. You grabbed the wheel and drove."

The waiter brought the tray. He had on a spotless white jacket and an empty expression. I couldn't tell him apart from the station attendant.

Elizabeth glanced at the waiter and adjusted the shoulder strap of her black sheath of an evening dress. She adjusted it down. The valley between blue-traced ivory curves showed pink.

The waiter finished the table setting and went away.

Elizabeth did not look after him.

"I felt like driving," she informed me.

"You never felt much like doing anything back on Earth," I observed.

She shrugged and rested her chin on her palm. "That was back there. Things are different here."

I nodded. "They are," I said.

"You sound awfully grim about that."

(I had a lot of reasons to be grim. For one thing, my wife was sitting across the table from me looking beautiful and desirable and I couldn't do a thing about it on Mars, not a thing. I hope I'm not shocking you, Mrs. Halloran. On the other hand, why be hypocritical about it? I don't give a continental corps of drum boys if I am shocking you. Don't just giggle. Have another drink.)

"You know more about this than I do," I said to Elizabeth without wanting to say it.

Her eyelids didn't flutter. "About *what*, Doug? I didn't think you thought I knew more about anything than you."

I made my hands steady and uncovered the dishes. I served Elizabeth and myself. I started to take a bite, then decided against it. The hunger inside me raised to another plateau and I ate.

"Elizabeth, don't make me think you are against me too." I was begging her, chewing my food carefully and begging her.

Her fine hands were dissecting the steak with silver. They paused. She looked up. "Against you? *Too?*"

I couldn't look her in the eyes. It suddenly seemed foolish.

"It probably is just some—*xenophobia*. Fear of the alien. But I get feelings of persecution. As if everybody were in some giant conspiracy against me."

"Doug," she said. It started out as a joke but there was sympathy in it.

"And I can't remember things," I said, having to finish it now that I had started.

"Absent-mindedness is standard equipment for professors," she said, laughing gently. "I forget where I put things, darling. We all do."

The back of my neck seemed to need rubbing with my hand. "It's more than that. How did we get here? To Mars? *Mars.*"

"By spaceship, of course," she said.

"Of course. How else could you get to Mars? But Elizabeth," I said, "I don't remember being on a spaceship. In fact I don't remember that there *are* any spaceships. The last I can remember, spaceships were only in magazines and comic strips."

Elizabeth looked worried. "Doug, I don't know about this. I don't know how often these kind of lapses occur. You had better see a good doctor when we get back."

I drained my water glass and refilled it from the pitcher. "Yes," I grunted.

"We shouldn't have come to Mars in the off season." She ran her fingers through her thick hair in agitation. "It is sort of lonely. It would be better with more people around."

"Yes," I said again.

Elizabeth dropped her spoon into her half-empty dessert.

"Let's go up to our room," she said to me.

What for? I thought. I walked around the table and held her chair. "Elizabeth, we go upstairs every night. We drive through the day, eat in the evening and go to bed at night. Let's do it different tonight. Let's get out the runabout and see what Mars looks like by twin moonlight."

Elizabeth looked at me. '*No.*" She added something: "It's too cold." She tried again: "I don't feel like it tonight, Doug."

I nodded. She was right.

But tomorrow we will do something different, I decided.

We went upstairs.

* * *

The world itself was different the next morning.

Something was changing.

We stood before our runabout and shivered in the difference of sensation. It was not really a difference in temperature, of hot and cold. Still I had put on a tweed jacket and Elizabeth had slipped into her pony-skin coat.

I looked at Elizabeth's profile, too sharp against the white sunlight. "I don't want to go out today," I said.

Elizabeth smiled fleetingly, eyes fast to the blank horizon. "I'd like to," she whispered. "It will do us—good, Doug."

I stood there quietly and once and for all, finally, at last, I had the guts to reject pretense. "I don't want to, but we'll go," I told her. *"We have to."*

She didn't say anything more. We got into the car and I took the wheel. I drove and because the mind is so kind to itself, because it protects itself so well, I didn't think for a long time.

Today was different.

The difference invaded my peace irrevocably. Before, there had been nothing to see on the desert. But today I had the intense impression that there was something to see if only I was fast enough. If only I could turn my head fast enough to catch what lurked at the furthest, blurred edge of the tunnel of my vision I would see something significant.

Whatever it was, it was just beyond the nearest rise of sand, or perhaps just behind the bottom rim of the bowl of the sky.

Then it seemed much closer. It seemed to be in the car with Elizabeth, with me.

My scalp tingled delicately and hair crept on the top of my head and stiffened at the base of my neck. I turned my eyes slowly towards Elizabeth but I looked back before my gaze reached her.

I tried again to look at her, and again, and finally I turned my eyes and my head and I looked at her.

And I saw her coat.

I wanted to scream but some civilized part of my mind made me ashamed to scream in front of my wife, so I just screamed inside. It isn't good that way. It's better to scream outside yourself.

I stopped the car and very gently I took hold of Elizabeth's coat and started to pull it off her. She looked at me once as if to protest but something stopped her.

I smiled at her reassuringly and I saw her white teeth clamp down on her full, pink lower lip. I made myself stop smiling.

The sand gritted under my shoes as I walked away from the car, carrying the coat.

There was no graduation between the metronome of normalcy and the trip-hammer of agony.

I was breathing all right one second and the next I was on my knees dying of suffocation.

I waited impatiently for the air starvation to end as it had the day before in the car, but it held on, continued evenly. I fell, sand biting cheek, and it got worse.

Dimly, without thinking, only by instinct and even it was blurring, I scrambled around and crawled back towards Elizabeth and the car, dragging the coat behind me.

She was in the seat waiting for me.

"Why didn't you come?" I croaked at her.

She didn't say a word. I think she wondered about it, but she didn't say a word.

I lurched to my feet and started to get back into the car. I stopped. I held the coat out at arm's length.

I laughed, and I squeezed the coat up against my chest. Why had I ever wanted to get rid of the coat? It was dead. Killed by man. The hide had been shaped by man to his own uses. It was nothing.

Except, perhaps, a pony-skin symbol.

I rested my spine against the edge of the car door and looked across the desert.

My hands were abruptly patting down my pockets and I wondered what I was looking for. I found it. It was an accordion-fold unit of post-cards—the inn supplied them free to guests. I had scribbled a few lines to Elizabeth's mother politely in the tiny message box that bravely invaded the domain of those who liked to look at pictures. I had done it some-time—days?—before. Now I would use it.

I walked back towards the place where my tracks stopped and blurred back, holding my breath the last few feet. Just before the imprint of my steps began to waver, I halted and struck a match to the shiny paper of the folder. It flared orange and I threw it past the furthest mark I had made in the Martian sand.

The fire turned to a deep, deep laboring red and died.

I returned to the car and Elizabeth.

* * *

Elizabeth sat across from me on the other side of the polished and gleaming table top. She had on a different gown than the night before, blue with a faint gunmetal figure. I still wore my tweeds of the morning. They were spotless and unsweated.

I watched the waiter carefully as he brought the food. I saw him and I saw Elizabeth's coquettish attitude towards him. Most of all, I saw that he had no nose.

After he had gone, I said, "They give us our air, Elizabeth."

She lifted her handsome shoulders. "What of that?"

I reached over the table and took her wrist.

"Don't you see?" I asked her. "They could cut it off anytime they liked. *They do*—when we do something they don't like."

Her light brown eyes darted.

"When *you* do something they don't like?" she said fiercely.

I ignored that. "Elizabeth, we have to take the next rocket back to Earth. I tell you it isn't safe among these people . . . or whatever they are."

She looked at me for a lingering second. *"You fool,"* she said. Her pulse was hammering under my fingertips. She jerked her wrist away.

Her breathing became shallower. "Why do you want to go back, Doug? To make money? To earn a living? Do you know how *disgusting* and degrading that is to me? Making a living is *dirty*. I hate it."

"Maybe that's why you married me," I said, without wanting to.

"Don't be so smug," Elizabeth said evenly. "I do as much to earn your salary as you do, darling. You would be eaten alive by campus politicians if it weren't for me."

"That's a lie," I said because I knew it was true.

I thought perhaps I saw a slight tic in her right cheek but I may have been wrong. She looked down and continued eating. I did too. The hunger we got at five-thirty was too strong to ignore.

"I want to go home because," I said carefully, "I can't love you here. They don't want me to."

"You should see some type of doctor, Doug."

I made myself stop eating. I didn't ask her what type. "You like things just the way they are?"

Elizabeth continued eating.

"Don't you—care for me at all?" I asked, a character in a Victorian drama.

She looked up finally. "I love you, you idiot." She sounded tired. Tired. "But it's so *tranquil* this way. It isn't like the pointless, circular rat-race on Earth. There's time for contemplation, time to think, make decisions . . . "

I got up from the table.

"What are you going to do with all your decisions?" I asked her. "Check them at the gate along with my—"

I headed upstairs. It was time to sleep. In the morning, Elizabeth and I would go for another sightseeing tour. In the evening, we would have dinner in the big, empty dining room once more.

It was a great life, but I was weakening.

* * *

Our air extended for a radius of thirty feet from the runabout, as nearly as I had been able to judge from my experiment. The paper wouldn't burn beyond that point. There wasn't enough oxygen to support combustion.

Martians didn't breathe, I decided. I had finally seen why the faces of the station attendant and the waiter and the others looked so flat and expressionless. They didn't have noses. Those were the facts I had to work on. I worked on them until I had a plan. My plan was primitive but I had a sound background in primitive traditions.

I drove across the desert and Elizabeth sat beside me, saying nothing.

The Change, the Difference, that was about us had not progressed. It was the same. The Difference was becoming familiar. Somehow that made it worse.

After a time, with power failing, I steered into a bright red station. I couldn't tell them apart. Maybe it was the same one. Maybe there was only one. If so, it was always just where we needed it.

The attendant shuffled out and attached our power cable to one of the spirals, flipping an external twist of metal on the column. He looked exactly like the waiter.

He bent down and inspected our wheels.

It was when he was examining the right front wheel and Elizabeth had gotten out and was quietly staring at the featureless landscape that I took from beneath my jacket the chair arm I had broken off and burned to a point.

I stepped out of the car in one movement and got the shaft of the arm under his chin. I reached around him and touched the stake to his heart. He was close to me to but he had no odor except one of oil and sand.

"Send us back home, to our world," I told him, laughing.

His body spasmed against me.

"No, Doug, no," Elizabeth cried. "They gave us the world—their world—don't make them take it away from us."

I stopped laughing. It sounded pretty bad, uncomfortably over the line.

"Baby, do you think they have given us Cloudcuckooland? Utopia?" I said loudly. "All they gave us is the works. We're in their *zoo*."

"*But—we're—free*," she said.

"Free? Free to get violently hungry at five-thirty? Free of having to worry about increasing our numbers? That's their worry. They will replace their specimens as needed. In the meantime they don't want to strain their facilities."

Elizabeth turned, mouth opening, soft eyes on the runabout.

"We had movement, not freedom," I told her fast, my grip on the attendant. "Remember Kenya State Park? The Martians refined it. They give the animals the cars and let them drive around showing themselves off. Maybe that's how the lions in Kenya feel."

The attendant began squirming spiritedly. I took a deep breath and held it. I wondered why they hadn't cut off the oxygen before this. I pressed the point of my stake deeper. "Send us home," I rasped.

The attendant began moving. I couldn't stop him. He dragged me along.

He checked the cable connection with the spiral and flipped the outside twist of metal. He turned. He checked the cable connection with the spiral . . .

I hit him on the shoulder with my stake. He flipped the outside twist of metal, disconnected the cable, and stowed it back in our runabout. He shuffled back inside the station.

I turned to Elizabeth. She was staring, chewing on the back of her hand, sobbing inside her throat.

"We don't have to worry about him," I said. "He just works here."

The horses trotted up and looked at us.

I dropped my eyes to the foolish stake gripped in my hand. I was a rube who had mistaken the trained monkey in the cage outside the gates for the zookeeper.

I looked at Elizabeth. She had sensed all along that the waiter and the attendant, if there were more than one, were in no remote way human. That was why, perhaps without thinking, she had tried so hard to get a normal, masculine response out of them.

The horses or what looked like horses were still observing me.

They didn't look like intelligent creatures, but did I, with my charred stake?

Elizabeth and I were trapped in the zoo, all reason said. So naturally I discarded reason as useless, and charged the beasts with my weapon and an enraged bellow.

A sharper sound cut across my yell as, dispassionately and with a startling new-found facility, I lined up the thrust of my sharp instrument with the heavy chest muscles of a big bay. I was choked with air starvation but I didn't care.

The sound was a whinny of terror . . . and I got a message, somewhere in here. It was not a compliment. Even after I got it, I held on to my stake, and that clinched it.

I took Elizabeth's limp, almost dead hand and led her back to the runabout. She didn't drive. I didn't either. It headed back toward the Inn.

"They are sending us home," I said.

Even after centuries of dealing with Earthmen, the Martians were not able to cope with beings who, even deprived of the common processes of life and therefore dead unless they stopped resisting, continued to resist. Their horror and fear and disgust demanded that they rid themselves of at least these particular specimens of the species.

"We're going home," I repeated for my wife.

"How?" Elizabeth asked, almost as if she were interested.

"The same way we came," I said, "The same way that nobleman in the Charles Fort book you used to like so well came."

Elizabeth finally presented me with her gaze.

"We will walk around the horses," I told her.

* * *

So have another drink, Mrs. Halloran. To tell you the God's truth, I don't usually drink like this, but when I drink like this, Mrs. Halloran, I tell you the God's truth. And *that*, Mrs. Halloran, is that I wasn't glad to see you at all like I said I was. Horse wipes off on people like you. You look like horse. You smell like horse. When you came prancing and whinnying in here and reared up and put your fetlocks on the bar here, Mrs. Halloran, frankly, you gave me the heaves. I didn't want to tell you that story. I wanted to forget that story.

But anyway, have another drink . . . Eddie! Fill us up.

Oh . . . She did, huh? Oh.

Well, give me one then, and one for yourself, Eddie, and hooray for Henry Ford.

AFTERWORD

I had originally submitted this story to *Fantasy and Science Fiction*, but I was asked if I would be willing for it to be used in their new companion magazine, *Venture*. I agreed, hoping that the next sale would be to the more prestigious *F&SF* (as it turned out to be). Then I was asked if I minded a few little changes being made by Theodore Sturgeon. I said no, I wouldn't mind. At that time, Sturgeon would be on many people's list of the top three science fiction writers, and just about everybody's list of the top six. I read the revised version and I could see Sturgeon had improved the story.

Often, a writer is asked to make changes in a story or they are made for him. I have found that those changes may be what I consider for the worst, or are simply a different way of doing it, no better, no worse. Very seldom do I find the changes really constitute an improvement. If you are trying to make a living from writing, and are not as fearless as, say, Harlan Ellison, you will put up with it. But with Sturgeon's changes, there was no argument.

Then I was asked if I would share a byline with Sturgeon. I agreed. It certainly could do me no harm to be associated with so important a name. But finally, Sturgeon decided he did not have enough input to deserve a byline. I would have been more than willing, but I would say Sturgeon's contributions constituted no more than twenty per cent of the story.

Unlike Isaac Asimov, Robert Bloch, and a number of other SF writers I knew well, I had only spoken to Sturgeon a few times at conventions. Still I was pleased that we had our little collaboration together.

THE PLACE WHERE CHICAGO WAS

It was late December of 1983. Abe Danniels knew that the streets and sidewalks of Jersey City moved under their own power and that half the families in America owned their own helicopters. He was pleased with these signs of progress. But he was sweating. He thought he was getting athlete's foot instead of athletic legs from walking from the New Jersey coast to just outside of Marshall, Illinois.

The heat was unbearable.

The road shimmered before him in rows of sticky black ribbon, on which nothing moved. Nothing but him.

He passed a signal post that said "Caution—Slow" in a gentle but commanding voice. He staggered on toward a reddish metallic square set on a thin column of bluish concrete. It was what they called a sign, he decided.

Danniels drooped against the sign and fanned his face with his sweat-ringed straw cowboy hat. The thing seemed to have something to say about the mid-century novelist, James Jones, in short, terse words.

The rim of the hat crumpled in his fist. He stood still and listened.

There *was* a car coming.

It would almost *have* to stop, he reasoned. A man couldn't stand much of this Illinois winter heat. The driver might leave him to die on the road if he didn't stop. Therefore he would stop.

He jerked out the small pouch from the sash of his jeans. Inside the special plastic the powder was dry. He rubbed some between his hands briskly, to build up the static electricity, and massaged it into his hair.

The metal of the Jones plaque was fairly shiny. Under the beating noon sun it cast a pale reflection back at Danniels. His hair looked a reasonably uniform white now.

He started to draw the string on the pouch, then dipped his hand in and scooped his palm up to his mouth. He chewed on the stuff while he was securing the nearly flat bag in his sash. He swallowed the dough; the powder had been flour.

Danniels took the hat from beneath his arm, set it to his head and at last faced the direction of the engine whine.

The roof, hood and wheels moved over the curve of the horizon and Danniels saw that the car was a brandless classic which probably still had some of the original, indestructible Model A left in it.

He pondered a moment on whether to thumb or not to thumb.

He thumbed.

The rod squealed to a stop exactly even with him. A door unfolded and a voice like a stop signal said flatly, "Get in."

Danniels got in. The driver was a teen-ager in a loose scarlet tunic and a spangled W.P.A. cap. The youth wouldn't have been bad-looking except for a sullen expression and a rather girlish turn of cheek, completely devoid of beard line. Danniels wrote him off as a prospective member of the Wolf Pack in a year or two.

But not just yet, he fervently hoped.

"Going far? I'm not," said the driver.

Danniels adjusted the knees of his trousers. "I'm going to—near where Chicago used to be."

"Huh?"

Danniels had forgotten the youth of his companion. "I mean I'm going to where you can't go any further."

The driver nodded smugly, relieved that the threat to the vastness of his knowledge had been dismissed. "I get you, Pop. I guess I can take you close to where you're headed."

They rode on in silence, both relieved that they didn't have to try to span the void between age and position with words.

"You aren't anywhere near starvation, are you?" the driver said suddenly, uneasy.

"No," Danniels said. "Anyway I've got money"

"Woodrow Wilson! I'll pull in at the next joint."

The next joint was carved out of the flat cross-section of hill that looked unmistakably like a strip ridge of a Colorado copper mine, but wasn't . . . even barring the fact that this was Illinois. The rectangle of visible dinner was color-fused aluminum from between No. Two and Korea.

Danniels was glad to get into the shockingly cold air-conditioning. It was constant, if unhealthy. The chugging unit in the car failed a heartbeat every now and then for a sickening wave of heat.

The two of them pulled up wire chairs to a linoleum-top table in a mirrored corner. A faint purple hectographed menu was stuck between appropriately colored plastic squeeze bottles labeled **MUSTARD** and **BLOOD**.

Danniels knew what the menu would say but he unfolded it and checked.

Steaks

Plankton 90
Juicy, rich-red tantalizing hamburger 17

Accessories

Mashed potatoes 40
Delectable oysters, all you can eat 09
Peas 35
Rich, fragrant cheese, large slice 02

Drinks

Coke 50
Milk, the forbidden wine of nature 01
Coffee (without) 50
Coffee (with) 02

A fat girl in white came to the table.

Danniels tossed the menu on the table. "I'll take the meat dinner," he said.

The teen-ager stared hard at the table top. "So will I."

"Good citizens," the waitress said, but the revulsion crept into her voice over the professional hardness.

Danniels looked carefully at his companion. "You aren't used to ordering meat."

"Pop," the youth began. Danniels waited to be told that being short of cash was none of his business. "Pop, on my leg. Kill it, kill it!"

Danniels leaned over the table startled and curious. A cockroach was feeling its way along a thin meridian of vari-colored jeans. Danniels pinched it up without injuring it and deposited it on the floor. It scurried away.

"Your kind make me sick," the driver said in lieu of thanks. "You act like a Fanatic but you're a Meat-Eater. How do you blesh that?"

Danniels shrugged. He did not have to explain anything to this kid. He couldn't be stranded.

The kid was under the same encephalographic inversion as the rest of the world. No human being could directly or indirectly commit murder, as long as the broadcasting stations every nation on earth maintained in self-dense continued to function.

These mechanical brain waves coated every mind with enforced pacifism. They could have just as easily broadcast currents that would have made minds swell with love or happiness. But world leaders had universally agreed that these conditions were too narcotic for the common people to endure.

Pacifism was vital to the survival of the planet.

War could not go on killing; but governments still had to go on winning wars. War became a game. The International War Games were held every two years. With pseudo-H bombs and mock-germ warfare, countries still effectively eliminated cities and individuals. A "destroyed" city was off-1imits for twenty years. Nothing could go in or out for that period. Most cities had provided huge food deposits for emergencies.

Before the Famine.

Some minds were more finely attuned to the encephalographic inversion than others. People so in tune with the wavelength of pacifism could not only not kill another human being, they could not even kill an animal. Vegetarianism was thrust upon a world not equipped for it. Some—like Danniels—who could not kill, still found themselves able to eat what others had killed. Others who could not kill or eat any once-living thing—even plants—rapidly starved to death. They were quickly forgotten.

Almost as forgotten as the Jonahs.

The War Dead.

Any soldier or civilian "killed" outside of a major disaster area (where he would be subject to the twenty years) became a man without a country—or a world. They were tagged with green hair by molecular exchange and sent on their way to starve, band together, reach a disaster area (where they would be accepted for the duration of the disaster), starve, or starve.

Anyone who in anyway communicated with a Jonah or even recognized the existence of one automatically became a Jonah himself.

It was harsh. And if it wasn't better than war it was quieter.

And more permanent.

The counterman with a greasy apron and hairy forearms served the plates. The meat had been lightly glazed to bring out the aroma and flavor but the blood was still a pink sheen on the ground meat. There were generous side dishes of cheese and milk. Even animal by-products were passed up by the majority of vegetarians. Eggs had been the first to be dropped—after all, every egg was a potential life. Milk and associated products came to be spurned through sheer revulsion by association. Besides, milk was intended only to feed the animal's own offspring, wasn't it?

Danniels squirted blood generously from its squeeze bottle. Even vegetarians used a lot of it. It gave their plankton the gory look the human animal craved. Of course it was not really blood, only a kind of tomato paste. When Danniels had been a boy people called it catsup.

He tried to dig into his steak with vengeance but it tasted of ashes. Meat was his favorite food; he was in no way a vegetarian. But the thought of the Famine haunted him. Vegetable food was high in price and ration points. Most people were living on 2500 calories a day. It wasn't quite starvation and it wasn't quite a full stomach. It was hard on anybody who did more than an average amount of work. It was especially hard on children.

The Meat-Eaters helped relieve the situation. Some, with only the minimum of influence from the Broadcasters, ate nothing but meat. They were naturally aggressive morons who were doing no one favors, potential members of a Wolf Pack.

Danniels knew how to end the Famine.

The mob that was the men he had commanded had hunted him in the hills below Buffalo, and he had been hungry, with no time to eat, or rest, or sleep. Only enough time to think. He couldn't stop thinking. Panting over a smothered spark of campfire, smoldering moss and leaves, he thought. Drinking sparkling but polluted water from a twisting mountain stream and trying unsuccessfully to trap silver shavings of fish with his naked hands, he thought.

His civilian job was that of a genopseudoxenobeastimacrobiologist, a specialized field with peacetime applications that had come out of the War Games—specialized to an almost comic-opera intensity. He knew virtually everything about almost nothing at all. Yet, delirious with hunger, from this he fashioned in his mind a way to provide food for everybody. Even Jonahs.

After they caught him—weeks before the Tag spot would have faded off—he wasn't sure whether his idea had been a sick dream or not. But he intended to find out. He wouldn't let any other mob stop him from that.

Danniels had decided he was against mobs, whether their violence and stupidity was social or anti-social. People are better as individuals.

The driver of the hot-rod was also picking at his food uncertainly. Probably a social vegetarian, Danniels supposed. An irresponsible faddist.

The counterman stopped staring and cleared his throat apologetically. "This ain't the Ritz but it don't look good for customers to sit with hats on."

Danniels knew that applied to only non-vegetarians, but he put his Stetson, reluctantly, on an aluminum tree.

The teen-ager looked up. And did not go back to the food.

Danniels knew that he had been found out.

The counterman went back to wiping down the bar.

The youth was still looking at Danniels.

"You better eat if you don't want me to be discovered," Danniels said gently.

Young eyes moved back and forth, searching, not finding.

"It won't do you any good to run," Danniels continued. "The waitress and the counterman will swear they had nothing to do with me. But you were driving me, eating with me."

"You can't let even a Jonah die," the youngster said in a hoarse whisper that barely carried across the table.

Danniels shook his head sadly. "It won't work. You might have slowed down enough to let me grab onto the rear bumper or tossed me out some food. But you took me into your car, sat down at a table with me."

"And this is the thanks I get!"

Danniels felt his face flush. "Look, son, this isn't a game where you can afford to play by good sportsmanship. That's somebody else's rules, designed to make sure you get at least no better a break than anyone else. You have to play by your rules—designed to give you the best possible break. Let's get out of here."

He wolfed the last bite and jammed his hat back on his head, pulling it down about his ears. The sweat band had rubbed the flour off his hair in a narrow band. A band of green. The mark of the Jonah.

In the last war games, Danniels had come into the sights of a Canadian's diffusion rifle. For six months he had worn a cancerous badge of luminosity over his heart. Until his comrades had trapped him and through a system similar to the one their rifles employed turned his hair to green and cast him out.

Danniels scooped up both checks and with deep pain paid both of them to save time. He wanted to get his companion out of there before he broke.

The heat struck at their faces like jets of boiling water. The authorities said nuclear explosion had had nothing to do with changing climatic conditions so radically, but *something* had.

The two of them were walking towards the parked car when the Wolf Pack got to them.

II

The horrible part was that Danniels knew they wouldn't kill him. No one could kill.

But the members of the Wolf Packs wanted to. They were the professional soldiers, policemen, prizefighters and gangsters of a society that had rejected them. They were able to resist some of the pacifism of the Broadcasters. In fact, they were able to resist quite a lot.

The first one was a round shouldered little man with silver spectacles. He kicked Danniels in the pit of the stomach with steel-shod toes. A clean-cut athletic boy grabbed the running teen-ager and ripped the red tunic halfway off. From the pavement Danniels at last isolated the doubt that had been nagging him. His companion wore a tight tee-shirt under the coat. She was a girl.

Danniels saw a heavy shoe aimed at his face but it went far afield. Running feet went past him completely.

He was left alone, unharmed, with only the breath knocked out of him momentarily.

They were closing in on the girl who had picked him up.

This Pack was all men, although there were female and co-ed groups just as vicious. Beating up a girl, Danniels knew, would give an added sexual kick to their usual masochosadism.

They were a Pack. A mob. They were like the soldiers who had hunted him down and had him permanently tagged a Jonah. His men had been looked upon favorably by his society, while the Wolf Pack was so ill-favored it was completely ignored in absolute contempt. But they were the same in the essentials: a mob.

And once again Danniels, who was incapable of harming the smallest living creature, wanted to kill men. But he couldn't.

All his life he had experienced this mad fury of desire and it shamed him. He wanted to destroy men of stupidity, greed and brutality on sight. Any other kind of conflict with them was weak compromise.

At times, he wondered if this atavistic if pro-survival trait had not shamed him so much that he over-compensated for it by violently refusing to take any kind of life. Like all men of his time, he asked himself: how much of my mind is the Broadcasters' and how much me?

If he couldn't destroy, he could defend.

With the idea still only half-formed, he lurched to his feet and stumbled into the side of the hot-rod. He fumbled open the heated metal door and slid under the wheel.

He thumbed the drive on savagely and roared down on the mob.

Rubber screamed, whined and smelled as he applied the brakes just soon enough for the men to jump out of the way—away from the girl.

He folded back the door he hadn't latched, leaned down, grabbed the teen-ager by the leg and dragged her bruised form bumping up into the car.

The little man with silver glasses tried to reach into the car.

Danniels swung the door back into his face.

The glasses didn't break; but everything else did.

With one foot under the girl and the other on her, Danniels tagged the illegal acceleration wire most cars had rigged under the dashboard and raced away into the brassy sunshine.

She was slouched against his shoulder when the stars blazed out in the moonless night.

Tires hummed beneath them and their headlights ate up the white-striped typewriter ribbon before them.

The girl opened her eyes, hesitated as they focused on the weave pattern of denim in his shirt, and said, "Where are they?"

"Back there some place," Danniels told her. "They followed in their cars, a couple on motorcycles. But they must have been scared of traffic cops on the main highway. They dropped out."

She sat up and ran her fingers through her cropped mouse-colored hair. Her quick glance at him was questioning; but she answered her own question and reluctantly absorbed the truth of it. She knew he knew.

The girl huddled in the tatters of her bright tunic.

"Just what do you expect to get out of helping me?" she asked.

Danniels kept his eyes on the road. "A free trip to Chicago."

"You'll get us both arrested!" she shrilled. "Nobody can get past those roadblocks."

He nodded to himself, not caring if she saw the gesture in the uncertain light from the auto gauges.

"All right," she admitted. "I know what Chicago is. That's no crime."

"You ought to," Danniels said. "You're from there."

She was tired. It was a moment before she could continue fighting. "That's foolish—"

He hadn't been sure. If she hadn't hesitated he might have given up the notion.

"That getup was what was foolish," Danniels snorted. "Anybody would know you were trying to hide something as soon as they found out the masquerade."

"You wouldn't have found it out," she said, "if one of that Pack hadn't torn my jacket off."

"I really don't know. It might be animal magnetism, if there is such a thing. But I can't be around a woman for long without knowing it. I repeat: why?"

"I—I didn't know what they would do to a girl outside."

"For Peace sake, why did you have to come out at all?"

The girl was silent for a mile. "Most Chicagoans think the rest of the world has reverted to barbarism," she told him.

"A common complaint of city dwellers," he observed.

"Don't joke!" she demanded.

"Our food is running out. We have enough to last five more years if the present birth-death cycle maintains itself."

Danniels whistled mournfully.

"And you have—let's see —about seven more years to go."

She nodded.

"I came out to see what chance there was of ending this senseless blockade."

"None at all," he snapped. "No one is going to risk breaking the rules of the War Games just to save a few million lives."

"But they will have to! The Broadcasters will make them."

"You would be surprised at how much doublethink people can practice about not killing," he assured her from bitter, personal experience. "They don't know for certain that you will be starving in there, so they will be free to keep you inside."

The girl straightened her shoulders, emphasizing the femininity of her slender form.

"We'll tell them," she said. "*I'll* tell them."

Danniels almost smiled, but not quite. His hands tightened on the steering wheel and he kept his eyes to the moving circle of light against the night.

"You open your mouth about Chicago to the authorities or anyone else and they will slap you under sedation and keep you there until you die of old age. They used to drop escapees back into the cities by parachute. But too many of them were inadvertently killed; they are more subtle these days. By the way," he said very casually, "how did you escape?"

She told him where to go in a primitive, timeless fashion.

"No," Danniels said. "I'm going to Chicago."

"Not with me," the girl assured him quietly. "We have enough to feed without bringing in another Jonah. Besides you might be an F.B.I. man or something trying to find our escape route."

"I'd be a Mountie then. The F.B.I. has deteriorated pretty badly. Spent itself on political security. The Royal Canadian Mounted Police lends us men and women during peacetime. Up until the War Games anyway—even though Britain would like to see us constantly disrupted. But," he said heavily, "I am not a government agent of any kind. Just the Jonah I appear to be."

She shivered. "I can't take the responsibility. I can't either expose our escape route—or bring in another mouth, to bring starvation a moment closer."

"Look, what can I call you?" he demanded in exasperation.

"Julie. Julie Amprey."

"Abe Danniels. Look, Julie—"

"You were named after Lincoln?" she asked quietly.

"A long time after. Look, Julie, I want to get into Chicago because of the old Milne Laboratories." He caught his breath for a long second. "They are still standing?"

Julie nodded and looked ahead, through the insect-spotted windscreen. "Partial operation, when I left."

Danniels gave a low whistle.

"Lord, after all these years!"

"We manage."

"Fine! Julie, I'm sure that if I can get back in a laboratory I can find a way of ending this condemned Famine—inside Chicago and outside."

"That sounds a little like delusions of grandeur to me," the girl said uncertainly.

"It was my field for ten years. Before the last War Games. I had time to think while my platoon was hunting me down, after I had been tagged out. I thought faster than I ever thought before."

Julie studied his face for a long moment.

"What was your idea?"

"The encephalographic inversion patterns of the Broadcasters," he said quickly, "can be applied to animals as well as human beings, on the right frequencies. Even microscopic animals. Bacteria. If you control the actions of bacteria, you control their reproduction. They could be made to multiply and assume different forms—the form of food, for example."

Danniels took a deep breath and plunged into his idea as they drove on through the deepening night. He talked and explained to her, and, in doing so, he clarified points that he hadn't been sure of himself.

He stopped at last because his throat was momentarily too dry to continue.

"It's too big a responsibility for me," Julie said.

Defeat stung him so badly he was afraid he had slumped physically. But it won't be permanent defeat, he told himself. I've come this far and I'll find some other way into Chicago,

"I haven't the right to turn down something this big," Julie said. "I'll have to let you put it to the mayor and the city council."

He relaxed a trifle, condemning himself for the weak luxury. He couldn't afford it yet. He ran his fingers through his flour-dusted green hair and the electricity of the movement dragged off much of the whiteness. His skin, like that of most people, had been given a slight negative charge by molecularization to repel dirt and germs. The powder was anxious to remove itself and dye or bleach refused to take at all.

"We're nearing the rim of the first blockade zone," Danniels told the girl. "Where to?"

"Circle around to first unrestricted beach of the lake shore."

"And then?"

"Underwater."

Illegal traffic in and out of Disaster Areas was not completely unheard of. There was a small but steady flow both ways that the authorities could not or would not completely check. The patrols seemingly were as alert as humanly possible. Capture meant permanent oblivion for Disaster Residents under sedation, while Outsiders got prescribed periods of Morphinvertinduced antipode depression of the brain, a rather sophisticated but effective form of torture. A few minutes under the drug frequently had an introspective duration of years. Therefore, under the typical sentence of three months, a felon lived several lifetimes in constant but varying stages of acute agony and post-hysteric terror.

While few personalities survived, many useful human machines were later salvaged by skillful lobotomies.

Lake Michigan beaches were pretty good, Danniels observed. Better than at Hawaii. This one had been cleaned up for a subdivision that had naturally never been completed. It had been christened Falstaff Cove, although it was almost a mathematically straight half mile of off-white sand.

He had shifted to four-wheel drive at the girl's direction and bored through the sand to the southernmost corner of the beach, where it blurred into weeds, rocks, dirt and incredible litter. He braked. The car settled noticeably.

"There's a two-man submarine out there in the water under the overhang," Julie said without prompting. "We got it from the Armed Forces Day display at Soldier's Field."

"What I'd like to know is how you get the car in and out of it?" Danniels said.

Anger, disgust and fatigue crossed the girl's face. It was after all, a very young face, he thought. "We have Outside contacts of sorts," she said. "Nobody trusts them very much."

He nodded. There was a lot of money in the Federal Reserve Vaults inside the city.

The two of them got out of the car.

Julie stripped off her jeans, revealing the bottom half of a swimsuit and nicely turned, but pale, legs. "We'll have to wade out to the sub."

"What about the car?" Danniels asked. "Is your friend going to pick it up?"

"No! They don't know about this place."

He reached in the window and turned the ignition. "Want me to run it off into the water? You don't want to tag this spot for the authorities."

"No, I-I guess not. I don't know what to do! I'm not used to this kind of thing. I don't know why I ever come. We paid an awful lot for the car . . ."

He found the girl's wailing unpleasant. "It's your car, but take my advice. Let me get rid of it for you.

"But," she protested, "if you run it into the water they can see from the air in daylight. I know. They used to spot our sub. Why not run it off into those weeds and little trees? They'll hide it and maybe we could get it later."

It wasn't a bad idea but he didn't feel like admitting it. He gunned the rod into the tangle of undergrowth.

Danniels came back to the girl with his arms and face laced with scratches from the limbs.

He tried to roll his trousers up at the cuff but they wouldn't stay. So he would spend a soggy ten minutes while they dried.

He told the girl to go ahead and he went after her, marking the spongy wet sand and slapping into the white-scummed, very blue water.

The tiny submarine was just where Julie had said it would be. He waited impatiently as she worked the miniature airlock.

They squeezed down into the metallic hollowness of the interior and Julie screwed the hatch shut, a Mason lid inappropriately on a can of sardines.

There were a lot of white-on-black dials that completely baffled Danniels. He had never been particularly mechanically minded. His field was closer to pure science than practical engineering. Because of this, rather than in spite of it, he had great respect for engineering.

It bothered him being in such close quarters with a woman after the months of isolation as a Jonah, but he had enough of the conventions of society fused into him and enough other problems to attempt easing his discomfort.

"It isn't much further," Julie at last assured him.

He was becoming bored to the point of hysteria. For the past several months he hadn't had much diversion but he had not been confined to what was essentially an oil drum wired for light and sound.

One of the lights changed size and pattern.

He found himself tensing. "That?" He pointed.

"Sonadar," Julie hissed. "Patrol boat above us. Don't make any noise."

Danniels pictured the heavily equipped police boat droning past above them and managed to keep quite silent.

Something banged on the hull.

It came from the outside and it rang against the port side, then the starboard. The rhythm was the same, unbroken. Danniels knew somehow the noise from both sides were made by the same agency. Something with a twelve-foot reach.

Something that knew the Morse code.

Da-da-da. Dit-dit-dit. Da-da-da.

S.O.S.

Help.

"It's not the police," Julie said. "We've heard it before."

She added, "They used to dump non-dangerous amounts of radioactives into the lake," as she decided the police boat had gone past and started up the engines again.

Danniels never forgot that call for help. Not as long as he lived.

III

The electron microscope revealed no significant change in the pattern of the bacteria.

Danniels decided to feed the white mice. He got out of his plastic chair and took a small cloth bag of corn from the warped, sticking drawer of the lab table.

Rationing out a handful of the withered kernels, he went down the rows of cages. A few, with steel instead of aluminum wiring, were flecked with rust. The mice inside were all healthy. Danniels was not using them in experiments; he was incapable of taking their lives. But some experimenter after him might use them. In any case, he was also incapable of letting them starve to death.

He had been out of jail less than two weeks.

The city council had thrown him into the Cook County lockup until they decided what to do with him. He hadn't known what happened to the girl, Julie Amprey, for bringing him back with her.

He was surprised to see Chicago functioning as well as it was after thirteen years of isolation. There were still a few cars and trucks running here and there, although most people walked or rode bicycles. But the atmosphere seemed heavy and the buildings dirtier than ever. The city had the aura of oppression and decay he thought of as belonging to nineteenth century London.

Danniels had waited out New Year's and St. Valentine's in a cell between a convicted burglar and an endless parade of drunks. Finally, two weeks ago the mayor himself came, apologizing profusely but without much feeling. Danniels was escorted to the old Milne Laboratory buildings and told to go to work on his idea. He had, they said, two weeks to produce. And he was getting nowhere.

His deadline was up. The deadline of the real world. But the one he had given himself was much, much more pressing.

"You'll kill yourself if you don't get some sleep," the girl's voice said behind his back.

Danniels closed the drawer on the nearly depleted sack of grain. It was the girl. Julie Amprey. He had been expecting her but not anticipating her. He didn't like her very much. The only reason he could conceive for her venture Outside was a search for thrills. It might be understandable, if immature, in a man; but he found it unattractive in a woman. He had no illusions about masculine superiority, but women were socially, if not physically and emotionally, ill-equipped for simple adventuring.

Julie was more attractive dressed in a woman's clothes, even if they were a dozen years out of style. Her hair had a titian glint. She was perhaps really too slender for the green knit dress.

"It's a big job," he said. "I'm beginning to think it's a lifetime job."

He half-turned and motioned awkwardly at the lab table and the naked piece of electronics.

"That's the encephalographic projector I jury-rigged," he explained.

"You can spare me the fifty-cent tour," Julie said.

He wondered how she had managed to get so irritating in such a short lifetime. "There's not much else to see," Danniels grunted. "I've got some reaction out of the bacteria, but I can't seem to control their reproduction or channel them into a food-producing cycle."

Julie tossed her head.

"Oh, I can tell you why you haven't done that," she said.

He didn't like the way she said that. "Why?"

"You don't *want* to control them," Julie said simply. "If you really control them, you'll cause some to be recessive. You'll breed some strains out of existence. You'll *kill* some of them. And you don't want to kill any living thing."

She was wrong.

He wanted to kill her.

But he couldn't. She was right about the bacteria. He should have realized it before. He had planned for almost a year, and worked for two weeks; and this girl had walked in and destroyed everything in five minutes. But she was right; he spun towards the door.

"Where are you going?" she demanded.

"I'm leaving. See what somebody else can do with the idea."

"But where are you going?" Julie repeated.

"Nowhere."

And he was absolutely right.

Danniels walked aimlessly through the littered streets for the rest of the day and night. He couldn't remember walking at night, but neither could he remember staying anywhere when he discovered dawn in the sky.

It was that time of dawn that looks strangely like an old two-color process movies that they show on TV occasionally all orange and green, with no yellow to it at all, when even the truest black seems only an off-brown—or a sinister purple.

He shivered in the chill of morning and decided what to do.

He would have to walk around for a few hours even yet.

The drink his friend, Paul, placed before him was not entirely distinct. Neither were the bills he had in his hand. It was money the mayor's hireling had given him to use for laboratory supplies. Danniels peeled off a bill of uncertain denomination and gave it to his friend. Paul seemed pleased. He put it into the pocket of his white shirt, the pocket eight inches below and slightly to the left of the black bow tie, and polished the bar briskly.

Danniels picked up the glass and sipped silently until it was empty.

"Do you want to talk about anything, Abe?" Paul asked solicitously.

"No," Danniels said cheerfully. "Just give me another drink."

"Sure thing."

Danniels studied his green hair in the glass. Here, the mark of the Jonah wasn't important. Not yet. But he would be unwelcome even here after the time of Disaster ran out. He would have to move on sooner or later. Eventually—why not now? That slogan went better than the one in pink light over the mirror—**The Beer That Made Milwaukee Famous.** There hadn't been any Milwaukee beer here for thirteen years. Most of the stuff came out of bathtubs.

Why not now?

He smoothed another bill on the damp polished wood and negotiated his way through the hazy room.

Outside, he turned a corner and the city dropped away from him. He seemed to be in a giant amusement park with acres of empty ground patterned off in squares by unwinking dots of light.

He grinned to himself, changed direction with great care, and started down the one-way street to the lake front.

He heard the footsteps behind him.

Danniels put his palm to the brick wall, scaling posters, and turned.

The clean-cut young man smiled disarmingly. "I saw you in at Paul's. You'll never make it home under your own power. Better let me take you in my cab."

Danniels knocked him out on his feet with a clean right cross.

He blinked down at the boy. Self-preservation had become instinctive with him during his months as a wandering Jonah.

Gnawing at his under lip, he studied the twisted way the supposed cabbie lay. If he really were . . . Danniels patted the man down and brought something out of a hip pocket.

He inspected the leather blackjack, weighing it critically in his hand.

It slid out of his palm and thudded heavily on the cracked sidewalk.

Danniels shrugged and grinned and moved unsteadily away. Towards the lake.

The lake looked gray and winterish.

There was no help for it.

Danniels swung his leg over the rust-spotted railing and looked down to where the water lapped at crumbling bricks blotched with green. He peered out over the water. Only a few miles to the beach where he had left the car parked in the undergrowth. He would have preferred to use the little sub, but he could swim it if he had to.

The surface below showed clearly in the globe lights.

Danniels dived.

Before he hit the water, he remembered that he should have taken off some of his clothes.

When he parted the icy foam with his body, he knew he had committed suicide. And he realized that that had been what he intended to do all along.

There was something in the lake holding him, and it had a twelve-foot reach.

It kept holding on to him under the surface of green ice and begging him for help. He couldn't breathe, and he couldn't help. Of the two, not being able to help seemed the worse. Not breathing wasn't so bad . . . It hurt to breathe. It choked him. It was very unpleasant to breathe. He had much preferred not breathing to this.

Some time later, he opened his eyes.

A small, round-faced man was staring down at him through slender-framed spectacles. For a moment he thought it was the man in whose face he had smashed the car door at the diner weeks before. But this man was different—among other things his glasses were gold, not silver. Yet he was also the same. Danniels knew the signs of the Wolf Pack.

"How's your foot?" the little man asked in a surprisingly full-bodied voice.

Danniels instantly became aware of a dull sub-pain sensation in the toes of his left foot. He looked over the crest of his chest and saw the foot, naked below the cuff of his wrinkled trousers. The three smaller toes were red. No, maroon. A red so dark it was almost black. Fainter streaks of red shot away from the toes, following the tendon.

Danniels swallowed. "The foot doesn't feel so bad, but I think it is."

"We may have to operate," the small man said eagerly.

"How did I get out of the lake?"

"Joel. The man you knocked out. He came to and followed you. Naturally, he had to save your life. He banged your foot up dragging you ashore."

Or afterwards, Danniels thought.

Abruptly, the stranger was gone and a door was closing and latching on the other side of the room.

Danniels tried to rise and fell back, his head floating around somewhere above him. Maybe a Wolf Pack member would have to save his life but he wouldn't have to bring him home and nurse him back to health.

Why?

He fell asleep without even trying to guess the answer.

He woke when they brought food to him.

Danniels finished with the tray and sat it aside.

The small man who had identified himself as Richard beamed. "I think you are strong enough to attend the celebration tonight."

Danniels did feel stronger after rest and food, but at the same time he felt vaguely dizzy and his leg was beginning to hurt. "What kind of a celebration?" he asked.

Richard chuckled. "Don't worry. You'll like it."

Danniels had seen the same expression of the faces of hosts at stag dinners; but with a Wolf Pack it was hard to know what to expect.

IV

The place he was in did not seem to be a house after all. Danniels leaned on the shoulder of Richard, who helped him along solicitously. They entered a large chamber nearly a hundred feet wide. There were people there. It wasn't crowded but there were many people standing around the walls. A lot of them were holding three-foot lengths of wood.

Richard led him to a chair, the only one apparent in the room.

"I'll go tell 'em we're ready now," the small man said, chuckling.

Danniels looked around slowly at the shadowed faces. Of those holding clubs, he knew only the man Richard had told him was Joel, the man who had pulled him from Lake Michigan. Apparently the ones with clubs were members of the Pack, while the others were observers and potential members. Among these, he spotted a member of the city council.

And Julie.

She stood in a loose sweater and skirt, her hands hugging her elbows, eyes intent on the empty center of the room. Danniels was reminded of some of the women he had seen at unorthodox political meetings.

Danniels was surprised to find that he wanted to talk to her. He might try hobbling over to her or calling her over to him. But with the instinct he had developed while being hunted, he knew it was wrong to call attention to the two of them together.

He noticed that he was in line with the door. Julie would have to pass by him when she left . . . after the celebration.

"The celebration begins in five minutes."

Someone he hadn't seen had shouted into the big room. The words bounced back slightly and hung suspended.

The people's waiting became an activity. Tension lived in the room.

And then the cat was released.

The Pack members moved apart from the rest and struck at the scrawny yellow beast. The cat didn't make it very far down the line. The men from the other end of the room moved up quickly to be in on the kill.

The clubs rose and fell even after it was clear there was no reason for it.

Their ranks parted and they left their handiwork where it could be admired.

It must be hard to find animals in a closed city like this, Danniels thought. It must be quite a treat to find one to beat to death.

He sat and waited for them to leave. But he found the Celebration was just beginning. The group was laughing and talking. Now that it was over they wanted to talk about it the rest of the evening. They had created death.

He searched out Julie Amprey again. She was looking at what they did. He thought she was sick at first. His lips thinned. Yes, she was sick.

Her eyes suddenly met his. Shock washed over her face, and in the next moment she was moving to him.

"So," she said coolly, "you found out my little secret. This is where I get my kicks."

He nodded, thinking of nothing to say.

"Did you ever read them?" she asked breathlessly. "All the old banned books—Poe and—Spillane and Proust. The pornography of death. I grew up on them, so you see there's no harm in them. Look at me."

"You want to kill?" Danniels asked her.

She lit an expensive king-size cigarette. "Yes," she exhaled. "I thought I might join a Pack on the Outside. But, you'll remember, I didn't quite make it. I couldn't even kill a cockroach. I want to, but the damned Broadcasters keep interfering with me."

Richard came back, smiling broadly. "Well, Abe, has Miss Amprey been telling you of our plans to ruin the planet?"

Danniels was incredibly tired. He had been listening and arguing for hours.

"You're a scientist," Joel persisted. "Help us."

"There are different kinds of scientists," Danniels repeated. "I'm not a nuclear physicist."

"Right there." Richard tapped the pink rubber of his pencil against the map of Cook County. "Right there. An Armory no one else knows anything about. Enough H-bombs to wipe out human life on the planet. And rockets to send them in."

"The councilman may be lying," Danniels said. "How do you think he should happen to find it and no one else?"

"The information was in the city records," Richard said patiently, "but buried and coded so it would take twenty years to locate. Bureaucracy is an insidious evil, Abe."

Danniels rubbed his face with his palms. "I'm not even sure if I understand what you mean to do. You want to rocket the H-bombs out almost but not quite beyond Earth's gravitation and explode them so the fallout will be evenly distributed over the surface of the planet. You think it will cause no more than injury and destruction—"

"That's all," Joel said sharply.

Richard gave an eager nod.

They had had to convince themselves of that, he knew. "But why do you want to do anything as desperate as that?"

"Simple revenge." Richard's tone was even and cold. "And to show them what we can do if they don't cut off the Broadcasters." The small man's liquid brown eyes softened. "You've got to understand that we really don't want to kill people. Our actions are merely necessary demonstrations against insane visionary politics. I only want the Broadcasters shut off so I can do efficient police work—Joel, so that he can fight in the ring with the true will to win of a sportsman. The rest of us have equally good reasons."

"I think I understand," Danniels said. "I'll do what I can to help you."

Danniels was not surprised when Julie Amprey was in the raiding party. He was past the capacity for surprise.

He was getting around on his own today only because he was learning to stand the pain. It was worse. And he was weak and dizzy from a fever.

They had all managed to produce bicycles. Richard had even managed to find one for him with a tiny engine powered by solar-charged batteries.

Julie looked crisp and attractive in sweater and jeans. Joel was strikingly handsome in the clear sun, and even Richard looked like a jolly fatherly type.

As they wheeled down the street, Danniels was afraid only he with his wet, tossed green hair and drooping cheeks warped the holiday mood of those who in some other probability sequence were happy picnickers.

When they reached the place, Richard giggled nervously.

"It takes a code to open the hatch," he explained. "If Aldrich didn't decode it correctly there will be a small but effective chemical explosion in this area.

Danniels leaned against a maple, watching. The bicycles were parked in the brush and a shallow hole had been dug at an exact spot in the suburban park. Only a few inches below ground was the gray steel door flush with the level of grass.

Richard hummed as he worked a prosaic combination dial.

Finally there was a muffled click and a churning whine began.

The hatch raised jerkily and latched at right angles.

The Pack milled about the opening, excited. Joel got the honor of going down first. Richard seemed to fumble his chance for the glory, Danniels observed. The other men went down, one and one. And finally only Julie and Richard were left. He supposed that this meant the girl had been accepted as a full member of the Wolf Pack. That would change the whole character of the organization. He vaguely wondered who her sponsor was. Joel?

Julie and the little man came to him. They started to help him down into the opening and suddenly he was at the bottom of a ladder. Things were beginning to seem to him as if they were taking place underwater.

They walked down a corridor of shadow, lit only by tarnished yellow from red sparks caught on the tips of silver wire inside water-clear bulbs recessed in the concrete ceiling.

When they passed a certain point sparks showered from slots in opposite walls. They burned out ineffectively before they reached the floor of cross-hatched metallic mats.

"Power failing," Richard observed with a chuckle. "Congress should investigate the builders."

There was a large, sliding door many feet thick but so well-balanced it slid open easily. And they were there.

It was a big room full of many little rooms. Each little room had a door that a man could enter by stooping and a chair-ledge inside for him to sit and read or adjust instruments. The outside of the rooms were finished off cleanly in shining metal with large, rugged objects fitted to all sides. These were hydrogen bombs.

The Wolf Pack ranged joyously through the maze.

Danniels found one of several stacks of small instruments and sat down on it. The things looked like radios but obviously weren't.

Richard came to him, wringing his hands. "These bombs seemed to be designed to be dropped from bombers. There are supposed to be rockets here too. I hope the H-bombs will fit. They seem so bulky . . . "

"Perhaps the rockets have self-contained bomb units," Danniels suggested.

"Perhaps. We're all going off and try to find the rockets. You'd be amazed at all the cutoffs down here. I'll leave Joel here to look after you."

Danniels sat on the instruments. Joel stayed several hundred feet away, an uncertain shadow in the light, smoking a red dot of a cigarette. Somehow Danniels associated fire and munitions instead of atomics and felt uneasy.

He discovered Julie Amprey at his side. She didn't say anything. She seemed to be sulking. Like a spoiled brat, he thought.

He fingered one of the portable instruments from an open crate beside him. "Wonder what these are?" he said to break up the heavy silence.

"Pseudo-H Bombs," the girl snapped.

Of course. Just as money had to be backed by gold or silver reserves, every pseudo bomb or mock-gas had to be backed by the real thing which, after its representative had been used, was dismantled, neutralized or retired. International inspection saw to that.

"There's enough here to blow up the whole world . . . if they were real," Danniels said.

The girl pointed out into the chamber. "Those are real."

Each nation had many times over the nuclear armament necessary to destroy human life. There was enough for that right in this vault—both in reality and in the Games.

Danniels stopped drifting and took a course. He stopped observing and began to act. There was a mob in action.

Even if they did somehow manage not to kill off the population with the fallout they were engineering, they would ruin farmland, create new recessive mutations.

Famine would cease to be a psychological affliction for half the world and become a physiological reality instead . . . for all the world.

He had failed in his plans to end the psychological Famine because of his own attunement to the Broadcasters. He wouldn't fail in stopping the new physiological Famine.

V

"Put that thing down," Joel said. "I don't trust you any further than I can spit, and that looks like a radio. You trying to warn the city council?"

Danniels put down the instrument. One wouldn't do it, and he could tell from Joel's eyes that he would get a very bad experience out of disobeying him.

"You were going to do something," Julie said. "What were you trying to do with that pseudie?"

"How do you know so much about this stuff?" Danniels demanded.

"My father told me all he found out from the records. He's Councilman Aldrich."

He rested his eyes for a second. "But your name —?" he heard himself say.

"My stepfather, I should have said. Mother married him when I was two. *What were you going to do?*"

"I," he said, "intended to end it all. All of this. All of it Outside. End everything."

The girl turned from him.

"Then why don't you do it?"

"You mean you don't want our friends to succeed in torturing a sick world?"

"I don't like pain," she said. "There's something clean, positive and challenging about killing. I'd like to kill. But pain seems so pointless. If you can stop them, go ahead. I'll help you.

He was exhausted and in fever. "Joel won't let me."

"Then—kill him," she said.

He knew it was all useless, tired, stale, unrewarding. It was done. He was nothing, and the girl was less. The Pack would succeed and a tortured world would die of a greater famine because he had failed all down the line. And he blamed himself for making a mistake that actually was unimportant. For a moment, he had trusted the girl.

"You can kill him." Julie turned back and faced him. "How much do you think those Broadcasters can really control human beings? We aren't fighting wars because we don't want to. We've finally seen what war can do and we're scared. We've retreated. The human race is hiding just like you are now."

Danniels laughed.

She lunged forward, tense. For a moment he thought she had actually stamped her foot. "It's true, you fool! Doesn't the actions of these men prove it to you? They are going to risk destroying the planet. If pacifism really controlled them do you think they could do that?"

He mumbled something about Wolf Pack members.

"There's never been any law or moral credo that human beings couldn't break and justify within themselves some way," Julie intoned carefully. "People can do the same with the induced precepts of the Broadcasters. If you really want to stop them, you can—by killing Joel and going ahead."

"Maybe later," Danniels mumbled. "I'll think about it."

Julie slapped his face. He wondered why he didn't feel it.

"You don't have much time left," Julie whispered. "Don't you know what's wrong with your foot? *Gangrene.* You have to get those toes amputated soon or you'll die."

"Yes," he said numbly. "Must get amputation." But it didn't seem urgent. He felt he should get some rest first.

"It's too bad you can't allow the operation," the girl said sweetly. "You can't allow lives to be destroyed just to save your own personality."

"What lives?" he demanded.

"All the cells and microorganisms in your toes," Julie told him. "You know they'll *die* if you are operated on. Are they any worse than the little bacteria you refused to murder? I suppose it's just as well that you die. How can you stand it on your conscience to breathe all the time and burn up innocent germs in your foul breath?"

Danniels understood. To live was to kill.

Every instant he lived his old cells were dying and new ones being born. So Danniels, who thought he could not kill any living thing, finally accepted himself as a killer. It wasn't human life he was taking . . . but it was life.

If he could be wrong about taking any life at all—and he had always believed himself unable to kill anything—he might be wrong about being able to kill men. In spite of everything he had been taught and what he believed about the influence of the Broadcasters.

He studied Joel in the gloom. The man represented everything he loathed—stupidity, brutality, the mob. If I can kill anyone, he told himself, it should be Joel.

He could try. Yes, he could. And that was a victory in itself.

He moved, and that was another triumph over the physical defeat that was already upon him.

Joel looked up, narrow eyes widened, as Danniels came down on him.

Danniels caught him in the stomach with the flat of his palm and shoved up.

Joel gargled in the back of his throat and rammed his thumbs for the prisoner's eyes. Danniels nodded and caught the balls of the thumbs on his forehead. He brought his fist up sharply and hit Joel on the point of the chin. His head snapped but righted itself slowly. He lashed into Danniels's body with both eager hands and Danniels, weakened, went down before he had time to think about it.

From the crazy angle of the floor he saw far above him Joel's lips curl back and closer, further down, a shoe was lifted to kick. It was aimed at Danniel's swollen foot.

Danniels smiled. He shouldn't have done that. If he had acted like a man instead of an animal he would have been fine. But now . . . Danniels rolled over quickly against the one leg of Joel's firmly on the floor. Off balance, Joel fell backwards with a curse, the back of his skull ringing against the side of one of the bombs.

Exertion was painting red lines across his vision but Danniels climbed to his knees, put his hands to Joel's corded throat and squeezed.

Yes. He knew he could kill. A few more seconds and he would be dead.

Danniels stopped.

There was no need to kill the boy. He would be unconscious long enough for him to do his job. And he found that fear had left him. He was no longer afraid of killing small things, because he was no longer afraid of killing men.

He had been able to kill when he had to, but more important, he had been able to keep from killing when it wasn't needed. He didn't need to be afraid of the old blood-lust—because he knew now he could best it.

And Julie had seen. She had seen something she had never believed was possible. That a man could keep from being a savage without the restraints of the Broadcasters or of society.

He limped to the stacked pseudies and sat down. "Now we can make it clean, Julie. We can end the whole mess. Ready?"

"Yes," she told him.

He picked up a pseudie and threw the switch.

The radio signal went out, and all over the world receivers noted a pseudo explosion in the heart of a Disaster Area. Danniels could imagine the men in the council room in the heart of the city seeing the flash and feeling the doom of a renewed twenty years of isolation and heading for the exact spot of the flash.

More signals flashed. And flashed. And flashed.

And he thought of the people all over the world wondering about the devastating sneak attack on the United States, and the incredible readings of the instruments.

"Keep working," Danniels said. "The Wolf Pack or the officials from the city will be here soon. I hope it's a dead heat. But," he said, "I think we've done it. But we can keep working on the safety margin."

"What have we done, Abe?" Julie asked trustingly.

He was going to feel foolish saying it. "We have just blown up the world according to the official records of the War Games."

"Then they'll have to start over," she said.

"Maybe," Danniels whispered. "If they do, we'll all start even. Everybody's a Jonah. The world is a Disaster Area. Maybe they'll start the War Games over. Or maybe they'll try the real thing again, now that they've seen how easy it is with pseudies."

He felt the numb foot and knew he would have to have an emergency operation if he survived the mobs that were coming. But he had a way of surviving mobs. He looked at Julie. He would see that their children could eat.

"At least," he said, triggering another H-bomb for the world's records, "it isn't a bad day when the world has been given a fresh slate, a new start."

There were footsteps outside, coming closer.

AFTERWORD

The dates in this story have passed, but I hope the ideas are still worth thinking about. It has been anthologized several times, and there is something in it that seems to reach people.

There is a trade-off in the movie, *Fail-Safe*, of cities in an atomic accident. The United States accidentally nukes Moscow (oops, sorry about that) but gives them a wiped-out New York City in exchange. In this story, I suggest a more gamesman-like solution, perhaps one more appealing to those who play video games.

THE SPICY SOUND OF SUCCESS

There was nothing showing on the video screen. That was why we were looking at it so analytically.

"Transphasia, that's what it is," Ordinary Spaceman Quade stated with a definite thrust of his angular jaw in my direction. "You can take my word on that, Captain Gavin."

"Can't," I told him. "I can't trust your opinion. I can't trust anything. That's why I'm Captain."

"You'll get over feeling like that."

"I know. Then I'll become First Officer."

"But look at that screen, sir," Quade said with an emphatic swing of his scarred arm. "I've seen blank scanning like that before and you haven't—it's your first trip. This always means transphasia—cortex dissolution, motor area feedback, the Aitchell Effect—call it anything you like, it's still transphasia."

"I know what transphasia is," I said moderately. "It means an electrogravitational disturbance of incoming sense data, rechanneling it to the wrong receptive areas. Besides the human brain, it also effects electronic equipment, like radar and television."

"Obviously." Quade glanced disgustedly at the screen.

"Too obvious. This time it might not be a familiar condition of many planetary gravitational fields. On this planet, that blank kinescope may mean our Big Brother kites were knocked down by hostile natives."

"You are plain wrong, Captain. Traditionally, alien races never interfere with our explorations. Generally, they are so alien to us they can't even recognize our existence.

I drew myself up to my full height—and noticed in irritation it was still an inch less than Quade's. "I don't understand you men. Look at yourself, Quade. You've been busted to Ordinary Spaceman for just that kind of thinking, for relying on tradition, on things that have worked before. Not only your thinking is slipshod, you've grown careless about everything else, even your own life."

"Just a minute, Captain. I've never been 'busted.' In the Exploration Service, we regard Ordinary Spaceman as our highest rank. With my hazard pay, I get more hard cash than you do, and I'm closer to retirement."

"That's a shallow excuse for complacency."

"Complacency! I've seen ten thousand wonders in twenty years of space, with a million variations. But the patterns repeat themselves. We learn to know what to expect, so maybe we can't maintain the reactionary caution the service likes in officers."

"I resent the word 'reactionary,' Spaceman! In civilian life, I was a lapidary and I learned the value of deliberation. But I never got too cataleptic to tap a million-dollar gem, which is more than my contemporaries can say, many of 'em."

"Captain Gavin," Quade said patiently, "you must realize that an outsider like you, among a crew of skilled spacemen, can never be more than a figurehead."

Was this the way I was to be treated? Why, this man had deliberately insulted me, his captain. I controlled myself, remembering the familiarity that had always existed between members of a crew working under close conditions, from the time of the ancient submarines and the first orbital ships.

"Quade," I said, "there's only one way for us to find out which of us is right about the cause of our scanning blackout."

"We go out and find the reason."

"Exactly. We go. You and me. I hope you can stand my company."

"I'm not sure I can," he answered reluctantly. "My hazard pay doesn't cover exploring with rookies. With all due respect, Captain."

I clapped him on the shoulder. "But, man, you have just been telling me all we had to worry about was common transphasia. A man with your experience could protect himself and cover even a rookie, under such familiar conditions—right?

"Yes, sir, I suppose I could," Quade said, bitterly aware he had lost out somewhere and hoping that it wasn't the start of a trend.

Looks okay to me," I said. Quade passed a gauntlet over his faceplate. "It's real. I can blur it with a smudged visor. When it blurs, it's solid."

The landscape beyond the black corona left by our landing rockets was unimpressive. The rocky desert was made up of silicon and iron oxide, so it looked much the same as a terrestrial location. Yellowish-white sand ran up to and around reddish brown rock clawing into the pink sunlight.

"I don't understand it," Quade admitted. "Transphasia hits you as soon as you let it into the airlock."

"Apparently, Quade, *this* thing is going to creep up on us."

"Don't sound smug, Captain. It's pitty-pattying behind you too."

The keening call across the surface of consciousness postponed my reply.

The wail was ominously forlorn, defiant of description. I turned my head around slowly inside my helmet, not even sure that I had heard it.

But what else can you do with a wail but hear it?

Quade nodded. "I've felt this before. It usually hits sooner. Let's trace it."

"I don't like this," I admitted. "It's not at all what I expected from what you said about transphasia. It must be something else."

"It couldn't be anything else. I know what to expect. You don't. You may begin smelling sensations, tasting sounds, hearing sights, seeing tastes, touching odors—or any other combination. Don't let it bother you."

"Of course not. I'll soothe my nerves by counting little shocks of lanolin jumping over a loud fence."

Quade grinned behind his faceplate. "Good idea."

"Then you can have it. I'm going to try keeping my eyes open and staying alive.

There was no reply.

His expression was tart and greasy despite all his light talk, and I knew mine was the same. I tested the security rope between our pressure suits. It was a taut and virile bass.

We scaled a staccato of rocks, our suits grinding pepper against our hides.

The musk summit rose before us, a minor-key horizon with a shifting treble for as far as I could smell. It was primitive beauty that made you feel shocking pink inside. The most beautiful vista I had ever tasted, it couldn't be dulled even by the sensation of beef broth under my skin.

"Is this transphasia?" I asked in awe.

"It always has been before," Quade remarked. "Ready to swallow your words about this being something an old hand wouldn't recognize, Captain?"

"I'm swallowing no words until I find out precisely how they taste here."

"Not a bad taste. They're pretty. Or haven't you noticed?"

"Quade, you're right! About the colors anyway. This reminds me of an illiscope recording from a cybernetic translator."

"It should. I don't suppose we could understand each other if it wasn't for our morphistudy courses in reading cross-sense translations of Centauri blushtalk and the like."

It became difficult to understand him, difficult to try talking in the face of such splendor. You never really appreciate colors until you smell them for the first time.

Quade was as conversational as ever, though. "I can't see irregularities occurring in a gravitational field. We must have compensated for the transphasia while we still had a point of reference, the solid reality of the spaceship. But out here, where all we have to hang onto is each other, our concept of reality goes *bang* and deflates to a tired joke."

Before I could agree with one of his theories for once, a streak of spice shot past us. It bounced back tangily and made a bitter rip between the two of us. There was no time to judge its size, if it had size, or its decibel range, or its caloric count, before a small, sharp pain dug in and dwindled down to nothing in one long second.

The new odor pattern in my head told me Quade was saying something I couldn't quite make out.

Quade then pulled me in the direction of the nasty little pain.

"Wait a minute, Spaceman!" I bellowed. "Where the devil do you think you're dragging me? Halt! That's a direct order."

He stopped. "Don't you want to find out what that was? This is an exploration party, you know, sir."

"I'm not sure I do want to find out what that was just now. I didn't like the feel of it. But the important thing is for us not to get any further from the ship."

"That's important, Captain?"

"To the best of my judgment, yes. This—condition—didn't begin until we got so far away from the spacer—in time or distance. I don't want it to get any worse. It's troublesome not to know black from white, but it would be a downright inconvenience not to know which way is up."

"Not for an experienced spaceman," Quade griped. "I'm used to free-fall."

But he turned back.

"Just a minute," I said. "There was something strange up ahead. I want to see if short-range radar can get through our electrogravitational jamming here."

I took a sighting. My helmet set projected the pattern on the cornea. Sweetness building up to a stab of pure salt—those were the blips.

Beside me, there was a thin thread of violet. Quade had whistled. He was reading the map too.

The slope fell away sharply in front of us, becoming a deep gorge. There was something broken and twisted at the bottom, something we had known for an instant as a streak of spice.

"There's one free-fall," I said, "where you wouldn't live long enough to get used to it."

He said nothing on the route back to the spacer.

"I know all about this sort of thing, Gav," First Officer Nagurski said expansively. He was rubbing the well-worn ears of our beagle mascot, Bruce. A heavy tail thudded on the steel deck from time to time.

My finger could barely get in the chafing band of my regulation collar. I was hot and tired, fresh—in only the chronological sense—from a pressure suit.

"What do you know all about, Nagurski? Dogs? Spacemen? Women? Transphasia?"

"Yes," he answered casually. "But I had immediate reference to our current psychophysiological phenomenon."

I collapsed into the swivel in front of the chart table. "First off, let's hear what you know about—never mind, make it dogs."

"Take Bruce, for example, then—"

"No, thanks. I was wondering why *you* did."

"I didn't." His dark, round face was bland. "Bruce picked me. Followed me home one night in Chicago Port. The dog or the man who picks his own master is the most content."

"Bruce is content," I admitted. "He couldn't be any more content and still be alive. But I'm not sure that theory works out with men. We'd have anarchy if I tried to let these starbucks pick their own master."

"I had no trouble when I was a captain," Nagurski said. "Ease the reins on the men. Just offer them your advice, your guidance. They will soon see why the service selected you as captain; they will pick you themselves."

"Did your crew voluntarily elect you as their leader?"

"Of course they did, Gav. I'm an old hand at controlling crews."

"Then why are you First Officer under me now?"

He blinked, then decided to laugh. "I've been in space a good many years. I really wanted to relax a little bit more. Besides, the increase in hazard pay was actually more than my salary as a captain. I'm a notch nearer retirement too."

"Tell me, did you always feel this way about letting the men select their own leader?"

Nagurski brought out a pipe. He would have a pipe, I decided.

"No, not always. I was like you at first. Fresh from the cosmic energy test lab, suspicious of everything, trying to tell the old hands what to do. But I learned that they are pretty smart boys; they know what they are doing. You can rely on them absolutely."

I leaned forward, elbows on knees. "Let me tell you a thing, Nagurski. Your trust of these damn-fool spacemen is why you are no longer a captain. You can't trust anything out here in space, much less human nature. Even I know that much!"

He was pained. "If you don't trust the men, they won't trust you, Gav."

"They don't have to trust me. All they have to do is *obey* me or, by Jupiter, get frozen stiff and thawed out just in time for court-marshal back home. Listen," I continued earnestly, "these men aren't going to think of me—of us, the officers, as their leaders. As far as the crew is concerned, Ordinary Spaceman Quade is the best man on this ship."

"He *is* a good man," Nagurski said. "You mustn't be jealous of his status."

The dog growled. He must have sensed what I almost did to Nagurski.

"Never mind that for now," I said wearily. "What was your idea for getting our exploration parties through this transphasia?"

"There's only one idea for that," said Quade, ducking his long head and stepping through the connecting hatch. "With the Captain's permission..."

"Go ahead, Quade, tell him," Nagurski invited.

"There's only one way to wade through transphasia with any reliability," Quade told me. "You keep some kind of physical contact with the spaceship. Parties are strung out on guide line, like we were, but the cable has to be run back and made fast to the hull."

"How far can we run it back?"

Quade shrugged. "Miles."

"How many?"

"We have three miles of cable. As long as you can feel, taste, see, smell or hear that rope anchoring you to home, you aren't lost."

"Three miles isn't good enough. We don't have enough fuel to change sites that often. You can't use the drive in a gravitational field, you know."

"What else can we do, Captain?" Nagurski asked puzzledly.

"You've said that the spaceship is our only protection from transphasia. Is that it?"

Quade gave a curt nod.

"Then," I told them, "we will have to start tearing apart this ship."

Sergeant-Major Hoffman and his team were doing a good job of ripping out the side of the afterhold. Through the portal I could see the suited men expertly guiding the huge curved sections on their ray projectors.

"Cannibalizing is dangerous." Nagurski put his pipe in his teeth and shook his head disapprovingly.

"Spaceships have parts as interchangeable as Erector sets. We can take apart the tractors and put our ship back together again after we complete the survey."

"You can't assemble a jigsaw puzzle if some of the pieces are missing."

"You can't get a complete picture, but you can get a good idea of what it looks like. We can take off in a reasonable facsimile of a spaceship."

"Not," he persisted, "if too many parts are missing."

"Nagurski, if you are looking for a job safer than space exploration, why don't you go back to testing cosmic bomb shelters?"

Nagurski flushed. "Look here, Captain, you are being too damned cautious. There is a way one handles the survey of a planet like this, and this isn't the way."

"It's my way. You heard what Quade said. You know it yourself. The men have to have something tangible to hang onto out there. One slender cable isn't enough of an edge on sensory anarchy. If the product of their own technological civilization can keep them sane, I say let 'em take a part of that environment with them."

"In departing from standard procedure that we have learned to trust, you are risking more than a few men—you risk the whole mission in gambling so much of the ship. A captain doesn't take chances like that!"

"I never said I wouldn't take chances. But I'm not going to take *stupid* chances. I *might* be doing the wrong thing, but I can see you *would* be doing it wrong."

"You know nothing about space, Captain! You have to trust *us*."

"That's it exactly, First Officer Nagurski," I said sociably. "If you lazy, lax, complacent slobs want to do something in a particular way, I know it *has* to be wrong."

I turned and found Wallace, the personnel man, standing in the hatchway.

"Pardon, Captain, but would you say we also lacked initiative?"

"I would," I answered levelly.

"Then you'll be interested to hear that Spaceman Quade took a suit and a cartographer unit. He's out there somewhere, alone."

"The idiot!" I yelped. "Everyone needs a partner out there. Send out a team to follow his cable and drag him in here by it."

"He didn't hook on a cable, Captain," Wallace said. "I suppose he intended to go beyond the three-mile limit as you demanded."

"Shut up, Wallace. You don't have to like me, but you can't twist what I said as long as I command this spacer."

"Cool off, Gav," Nagurski advised me. "It's been done before. Anybody else would have been a fool to go out alone, but Quade is the most experienced man we have. He knows transphasia. Trust him."

"I trusted him too far by letting him run around loose. He needs a leash in more ways than one, and I'm going to put one on him."

For me, it was a nightmare. I lay down in my cabin and thought. I had to think things through very carefully. One mistake was too many for me. My worst fear had been that someday I would overlook one tiny flaw and ruin a gem. Now I might have ruined an exploration and destroyed a man, not a stone, because I had missed the flaw.

No one but a reckless fool would have gone out alone on a strange planet with a terrifying phenomenon, but I'd had enough evidence to see that space exploration made a man a reckless fool by doing things on one planet he had once found safe and wise on some other world.

The thought intruded itself: *why* hadn't I recognized this before I let Quade escape to almost certain death? Wasn't it because I wanted him dead, because I resented the crew's resentment of my authority, and recognized in him the leader and symbol of this resentment?

I threw away that idea along with my half-used cigarette. It might very well be true, but how did that help now?

I had to *think*.

I was going after him, that was certain. Not only for humane reasons—he was the most important member of the crew. With him around, there were only two opinions, his and mine. Without him, I'd have endless opinions to contend with.

But it wouldn't do any good to go out no better equipped than he.

There was no time to wait for tractors to be built if we wanted to reach him alive, and we certainly couldn't reach him five or ten miles out with our three miles of safety line. We would have to go in spacesuits.

But how would that leave us any better off than Quade?

Why was Quade vulnerable in his spacesuit, as I knew from experience he would be?

How could we be less vulnerable, or preferably invulnerable?

"Captain, you got nothing to worry about," Quartermaster Farley said. He patted a space helmet paternally. "You got yourself a self-contained environment. The suit's eye looks into yours at the arteries in the back of your eyeball so it can read your amber corpuscles and feed you your oxygen in the right amounts; you're a bottle-fed baby. If transphasia gets you seeing limburger, turn on the radar and you're air-conditioned as an igloo. Nothing short of a cosmic blast can dent that hide. You got it made."

"You are right," I said, "only transphasia comes right through these air-fast joints."

"Something strange about the trance, Captain," Farley said darkly. "Any spaceman can tell you that. Things we don't understand."

"I'm talking about something we do understand—*sound*. These suits perfectly soundproof?"

"Well, you can pick up sound by conduction. Like putting two helmets together and talking without using radio. You can't insulate enough to block out all sound and still have a man-shaped suit You have—"

"I know. Then you have something like a tractor or a miniature spaceship. There isn't time for that. We will have to live with the sound."

"What do you think he's going to hear out there, Captain? We'd like to find one of those beautiful sirens on some planet, believe me, but—"

"I believe you," I said quickly. "Let's leave it at that. I don't know what he will hear; what's worrying me is *how* he'll hear it, in what sensory medium. I hope the sound doesn't blind him. His radar is his only chance."

"How do you figure on getting a better edge yourself, sir?"

"I have the idea, but not the word for it. Tonal compensation, I suppose. If you can't shut out the noise, we'll have to drown it out."

Farley nodded. "Neat. Like a telephone time signal?"

"That would do it."

"It would do something else. It would drive you nuts."

I shrugged. "It might be distracting."

"Captain, take my word for it," argued Farley. "Constant sonic feedback inside a spacesuit will set you rocking against the grain."

"Devise some regular system of interruptions," I suggested.

"Then the pattern will drive you crazy. Maybe in a few months, with luck, I could plan some harmonic scale you could tolerate—"

"We don't have a few months," I said. "How about music? There's a harmonic scale for you, and we can endure it, some of it. *Figaro* and *Asleep in the Cradle of the Deep* can compensate for high-pitched outside temperatures, and *Flight of the Bumble Bee* to block bass notes."

Farley nodded. "Might work. I can program the tapes from the library."

"Good. There's one more thing—how are our stores of medicinal liquor?"

Farley paled. "Captain, are you implying that *I* should be running short on alcohol? Where do you get off suggesting a thing like that?"

"I'm getting off at the right stop, apparently," I sighed. "Okay, Farley, no evasions. In plain figures, how much drinking alcohol do we have left?"

The quartermaster slumped a bit. "Twenty-one liters unbroken. One more about half full."

"Half full? How did that ever happen? I mean you had some *left*? We'll take this up later. I want you to run it through the synthesizer to get some light wine . . . "

"Light wine?" Farley looked in pain. "Not whiskey, brandy, beer?"

"Light wine. Then ration it out to some of the men."

"Ration it to the men!"

"That's an accurate interpretation of my orders."

"But, sir," Farley protested, "you don't give alcohol to the crew in the middle of a mission. It's not done. What reason can you have?"

"To sharpen their taste and olfactory senses. We can turn up or block out sound. We can use radar to extend our sight, but the Space Service hasn't yet developed anything to make spacemen taste or smell better."

"They are going to smell like a herd of winos," Farley said. "I don't like to think how they would taste."

"It's an entirely practical idea. Tea-tasters used to drink almond-and-barley water to sharpen their senses. I've observed that wine helps you appreciate culinary art more. Considering the mixed-up sensory data under transphasia, wine may help us to see where we are going.

"Yes, sir," Farley said obediently. "I'll give spacemen a few quarts of wine, telling them to use it carefully for scientific purposes only, and then they will be able to see where they are going. Yes, sir."

I turned to leave, then paused briefly. "You can come along, Farley. I'm sure you want to see that we don't waste any of the stuff."

"There they are!" Nagurski called. "Quade's footsteps again, just beyond that rocky ridge."

The landscape was rich chocolate ice cream smothered with chocolate syrup, caramel, peanuts and maple syrup, eaten while you smoked an old, mellow Havana. The footsteps were faint traces of whipped cream across the dark, rich taste of the planet.

I splashed some wine from my drinking tube against the roof of my mouth to sharpen my taste. It brought out the footsteps sharper. It also made the landscape more of a teen-ager's caloric nightmare.

The four of us pulled ourselves closer together by reeling in more of our safety line. Farley and Hoffman, Nagurski and myself, we were cabled together. It gave us a larger hunk of reality to hold onto. Even so, things wavered for me during a wisp of time.

We stumbled over the ridge, feeling out the territory. It was a sticky job crawling over a melting, chunk-style Hershey bar. I was thankful for the invigorating Sousa march blasting inside my helmet. Before the tape had cut in, kicked on by the decibel gauge, I had heard or felt something dark and ominous in the outside air.

"Yes, this is definitely the trail of Quail," Nagurski said soberly. "This is serious business. I must ask whoever has been giggling on his channel to shut up. Pardon me, Captain. You weren't giggling, sir?"

"I have never giggled in my life, Nagurski."

"Yes, sir. That's what we all thought."

A moment later, Nagurski added, "Anyway, I just noticed it was my shelf—my, that is, self."

The basso profundo performing *Figaro* on my headset climbed to a girlish shriek. A sliver of ice. This was the call Quade and I had first heard as we were about to troop over a cliff. I dug in my heels.

"Take a good look around, boys," I said. "What do you see?"

"Quail," Nagurski replied. 'That's what I see."

"You," I said carefully, "have been in space a *long* time. Look again."

"I see our old buddy, Quail."

I took another slosh of burgundy and peered up ahead. It was Quade. A man in a spacesuit, faceplate in the dust, two hundred yards ahead.

Grudgingly I stepped forward, out of the shadow of the ridge. A hysterically screaming wind rocked me on my toes. We pushed on sluggishly to Quade's side, moving to the tempo of *Pomp and Circumstance.*

Farley lugged Quade over on his back and read his gauges.

The Quartermaster rose with grim deliberation, and hiccuped. "Better get him back to the spaceship fast. I've seen this kind of thing before with transphasia. His body cooled down because of the screaming wind—psychosomatic reaction—and his heating circuits compensated for the cool flesh. The poor devil's got frostbite and heat prostration."

The four of us managed to haul Quade back by using the powered joints in our suits. Hoffman suggested that he had once seen an injured man walked back inside his suit like a robot, but it was a delicate adjustment, controlling power circuits from outside a suit. It was too much for us—we were too tired, too numb, too drunk.

At first sight of the spacer in the distance, transphasia left me with only a chocolate-tasting pink afterimage on my retina. It was now showing bare skeleton from cannibalization for tractor parts, but it looked good to me, like home.

The wailing call sounded through the amber twilight.

I realized that I was actually *hearing* it for the first time.

The alien stood between us and the ship. It was a great pot-bellied lizard as tall as a man. Its sound came from a flat, vibrating beaver tail. Others of its kind were coming into view behind it.

"Stand your ground," I warned the others thickly. "They may be dangerous."

Quade sat up on our crisscross litter of arms. "Aliens can't be hostile. Ethnic impossibility. I'll show you."

Quade was delirious and we were drunk. He got away from us and jogged toward the herd.

"Let's give him a hand!" Farley shouted. "We'll take us a specimen!"

I couldn't stop them. Being in Alpine rope with them, I went along. At the time, it even seemed vaguely like a good idea.

As we lumbered toward them, the aliens fell back in a solid line except for the first curious-looking one. Quade got there ahead of us and made a grab. The creature rose into the air with a screaming vibration of his tail and landed on top of him, flattening him instantly.

"Sssh, men," Nagurski said. "Leave it to me. I'll surround him."

The men followed the First Officer's example, and the rope tying them to him. I went along cheerfully myself, until an enormous rump struck me violently in the face. My leaded boots were driven down into fertile soil, and my helmet was ringing like a bell. I got a jerky picture of the beast jumping up and down on top of the others joyously. Only the stiff space armor was holding up our slack frames.

"Let's let him escape," Hoffman suggested on the audio circuit.

"I'd like to," Nagurski admitted, "but the other beasts won't let us get past their circle."

It was true. The aliens formed a ring around us, and each time a bouncing boy hit the line, he only bounced back on top of us.

"Flat!" I yelled. "Our seams can't take much more of this beating."

I followed my own advice and landed in the dirt beside Quade.

The bouncer came to rest and regarded us silently, head on an eighty-degree angle.

I was stone sober.

The others were lying around me quietly, passed out, knocked out, or taking cover.

The ring of aliens drew in about us, closer, tighter, as the bouncer sat on his haunches and waited for us to move.

"Feeling better?" I asked Quade in the infirmary.

He punched up his pillow and settled back. "I guess so. But when I think of all the ways I nearly got myself killed out there . . . How far have you got in the tractors?"

"I'm having the tractors torn down and the parts put back into the spaceship where they belong. We *shouldn't* risk losing them and getting stuck here."

"Are you settling for a primary exploration?"

"No. I think I had the right idea on your rescue party. You have to meet and fight a planet on its own terms. Fighting confused sounds and tastes with music and wine was crude, but it was on the right track. Out there, we understood language because we were familiar with alien languages changed to other sense mediums by cybernetic translators. Using the translator, we can learn to recognize all confused data as easily. I'm starting indoctrination courses."

"I doubt that that is necessary, sir," Quade said. "Experienced spacemen are experienced with transphasia. You don't have to worry. In the future, I'll be able to resist sensations that tell me I'm freezing to death—if my gauges tell me it's a lie."

I examined his bandisprayed hide. "I think my way of gaining experience is less painful and more efficient."

Quade squirmed. "Yes, sir. One thing, sir—I don't understand how you got me away from those aliens."

"The aliens were trying to help. They knew something was wrong and they were prodding and probing. When the first tractor pulled up and the men got out, they seemed to realize our own people could help us easier than they could."

"I am not quite convinced that those babies just meant to help us all the time."

"But they did! First, that call of theirs—it wasn't to lead us into danger, but to warn us of the cliff, the freezing wind. They saw we were trying to find out things about their world, so they even offered us one of their own kind to study. Unfortunately, he was too much for us. They didn't give us their top man, of course, only the village idiot. It's just as well. We aren't allowed to dissect creatures that far up the intelligence scale."

"But why should they want to help us?" Quade demanded suspiciously.

"I think it's like Nagurski's dog. The dog came to him when it wanted somebody to own it, protect it, feed it, love it. These aliens want Earthmen to colonize the planet. We came here, you see, same as the dog came to Nagurski."

"Well, I've learned one thing from all of this," Quade said. "I've been a blind, arrogant, cocksure fool, following courses that were good on some worlds, most worlds, but not good on *all* worlds. I'm ever going to be that foolhardy again."

"But you're losing *confidence*, Quade! You aren't sure of yourself any more. Isn't confidence a spaceman's most valuable asset?"

"The hell it is," Quade said grimly. "It's his deadliest liability."

"In that case, I must inform you that I am demoting you to Acting Executive Officer."

"Huh?" Quade gawked. "But dammit, Captain, you can't do that to me! I'll lose hazard pay and be that much further from retirement!"

"That's tough," I sympathized, "but in every service a chap gets broken in rank now and then."

"Maybe it's worth it," Quade said heavily. "Now maybe I've learned how to stay alive out here. I just hope I don't forget."

I thought about that. I was nearly through with my first mission and I could speak with experience, even if it was the least amount of experience aboard.

"Quade," I said, "space isn't as dangerous as all that." I clapped him on the shoulder fraternally. "You worry too much!"

AFTERWORD

I based this story submitted to *Galaxy* on a concept that the editor of that magazine, H.L. Gold, had previously used in a story he had written.

The concept was that a person could experience one kind of sensory input as another variety. One could hear colors, smell sounds, and so forth. Either Gold could think I was plagiarizing him or feel complimented by the imitation (the sincerest form of flattery). He apparently felt complimented. He accepted the story.

Originally I referred to the condition as the Aitchell Effect (for H.L.). I did it a number of times and Horace L. Gold cut them out. I think there may be one reference to this left, but on a casual re-reading of the story I could not find it.

CHARITY CASE

When he began his talk with "You got your health, don't you?" it touched those spots inside me. That was when I did it.

Why couldn't what he said have been "The best things in life are free, buddy" or "Every dog has his day, fellow" or "If at first you don't succeed, man"? No, he had to use that one line. You wouldn't blame me. Not if you believe me.

The first thing I can remember, the start of all this, was when I was four or five somebody was soiling my bed for me. I absolutely was not doing it. I took long naps morning and evening so I could lie awake all night to see that it wouldn't happen. It couldn't happen. But in the morning the bed would sit there dispassionately soiled and convict me on circumstantial evidence. My punishment was as sure as the tide.

Dad was a compact man, small eyes, small mouth, tight clothes. He was narrow but not mean. For punishment, he locked me in a windowless room and told me to sit still until he came back. It wasn't so bad a punishment, except that when Dad closed the door, the light turned off and I was left there in the dark.

Being four or five, I didn't know any better, so I thought Dad made it dark to add to my punishment. But I learned he didn't know the light went out. It came back on when he unlocked the door. Every time I told him about the light as soon as I could talk again, but he said I was lying.

One day, to prove me a liar, he opened and closed the door a few times from outside. The light winked off and on, off and on, always shining when Dad stuck his head inside. He tried using the door from the inside, and the light stayed on, no matter how hard he slammed the door.

I stayed in the dark longer for lying about the light.

Alone in the dark, I wouldn't have had it so bad if it wasn't for the things that came to me.

They were real to me. They never touched me, but they had a little boy. He looked the way I did in the mirror. They did unpleasant things to him.

Because they were real, I talked about them as if they were real, and I almost earned a bunk in the home for retarded children until I got smart enough to keep the beasts to myself.

My mother hated me. I loved her, of course. I remember her smell mixed up with flowers and cookies and winter fires. I remember she hugged me on my ninth birthday. The trouble came from the notes written in my awkward hand that she found, calling her names I didn't understand. Sometimes there were drawings. I didn't write those notes or make those drawings.

My mother and father must have been glad when I was sent away to reform school after my thirteenth birthday party, the one no one came to.

The reform school was nicer. There were others there who'd had it about like me. We got along. I didn't watch their shifty eyes too much, or ask them what they shifted to see. They didn't talk about my screams at night.

It was home.

My trouble there was that I was always being framed for stealing. I didn't take any of those things they located in my bunk. Stealing wasn't in my line. If you believe any of this at all, you'll see why it couldn't be me who did the stealing.

There was reason for me to steal, if I could have got away with it. The others got money from home to buy the things they needed—razor blades, candy, sticks of tea. I got a letter from Mom or Dad every now and then before they were killed, saying they had sent money or that it was enclosed, but somehow I never got a dime of it.

When I was expelled from reform school, I left with just one idea in mind—to get all the money I could ever use for the things I needed and the things I wanted.

It was two or three years later that I skulked into Brother Partridge's mission on Durbin Street.

The preacher and half a dozen men were singing *Onward Christian Soldiers* in the meeting room. It was a drafty hall with varnished camp chairs. I shuffled in at the back with my suitcoat collar turned up around my stubbled jaw. I made my hand shaky as I ran it through my knotted hair. Partridge was supposed to think I was just a bum. As an inspiration, I hugged my chest to make him think I was some wino nursing a flask full of Sneaky Pete. All I had there was a piece of copper alloy tubing inside a slice of plastic hose for taking care of myself, rolling sailors and the like. How bad the price of a bottle?

Partridge didn't seem to notice me, but I knew that was an act. I knew people were always watching every move I made. He braced his red-furred hands on the sides of his auctioneer's stand and leaned his splotched eagle beak toward us. "Brothers, this being Thanksgiving, I pray the good Lord that we all are truly thankful for all that we have received. Amen."

Some skin-and-bones character I didn't know struggled out of his seat, amening. I could see he had a lot to be thankful for—somewhere he had received a fix.

"Brothers," Partridge went on after enjoying the interruption with a beaming smile, "you shall all be entitled to a bowl of turkey soup prepared by Sister Partridge, a generous supply of sweet rolls and dinner, rolls contributed by the Early Morning Bakery of this city, and all the coffee you can drink. Let us march out to *The Stars and Stripes Forever*, John Philip Sousa's grand old patriotic song."

I had to laugh at all those bums clattering the chairs in front of me, scampering after water soup and stale bread. As soon as I got cleaned up, I was going to have dinner in a good restaurant, and I was going to order such expensive food and leave such a large tip for the waiter and send one to the chef that they were going to think I was rich, and some executive with some brokerage firm would see me and say to himself, "Hmm, executive material. Just the type we need. I beg your pardon, sir—" just like the razor-blade comic-strip ads in the old magazines that Frankie the Pig sells three for a quarter.

I was marching. Man, was I ever marching, but the secret of it was I was only marking time the way we did in fire drills at the school.

They passed me, every one of them, and marched out of the meeting room into the kitchen. Even Partridge made his way down from the auctioneer's stand like a vulture with a busted wing and darted through his private door.

I was alone, marking time behind the closed half of double doors. One good breath and I raced past the open door and flattened myself to the wall. Crockery was ringing and men were slurping inside. No one had paid any attention to me. That was pretty odd. People usually watch my every move, but a man's luck has to change sometime, doesn't it?

Following the wallboard, I went down the side of the room and behind the last row of chairs, closer, closer, and halfway up the room again to the entrance—the entrance and the little wooden box fastened to the wall beside it.

The box was old and made out of some varnished wood. There was a slot in the top. There wasn't any sign anywhere around it, but you knew it wasn't a mailbox.

My hand went flat on the top of the box. One finger at a time drew up and slipped into the slot. Index, fore, third, little. I put my thumb in my palm and shoved. My hand went in.

There were coins inside. I scooped them up with two fingers and held them fast with the other two. Once I dropped a dime—not a penny, milled edge—and I started to reach for it. No, don't be greedy. I knew I would probably lose my hold on all the coins if I tried for that one. I had all the rest. It felt like about two dollars, or close to it.

Then I found the bill. A neatly folded bill in the box. Somehow I knew all along it would be there.

I tried to read the numbers on the bill with my fingertips, but I couldn't. It had to be a one. Who drops anything but a one into a Skid Row collection box? But still there were tourists, slummers. They might leave a fifty or even a hundred. A hundred!

Yes, it felt new, crisp. It had to be a hundred. A single would be creased or worn.

I pulled my hand out of the box. I *tried* to pull my hand out of the box.

I knew what the trouble was, of course. I was in a monkey trap. The monkey reaches through the hole for the bait, and when he gets it in his hot little fist, he can't get his hand out. He's too greedy to let go, so he stays there, caught as securely as if he were caged.

I was a man, not a monkey. I knew why I couldn't get my hand out. But I couldn't lose that money, especially that century bill. Calm, I ordered myself. *Calm.*

The box was fastened to the vertical tongue-and-groove laths of the woodwork, not the wall. It was old lumber, stiffened by a hundred layers of paint since 1908. The paint was as thick and strong as the boards. The box was fastened fast. Six-inch spike nails, I guessed.

Calmly, I flung my whole weight away from the wall. My wrist almost cracked, but there wasn't even a bend in the box. Carefully, I tried to jerk my fist straight up, to pry off the top of the box. It was as if the box had been carved out of one solid piece of timber. It wouldn't go up, down, left or right.

But I kept trying.

While keeping a lookout for Partridge and somebody stepping out of the kitchen for a pull on a bottle, I spotted the clock for the first time, a Western Union clock high up at the back of the hall. Just as I seen it for the first time, the electricity wound the spring motor inside like a chicken having its neck wrung.

The next time I glanced at the clock, it said ten minutes had gone by. My hand still wasn't free and I hadn't budged the box.

"This," Brother Partridge said, "is one of the most profound experiences of my life."

My head hinged until it lined my eyes up with Brother Partridge. The pipe hung heavy in my pocket, but he was too far from me.

"A vision of you at the box projected itself on the crest of my soup," the preacher explained in wonderment.

I nodded. "Swimming right in there with the dead duck."

"Cold turkey," he corrected. "Are you scoffing at a miracle?"

"People are always watching me, Brother," I said. "So now they do it even when they aren't around. I should have known it would come to that."

The pipe was suddenly a weight I wanted off me. I would try robbing a collection box, knowing positively that I would get caught, but I wasn't dumb enough to murder. Somebody, somewhere, would be a witness to it. I had never got away with anything in my life. I was too smart to even try anything but the little things.

"I may be able to help you," Brother Partridge said, "if you have faith and a conscience."

"I've got something better than a conscience," I told him.

Brother Partridge regarded me solemnly. "There must be something special about you, for your apprehension to come through miraculous intervention. But I can't imagine what."

"I always get apprehended somehow, Brother," I said. "I'm pretty special."

"Your name?"

"William Hagle." No sense lying. I had been booked and printed before.

Partridge prodded me with his bony fingers as if making sure I was substantial. "Come. Let's sit down, if you can remove your fist from the money box."

I opened up my fingers and let the coins ring inside the box and I drew out my hand. The bill stuck to the sweat on my fingers and slid out along with the digits. A one, I decided. I had got into trouble for a grubby single. It wasn't any century. I had been kidding myself.

I unfolded the note. Sure enough, it wasn't a hundred-dollar bill, but it was a twenty, and that was almost the same thing to me. I creased it and put it back into the slot.

As long as it stalled off the cops, I'd talk to Partridge.

We took a couple of camp chairs and I told him the story of my life, or most of it. It was hard work on an empty stomach; I wished I'd had some of that turkey soup. Then again I was glad I hadn't. Something always happened to me when I thought back over my life. The same thing.

The men filed out of the kitchen, wiping their chins, and I went right on talking.

After some time Sister Partridge bustled in and snapped on the overhead lights and I kept talking. The brother still hadn't used the phone to call the cops.

"Remarkable," Partridge finally said when I got so hoarse I had to take a break. "One is almost—*almost*—reminded of Job. William, you are being punished for some great sin. Of that, I'm sure."

"Punished for a sin? But, Brother, I've always had it like this, as long as I can remember. What kind of a sin could I have committed when I was fresh out of my crib?"

"William, all I can tell you is that time means nothing in Heaven. Do you deny the transmigration of souls?"

"Well," I said, "I've had no personal experience—"

"Of course you have, William! Say you don't remember. Say you don't want to remember. But don't say you have no personal experience!"

"And you think I'm being punished for something I did in a previous life?"

He looked at me in disbelief. "What else could it be?"

"I don't know," I confessed. "I certainly haven't done anything that bad in *this* life."

"William, if you atone for this sin, perhaps the horde of locusts will lift from you."

It wasn't much of a chance, but I was unused to having any at all. I shook off the dizziness of it. "By the Lord, Harry, Brother, I'm going to give it a try!" I cried.

"I believe you," Partridge said, surprised at himself.

He ambled over to the money box on the wall. He tapped the bottom lightly and a box with no top slid out of the slightly larger box. He reached in, fished out the bill and presented it to me.

"Perhaps this will help in your atonement," he said.

I crumpled it into my pocket fast. Not meaning to sound ungrateful, I'm pretty sure he hadn't noticed it was a twenty.

And then the bill seemed to lie there, heavy, a lead weight. It would have been different if I had managed to get it out of the box myself. You know how it is.

Money you haven't earned doesn't seem real to you.

There was something I forgot to mention so far. During the year between when I got out of the reformatory and the one when I tried to steal Brother Partridge's money, I killed a man.

It was all an accident, but killing somebody is reason enough to get punished. It didn't have to be a sin in some previous life, you see.

I had gotten my first job in stacking boxes at the freight door of Baysinger's. The drivers unloaded the stuff, but they just dumped it off the truck. An empty rear end was all they wanted. The freight boss told me to stack the boxes inside, neat and not too close together.

I stacked boxes the first day. I stacked more the second. The third day I went outside with my baloney and crackers. It was warm enough even for November.

Two of them, dressed like Harvard seniors, caps and striped duffer jackets, came up to the crate I was dining off.

"Work inside, Jack?" the taller one asked.

"Yeah," I said, chewing.

"What do you do, Jack?" the fatter one asked.

"Stack boxes."

"Got a union card?"

I shook my head.

"Application?"

"No," I said. "I'm just helping out during Christmas."

"You're a scab, buddy," Long-legs said. "Don't you read the papers?"

"I don't like comic strips," I said.

They sighed. I think they hated to do it, but I was bucking the system.

Fats hit me high. Long-legs hit me low. I blew cracker crumbs into their faces. After that, I just let them go. I know how to take a beating. That's one thing I knew.

Then lying there, bleeding to myself, I heard them talking. I heard noises like *make an example of him* and *do something permanent* and I squirmed away across the rubbish like a polite mouse.

I made it around a corner of brick and stood up, hurting my knee on a piece of brown-splotched pipe. There were noises on the other angle of the corner and so I tested if the pipe was loose and it was. I closed my eyes and brought the pipe up and then down.

It felt as if I connected, but I was so numb, I wasn't sure until I unscrewed my eyes.

There was a big man in a heavy wool overcoat and gray homburg spread on a damp centerfold from the *News*. There was a pick-up slip from the warehouse under the fingers of one hand, and somebody had beaten his brains out.

The police figured it was part of some labor dispute, I guess, and they never got to me.

I suppose I was to blame anyway. If I hadn't been alive, if I hadn't been there to get beaten up, it wouldn't have happened. I could see the point in making me suffer for it. There was a lot to be said for looking at it like that. But there was nothing to be said for telling Brother Partridge about the accident, or murder, or whatever had happened that day.

Searching myself after I left Brother Partridge, I finally found a strip of gray adhesive tape on my side, out of the fuzzy area. Making the twenty the size of a thick postage stamp, I peeled back the tape and put the folded bill on the white skin and smoothed the tape back.

There was only one place for me to go now. I headed for the public library. It was only about twenty blocks, but not having had anything to eat since the day before, it enervated me.

The downstairs washroom was where I went first. There was nobody

there but an old guy talking urgently to a kid with thick glasses, and somebody building a fix in one of the booths. I could see charred matches dropping down on the floor next to his tennis shoes, and even a few grains of
white stuff. But he managed to hold still enough to keep from spilling
more from the spoon.

I washed my hands and face, smoothed my hair down, combing it with
my fingers. Going over my suit with damp toweling got off a lot of the dirt.
I put my collar on the outside of my jacket and creased the wings with my
thumbnail so it would look more like a sports shirt. It didn't really. I still
looked like a bum, but sort of a neat, non-objectionable bum.

The librarian at the main desk looked sympathetically hostile, or
hostilely sympathetic.

"I'd like to get into the stacks, miss," I said, "and see some of the old
newspapers."

"Which newspapers?" the old girl asked stiffly.

I thought back. I couldn't remember the exact date. "Ones for the first
week in November last year.

"We have the *Times* microfilmed. I would have to project them for you."

"I didn't want to see the *Times*," I said, fast. "Don't you have any newspapers on paper?" I didn't see what I wanted to read up on.

"We have the *News*, bound, for last year."

I nodded. "That's the one I wanted to see."

She sniffed and told me to follow her. I didn't rate a cart to my table, I
guess, or else the bound papers weren't supposed to come out of the
stacks.

The cases of books, row after row, smelled good. Like old leather and
good pipe tobacco. I had been here before. In this world, it's the man with
education who makes the money. I had been reading the Funk & Wagnalls
Encyclopedia. So far I knew a lot about Mark Antony, Atomic Energy,
Boron, Brussels, Catapults, Demons, and Divans.

I guess I had stopped to look around at some of the titles, because the
busy librarian said sharply, "Follow me."

I heard my voice say, "A pleasure. What about after work?"

I didn't say it, but I was used to my voice independently saying things.
Her neck got to flaming, but she walked stiffly ahead. She didn't say
anything. She must be awful mad, I decided. But then I got the idea she was
flushed with pleasure. I'm pretty ugly and I looked like a bum, but I was
young. You had to grant me that.

She waved a hand at the rows of bound *News* and left me alone with them. I wasn't sure if I was allowed to hunt up a table to lay the books on or not, so I took the volume for last year and laid it on the floor. That was the cleanest floor I ever saw.

It didn't take me long to find the story. The victim was a big man, because the story was on the second page of the Nov. 4 edition.

I started to tear the page out, then only memorized the name and home address. Somebody was sure to see me and I couldn't risk trouble just now.

I stuck the book back in line and left by the side door.

I went to a dry-cleaner, not the cheapest place I knew, because I wouldn't be safe with the change from a twenty in that neighborhood. My suit was cleaned while I waited. I paid a little extra and had it mended. Funny thing about a suit—it's almost never completely shot unless you just have it ripped off you or burned up. It wasn't exactly in style, but some rich executives wore suits out of style that they had paid a lot of money for. I remembered Fredric March's double-breasted in *Executive Suite* while Walter Pidgeon and the rest wore Ivy Leagues. Maybe I would look like an eccentric executive.

I bought a new shirt, a good used pair of shoes, and a dime pack of single-edged razor blades. I didn't have a razor, but anybody with nerve can shave with a single-edge blade and soap and water.

The clerk took my two bucks in advance and I went up to my room.

I washed out my socks and underwear, took a bath, shaved and trimmed my hair and nails with the razor blade. With some soap on my finger, I scrubbed my teeth. Finally I got dressed.

Everything was all right except that I didn't have a tie. They had them, a quarter a piece, where I got the shoes. It was only six blocks—I could go back. But I didn't want to wait. I wanted to complete the picture.

The razor blade sliced through the pink bath towel evenly. I cut out a nice modern-style tie, narrow, with some horizontal stripes down at the bottom. I made a tight, thin knot. It looked pretty good.

I was ready to leave, so I started for the door. I went back. I had almost forgotten my luggage. The box still had three unwrapped blades in it. I pocketed it. I hefted the used blade, dulled by all the work it had done. You can run being economical into stinginess. I tossed it into the wastebasket.

I had five hamburgers with, and five cups of coffee. I couldn't finish all of the French fries.

"Mac," I said to the fat counterman, who looked like all fat countermen, "give me a Milwaukee beer."

He stopped polishing the counter in front of his friend. "Milwaukee, Wisconsin, or Milwaukee, Oregon?"

"Wisconsin."

He didn't argue.

It was cold and bitter. All beer is bitter, no matter what they say on TV. I like beer. I like the bitterness of it.

I felt like another, but I checked myself. I needed a clear head. I thought about going back to the hotel for some sleep; I still had the key in my pocket (I wasn't trusting it to any clerk). No, I had had sleep on Thanksgiving, bracing up for trying the lift at Brother Partridge's. Let's see, it was daylight outside again, so this was the day after Thanksgiving. But it had only been sixteen or twenty hours since I had slept. That was enough.

I left the money on the counter for the hamburgers with and coffee and the beer. There was $7.68 left.

As I passed the counterman's friend on his stool, my voice said, "I think you're yellow."

He turned slowly, his jaw moving further away from his brain.

I winked. "It was just a bet for me to say that to you. I won two bucks. Half of it is yours." I held out the bill to him.

His paw closed over the money and punched me on the biceps. Too hard. He winked back. "It's okay."

I rubbed my shoulder, marching off fast, and I counted my money. With my luck, I might have given the counterman's friend the five instead of one of the singles. But I hadn't. I now had $6.68 left.

"I *still* think you're yellow," my voice said.

It was my voice, but it didn't come from me. There were no words, no feeling of words in my throat. It just came out of the air the way it always did.

I ran.

HAROLD R. THOMPKINS, 49, vice-president of Baysinger's, was found dead behind the store last night. His skull had been crushed by a vicious beating with a heavy implement, Coroner McClain announced in preliminary verdict. Tompkins, who resided at 1467 Claremont, Edgeway, had been active in seeking labor-management peace in the recent difficulties …

I had read that a year before. The car cards on the clanking subway and the rumbling bus didn't seem nearly so interesting to me. Outside the van, a tasteful sign announced the limits of the village of Edgeway, and back inside, the monsters of my boyhood went *bloomp* at me.

I hadn't seen anything like them in years.

The slimy, scaly beasts were slithering over the newspaper holders, the ad card readers, the girl watchers as the neat little carbon-copy modern homes breezed past the windows.

I ignored the devils and concentrated on reading the withered, washed-out political posters on the telephone poles. My neck ached from holding it so stiff, staring out through the glass. More than that, I could feel the jabberwocks staring at me. You know how it is. You can feel a stare with the back of your neck and between your eyes. They got one brush of a gaze out of me.

The things abruptly started their business, trying to act casually as if they hadn't been waiting for me to look at them at all. They had a little human being of some sort.

It was the size of a small boy, like the small boy who looked like me that they used to destroy when I was locked up with them in the dark. Except this was a man, scaled down to child's size. He had sort of an ugly, worried, tired, stupid look and he wore a shiny suit with a piece of a welcome mat or something for a necktie. Yeah, it was me. I really knew it all the time.

They began doing things to the midget me. I didn't even lift an eyebrow. They couldn't do anything worse to the small man than they had done to the young boy. It was sort of nostalgic watching them, but I really got bored with all that violence and killing and killing the same kill over and over. Like watching the Saturday night string of westerns in a bar.

The sunlight through the window was yellow and hot. After a time, I began to dose.

The shrieks woke me up.

For the first time, I could hear the shrieks of the monster's victim and listen to their obscene droolings. For the very first time in my life. Always before it had been all pantomime, like Charlie Chaplin. Now I heard the sounds of it all.

They say it's a bad sign when you start bearing voices.

I nearly panicked, but I held myself in the seat and forced myself to be rational about it. My own voice was always saying things everybody could hear but which I didn't say. It wasn't any worse to be the only one who could hear other things I never said. I was as sane as I ever was. There was no doubt about that.

But a new thought suddenly impressed itself on me.

Whatever was punishing me for my sin was determined that I turn back before reaching 1467 Claremont.

"Clarmont," the driver announced, sending the doors hissing open and the bus cranking to a stop.

I walked through the gibbering monsters, and passing the driver's seat, I heard my voice say, "Don't splatter me by starting up too soon, fat gut."

The driver looked at me with round eyes. "No, sir, I won't."

The monsters gave it up and stopped existing.

The bus didn't start until I was halfway up the block of sandine moderns and desk-size patios.

Number 1423 was different from the other houses. It was on fire.

One of the most beautiful women I've ever seen came running up to me. What black hair, what red lips, what sparkling eyes she had when I finally got up that far! "Sir," she said, "my baby brother is in there. I'd be so grateful—"

I grabbed for her. My hand went right on through. I didn't try grabbing her again. This time, I had, a feeling I would feel her. I didn't want to be *that* bad off.

I walked on, ignoring the flames shooting out of 1423.

As I reached the patio of 1467, the flames stopped. It was a queer kind of break. No fadeout, just a stoppage. I took a step backward. No flames this time, but the very worst and very biggest monster of them all. Coming suddenly like that, it got to my spine and stomach, even though I was pretty used to them. I stepped away from it and it was gone.

Number 1467 was different from the other houses, and it wasn't even on fire. It was on two lots, and it had two picture windows, but only one little porch and front door. I guess even the well-to-do have a hard time finding big houses and good building sites and the right neighborhood. The trouble is so many people are well-to-do and there just aren't enough old manses to go around.

I strolled up the stucco path and lifted the wrought iron knocker, which rang a bell.

The door opened and there was a girl there. She wasn't much compared to the one I put my hand through. But she was all right—brown hair, a nice face underneath the current shades of cosmetics, no figure for a stripper, but it would pass.

"You the maid?" I inquired.

"I am Miss Tompkins," she said,

"Oh. Any relation to Harold J. Tompkins?"

"My father. He died last year."

"Can I see your mother?"

"Mother died a few months after Daddy did."

"You'll do then."

I stepped inside. Miss Tompkins seemed too surprised to protest.

"I'm William Hagle," I said. "I want to help you."

"Mr. Hagle, whatever it is—insurance—"

"That's not it exactly," I told her. "I just want to help you. I only want to do whatever you want me to do."

She stared at me, her eyes moving too quickly over my face. "I've never even seen you before, have I? Why do you want to help me? How?"

"What's so damned hard to understand? I just want to help. I don't have any money, but I can work and give you my pay. You want me to clean up the basement, the yard? Got any painting to be done? Hell, I can even sew. Anything—don't you understand—I'll do *anything* for you."

The girl was breathing too hard now. "Mr. Hagle, if you're hungry, I can find something—no, I don't think there is anything. But I can give you some money to—"

"Damn it, I don't want your money! Here, I'll give you mine!" I wadded up the $6.38 cents I had left, plus one bus transfer, and put it on the top of a little bookcase next to the door. "I know it doesn't mean anything to you, but it's every penny I've got. Can't I do anything for you? Empty the garbage—"

"We have a disposal," she said automatically.

"Scrub the floors?'

"There's a polisher in the closet."

"Make the beds!" I yelled. "You don't have a machine for *that*, do you?"

The corners of Miss Tompkins' eyes drew up and the corners of her mouth drew down. She stayed like that for a full second, then smiled a strange smile. "You—you saw me on the street." She was breathing her words now, so softly that I could only just understand them. "You thought I was—stacked."

"To tell the truth, ma'am, you aren't so—"

"Well, sit down. Don't go away. I'll just go into the next room—slip into something comfortable—"

"Miss Tompkins!" I grabbed hold of her. She felt real. I hoped she was. "I want nothing from you. Nothing! I only want to do something for you, anything for you. I've got to help you, can't you understand? I KILLED YOUR FATHER."

I hadn't meant to tell her that, of course.

She screamed and began twisting and clawing the way I knew she would as soon as I said it. But she stopped, stunned, as if I'd slapped her out of hysterics, only I'd never let go of her shoulders.

She hung then, her face empty, repeating, *"What? What?"*

Finally she began laughing and she pulled away from me so gently and naturally that I had to let go. She sank down and sat on top of my money on the little bookcase. She laughed some more into her two open hands.

I stood there, not knowing what to do with myself.

She looked up at me and brushed away a few tears with her fingertips. *"You* want to get me off of your conscience, do you, William Hagle? God, that's a good one." She reached out and took my hand in hers. "Come along down into the basement, William. I want to show you something. Afterward, if you want to—if you really want to—you may kill me."

"Thanks," I said.

I couldn't think of anything else to say.

Down in the basement, the machinery looked complex, with all sorts of thermostats and speedometers.

"Automatic stoker?" I asked.

"Time machine," she said.

"You don't mean a time machine like H. G. Wells'," I said, to show her I wasn't ignorant.

"Not exactly like that, but close," she answered sadly. "This has been the cause of all your trouble, William."

"It has?"

"Yes. This house and the ground around it are the Primary Focus area for the Hexers. The Hexers have tormented and persecuted you all your life. They got you into trouble. They made you think you were going crazy—"

"I never thought I was going crazy!" I yelled at her.

"That must have made it worse," she said miserably.

I thought about it. "I suppose it did. What are the Hexers? What—for the sake of argument—have they got against me?"

"The Hexers aren't human. I suppose they are extraterrestrials. No one ever told me. Maybe they are a kind of human strain that went different. I don't really know. They want different things than we do, but they can buy some of them with money, so they can be hired. People in the future hire them to hex people in the past."

"Why would anybody up ahead there with Buck Rogers want to cause me trouble? I'm dead then, aren't I?"

"Yes, you must be. It's a long time into the future. But, you see, some of my relatives there want to punish you for—it must be for killing Father. They lost out on a chain of inheritance because he died when he did. They have money now, but they are bitter because they had to make it themselves. They can afford every luxury—even the luxury of revenge."

I suppose when you keep seeing monsters and hearing yourself say things you didn't say, you can believe unusual things easier. I believed Miss Tompkins.

"It was not murder," I said. "I killed him by accident."

"No matter. They would hex you if you had hit him with a car in a fog or given him the flu by sneezing in his face. I understand people are hexed all the time for things they never even knew they did. People up there have a lot of leisure, a lot of time to indulge their every irritation or hate. I think it must be decadent, the way Rome was."

"What do you—and the machine—have to do with my hex?" I asked.

"This is the Primary Focus area, I told you. It's how the Hexers get into this time hypothesis. They can't get back into this Primary itself, but they can come and go through the outer boundary. It's hard to set up a Primary Focus—takes a tremendous drain of power. They broke through into the basement of the old house before I was born and Daddy was the first custodian of the machine. He never knew that he was helping avenge his own death. They let that slip later, after—it happened."

"Why did they come to you? Why did you help them?"

She turned half away. "The custodian is well paid. My relatives preferred the salary to go to someone in the family, instead of an outsider. Daddy accepted the offer and I've carried on the job."

"Paid? You were paid?"

She brushed at her eyes. "Oh, not in United States currency. But—Daddy got to be president of the store. It was set up so he could make a fortune that they could inherit. All he left was his insurance, and that went to mother. She died a few months later and some of it went to me and the rest to her relatives."

"You mean my life has been like it has because some descendants of yours in the future hate me for an accident that deprived them of some money?"

She nodded enthusiastically. "You understand! And because I helped the Hexers they hired get to you. I was afraid you wouldn't believe me. Now"—she stopped to exhale—"do you want to kill me?"

"No, I don't want to kill you." I walked over and squinted at the machine. "Could I get into the future with this thing?"

"I don't know how you work the outer boundary. I think you need something else. There's an internal energy contact—you can talk to Communications." She raced through that. "You want to kill *them*, don't you? The Hexers and my relatives?"

"I don't want to kill anybody," I told her patiently. "I feel dirty just hearing how far some people can go for revenge. I just want them to let me alone. Why don't they kill me and get it over with?"

"They haven't a license to kill. Not yet. There's legislation going on."

"Listen," I said, listening to the idea coming into my head, "listen. These descendants of your mother's relatives—they *did* inherit money because your father died. Maybe they feel grateful to me. Maybe they would help me. Would you help me try to talk to them?"

"Yes," Miss Tompkins said, and she used a dial on the machine.

It was as simple as putting through a phone call.

"We really understand your situation," Mr. Grimes-Tompkins said. "But it would take quite a bit to buy off the Hexers. However, we certainly appreciate the killing you made for us."

"Couldn't you buy off the Hexers, then, with some of the money I brought to your side of the family?" I asked.

"We don't appreciate it that much."

"What? You aren't going to pay him back for killing my father?" Miss Tompkins cried, outraged.

"Look," I said, "if you had some money of mine, would you pay off the Hexers for me? You do still use money up there, don't you?"

"We certainly do, young man. Just what did you have in mind?"

"If I gave you authorization now to use any assets I have in your time, would it be legal?"

"Declarations by temporal transmission? Yes, of course. Routine transaction."

"Take any money I have and use it to pay off the Hexers. Will you do it?"

"I don't see why not, since our ancestor seems to approve."

Miss Tompkins regarded me solemnly. "What do you intend to do, William?"

"Banks are out," I said, thinking hard. "They don't let inactive accounts go on drawing interest more than twenty years, or something like that. But government bonds don't have to be converted when they mature. One bond can pile up a fantastic amount of interest for them to collect."

"You have government bonds, William?"

"Not yet."

Miss Tompkins stood close to me. "I have plenty of money, William. I'll give it to you. You can buy bonds in my name."

"No. I'll get my own money."

"Shall I destroy the machine, William? Of course they'll only open another Focus—"

"No, you would just get yourself hexed too."

"What can I do, William?" she asked. "All along, ever since I was a little girl, I've known I've been helping to torture somebody. I didn't even know your name, William, but I helped torture you—"

"Because I killed your father."

"—and I've got to make it up to you. I'll give you everything, William, everything."

"Sure," I said, "to take me off your conscience. And if I take your offer and you get hexed, what happens to my conscience? Do we go around again—me working my tail off to raise the dough to get you unhexed, and you buying the Hexers off me? Where would it stop? We're even right now. Let's let it go at that."

"But, William, if we've taken, now we can give to each other."

She looked almost pretty then, and I wanted her the way I'd always wanted women. But I knew better. She wasn't going to get me into any trouble.

"No, thanks. Good-by."

I walked away from her.

For the first time, I could see what my life would be like if I wasn't hexed. Now I could realize that I knew how to do things right if I was only let alone.

The intern took the blood smear. He reeled off a long string of questions about diseases I wasn't allowed to have.

"No," I said, "and I haven't given blood in the last thirty days."

He took my sample of blood and left.

I had to have eighteen dollars and seventy-five cents. They paid you twenty dollars a pint for blood here.

One government bond held for centuries would pile up a fortune in interest. The smallest bond you can buy is twenty-five dollars face value, and it costs eighteen seventy-five.

If I had kept that twenty, I would have had a buck and a quarter change. But if I hadn't have gotten cleaned up, the hospital might not have accepted me as a donor at all. They had had some bad experiences from old bums dying from giving too often.

I only hoped I could force myself to let that bond go uncashed through the rest of my life.

The intern returned, his small mustache now pointing down. "Mr. Hagle, I have some bad news for you. Very bad. I hardly know how to tell you, but—you've got lukemia."

I nodded. "That means you won't take my blood." Maybe it also meant that I would never be allowed to have eighteen dollars and seventy-five cents in one lump again as long as I lived.

"No," the intern finally managed. "We can't accept your blood—"

I waved him off. "Isn't there some fund to take care of lukemia victims? Feed them, house them, send them to Florida to soak up the sun?"

"Certainly there is such a fund, and you may apply, Mr. Hagle."

"I'd certainly benefit a lot from that fund. Doctor, humor me. Test me again and see if I still have lukemia."

He did. I didn't.

"I don't understand this," the intern said, looking frightened. "Transitory lukemia? It must be a lab error."

"Will you buy my blood now?"

"I'm afraid as long as there is some doubt—this must be something new."

"I suppose it is," I told him. "I have all sorts of interesting symptoms."

"You do?" The intern was vitally interested. "Feel free to tell me all about them."

"I see and hear things."

"Really?"

"Do you believe in ESP?"

"I've sometimes wondered."

"Test me as much as you like. You'll find that in any game of chance, I score consistently far below the level of wins I should get by the law of averages. I'm psionically subnormal. And that's just the beginning."

"This must be *really* new," the intern said, eyes shining.

"It is," I assured him. "And listen, Doctor, you don't want to turn something like me over to your superiors, to leave me to the mercies of the A.M.A. This can be big, Doctor, *big*."

They offered Hagle's Disease to a lot of comedians, but finally it was the new guy, Biff Kelsey, that got it and made it his own. He did a thirty-hour telethon for Hagle's Disease.

Things really started to roll then. Boston coughed up three hundred thousand alone. The most touching contribution came from Carrville.

I plugged away on the employ-the-physically-handicapped theme and was made president of the Foundation for the Treatment of Hagle's Disease. Dr. Wise (the intern) was the director.

So far, I had been living soft at Cedars, but I hadn't got my hands on one red cent. I wanted to get that government bond to buy off the Hexers, but at the same time it no longer seemed so urgent. They seemed to have given up, and were just sitting back waiting for their bribe.

One morning three months later, Doc Wise came worriedly into my room at the hospital.

"I don't like these reports, William," he said. "They all say there's nothing wrong with you."

"It comes and it goes," I said casually. "You saw some of the times when it came."

"Yes, but I'm having trouble convincing the trustees you weren't malingering. And, contrary to our expectations, no one else in the country seems to have developed Hagle's Disease."

"Stop worrying, Doc. Read the Foundation's charter. You have to treat Hagle's Disease, which means you can use that money to treat *any* disease of mine while we draw our salaries. I must have *something* wrong with me."

Wise shook his head. "Nothing. Not even dandruff or B.O. You are the healthiest man I have ever examined. It's *unnatural*."

Six months afterward, I had been walking all night in the park, in the rain. I hadn't had anything to eat recently and I had fever and I began sneezing. The money was still in the bank—no, not in my name—I couldn't touch it; Miss Tompkins' descendants couldn't touch it—just waiting for me to—

I started running toward the hospital.

I slammed my fists against Wise's door. "Obed up, Wise. Id's be, Hagle. I god a cold. *That's* a disease, is'd it?"

Wise threw back the door. "What did you say?"

"I said 'Open up, Wise. It's me, Hagle. I've got a cold' . . . Never mind, Wise, never mind."

But you don't want to hear about all that. You want to know about what happened in the relief office. There's not much to tell.

I picked up the check from the guy's desk and looked at it. Nine fifty-seven to buy food for two weeks. I griped that it wasn't enough—not enough to keep alive on and save eighteen seventy-five clear in a lifetime.

The slob at the desk said, "What have you got to complain about? You got your health, don't you?"

That's when I slugged him and smashed up the relief office, and that's why the four cops dragged me here, and that's why I'm lying here on your couch telling you this story, Dr. Schultz.

I had my health, sure, but I finally figured out why. If you believe any of this, you're thinking that the Hexers must have laid off me, which is why I'm healthy. I thought so too, but how would that add up?

Look, I tried every way I could to raise eighteen seventy-five to buy a government bond. I never made it. I never made it because I wasn't *allowed* to.

But I didn't know it because I'd been euchred into the Foundation for the Treatment of Hagle's Disease. Hundreds of thousands of dollars, all earmarked for one purpose only—treating my disease —and I haven't got any!

Or maybe you're figuring the way I did, that senility is a disease, and all I have to do is wait for it to creep up on me so I can get some of that Foundation money. But the Hexers have that fixed too, I'll bet. I'm not sure, but I think I'm going to live for centuries without a sick day in my life. In other words, I'm going to live that life out as poor as I am right now!

It's a fantastic story, Doctor, but you believe me, don't you? You *do* believe every word of it. You *have* to, Doctor!

Because a persecution complex is kind of a disease and I'd have to be treated for it.

Now will you let me out of this jacket so I can smoke a cigarette?

AFTERWORD

The world of books is full of rich heroes: Gatsby; Nick Charles, the Thin Man; Lamont Cranston, The Shadow; even Bruce Wayne, Batman. I thought I would at least do a short story about a poor man. I certainly could identify with my protagonist. We never had much money growing up, and for many years I did not earn much as a writer.

When I wrote this story I was living at home in Mount Carmel, Illinois. However, it reflects almost precognition on my part. I did live to actually encounter the skid row types I imagined, and rather correctly foresaw. After I moved to Los Angeles a publisher I had worked for allegedly went broke and refused to pay me for several paperback novels I had written. I had to take a job working as a telephone solicitor and many of my compatriots were down-and-outers similar to the ones in this story.

Most were alcoholics. I was given the job of office manager because I appeared to be the most sober (easy to do since I did not drink at all), not because of my salesmanship abilities.

I learned these people could be generous. One morning when I was feeling depressed by the job and my present circumstances, and admitted to feeling bad, one of my co-workers offered me a pull on his wine bottle, stuff that was life's blood to him. I turned it down, but I appreciated the generosity of the offer.

Then came the surprise. The publisher finally paid me for those books. I was back to living and writing in my Hollywood apartment. But I still was far from rich. I could now remember what I had only imagined in this story.

THE DEPTHS

"You don't know what feeling low means until you've been in the Depths," the beef-fed businessman told Amel Smith.

Smith smiled politely, gazed into the three dimensional mural of the Arizona desert on the bulkhead, and blotted the bloom of perspiration from his upper lip.

None of the other passengers seemed concerned. They sat in their seats as confidently as cavalrymen would sit saddles. The Light Brigade, for instance, he thought suddenly. *Into the Valley of Death, rode the six hundred . . .*

Can that! Smith warned himself. Cancan . . . No, they used plastic bags. He stripped the foil from the tip of a roll of mints and popped one into his mouth. Life-Saver. Really need a . . . Smith shut his eyes hard.

"I'm in steel," the businessman said. "What's your line?"

"I'm a cowboy," Smith informed him.

"Pardon?"

"Rodeo work. Competition. Riding broucs, Brahmas, that kind of thing. It's an organized sport, like baseball. I'm a professional player."

"Come from out west, I suppose?"

"Philadelphia," Smith explained.

"Well," said the businessman, "after riding broncs, you shouldn't let a little thing like this trip . . . *throw* you. Ha-ha. Now, don't take what I said at first about feeling 'low' too seriously. They exaggerate about the Depths."

"No, they don't," Smith said grimly, rubbing his palms over the bony ridges of his long legs. "We are about to descend into the Pit. We are about to experience every terror known to Man."

"All we're going to do, my friend," the beefy businessman said, "is take a simple inner-planetary trip. We are going to take a rocket through a tunnel bored completely through the Earth, from Chicago to Capetown. We are following a law of simple geometry—the shortest distance between two points is a straight line. All those boys making globes after Columbus threw us off but we finally got back on the right track. Every boy who ever tried to dig a hole through to China knew the right way to travel on this planet instinctively."

"Boys play with fire," Smith said, looking around uneasily at the completely windowless compartment.

"First trip jitters, that's all."

Smith felt a muscle jump in the hard ridge of his cheek, and pressed his fingers against it to stop it. "Don't you *see*? We are going *down*, as in going down for the third time. We are *falling* clean through the world. What greater terrors for an aquaphobe or an acrophobe? The oceans of the planet will be over us completely, and we'll be surrounded by the mass of millions of mountains, completely trapped. Alone. Yet with hundreds of people from whom we absolutely can not get away. What are we doing? The symbolic nature of our trip can not escape any student of Freud, or even the subconscious of those who *must* neurotically reject Freud. Where are we headed? According to almost all religions, those powerful primeval influences, we are heading straight for Hell!"

Smith leaned back on his contour seat, and stared ahead. "Such things as air and space travel can't touch inner-planetary travel for terror. It is the ultimate in human *fear*."

The businessman shifted in his seat. "I'm not so much afraid. Just kind of . . . depressed."

"Of course you feel low. You are sinking into the Depths."

"Look," the businessman said impatiently, "if you feel so dead set against Depth travel, why are you taking this trip?"

"I've got to get to Capetown before midnight tonight in order to collect an inheritance from the estate of an uncle. I've got to give up rodeo work. An allergy."

"Horses?" the businessman asked.

Smith shook his head. "Blood. Psychosomatic, not physiological, of course."

The businessman got up and changed seats.

A pretty blonde girl entered the compartment and sat down next to

Smith. Her nose, he observed, was too small.

"Aren't you filled with a feeling of mystical wonder?" the pretty blonde girl inquired of Smith.

"Really quite too small, he thought. "Not exactly," he said.

She turned towards him in furious intensity. "Doesn't traveling through the heart of the planet itself make you feel as one with Mother Earth and all her peoples?"

Smith shook his head.

"Then what does going underground make you think of?" she demanded.

"The grave," Smith said. "The walls will crush in upon us, making us one with Mother Earth indeed."

"The walls cannot crush in. They are firmly held back by force beams that would hold them back were they pressing together with ten times their urgency."

The two of them sat back and listened to the gentle blur of words from the driver filtering through the mesh of the speaker.

"Good evening. This is your driver. We will arrive in Capetown, eleven fifty, p.m., African Standard Time. The trip will take forty-four minutes. Inner-Planetary Lines have provided means of amusing yourselves for the duration, and we trust time will not hang heavy on your hands. Thank you."

"Miss," Smith said, "I think perhaps you'd better change your seat. I'm not at all sure I can control myself."

The girl looked at him, startled. "Surely you can, if you really try. I am a student of Eastern philosophy myself, and have complete authority over my impulses."

A muscle worked in Smith's angular jaw. "I have a horrible fear I am going to make a fool out of myself. I don't know what going into the Depths will do for me. I've always been alarmed at the idea. I may throw a fit. Or something."

"Is *that* all?" the girl said.

"All?" Smith faced her. "Young lady, I am Arizona Amel Smith. I make my living riding the backs of berserk animals, and all of the time, up in the stands, the audience is waiting for me to get thrown and have my head trampled into a bloody mess. It's not merely that they want to see me killed—I could forgive them a natural emotion like that—they want to see me *fall*, to be ingloriously thrown, to lose my dignity, like slipping on a banana peel. Nothing is so funny to them. I don't like to give people a laugh by shedding my blood. Neither do I want to lose my composure on this trip and be a laughing stock."

The girl looked at him steadily. "Mr. Smith, if you don't want that, it never has to happen. The human mind can achieve all it desires." Her gaze faltered. "You told me your name. Mine is Sarah Applewhite. I go to Hunter."

"Sophomore," he said.

"Yes. How did you know?" Before he could answer, Disaster struck.

The craft's automatic safety system called Disaster, after what it was supposed to prevent, went into action.

The craft jerked to an abrupt halt and the passengers rose from their seats, wafting on the air conduction.

"Null-gravity?" Smith murmured. "Are we at the center of the Earth?"

"Near enough," a junior officer said, kicking forward from the rear. "You've got a few ounces of weight, but it hardly matters. The currents from the forced air-vents will toss you around like feathers."

"I am no dandelion puff-ball," the businessman said. "Shut off the forced air."

"I don't think that would be wise, sir," the junior officer demured. "We should all suffocate in a few moments from the accumulation of carbon dioxide we breathe out."

"In that case," said the businessman, "perhaps you'd better not shut them off."

Smith was terrified, as he had expected to be. Yet, somehow the disaster was gratifying. It vindicated his superior judgement and intuition in expecting it.

He became aware of the girl floating beside him, her face a poem of rapture.

"Miss Applewhite, are you feeling well?" he asked.

"I feel *wonderful*," the girl breathed. "Have you ever known a more glorious sensation?"

"You haven't, obviously," Smith said.

The driver appeared in the compartment doorway, a white marble pillar in an ocean of chaos.

"Please keep calm, ladies and gentlemen. Our retro-rockets somehow fired prematurely. Certain adjustments will have to be made. We will be about twenty minutes late."

"That means," Smith said, "I will be five minutes after midnight arriving in Capetown. I'll lose a fortune."

"My wife's going to be angry waiting for me in that depot," the fat businessman observed.

"My husband's going to get suspicious, I don't show up on time," a woman with a British accent observed.

"There is a more urgent trouble," the Hunter sophomore said. "There is another rocket only fifteen minutes behind us in this tube. If we remain twenty minutes behind schedule, five minutes before Capetown, the second rocket will collide with us and we will be blown to Kingdom Come."

Howls of anguish, anger and fear tore through the confined atmosphere of the craft.

Smith nodded thoughtfully to himself. Just as he had expected.

The driver turned a face as stern as the one on an armed forces recruiting poster to the girl. "Miss, I don't really think it was wise to mention the rocket behind us. You seem to have produced rather a bit of stark panic."

"I believe in Truth, driver," she said. "We all have a right to it."

'The fools," the fat businessman observed, looking at the groaning faces about him. "They should know all you have to do is telephone back and have the second rocket fire its retros, too."

"Yes, sir, I'll tell them that in a moment, when they've calmed." The driver then muttered something to himself.

"What was that?" the businessman demanded.

"Nothing," the driver said.

"I know what it was," Sarah Applewhite of Hunter said. "I can read lips. He said, 'I wish it were true'."

"What?" the businessman shouted. "You mean you *can't* telephone back?"

The driver took the businessman's arm and eased him into his armchair. "It might be best if you remain seated. Just use your seatbelt so you don't float about so much. No, sir, it won't be possible to telephone back, Mr.—" he glanced at the illuminated seating chart overhead "—Bosley. The premature retroing caused us to skid against the tunnel wall, shredding the lines."

Businessman Bosley stared ahead numbly. "Why don't your damned Depth-craft carry radios anyway?"

"Sir," the driver said, "the tunnel is *theoretically* straight, but it takes much less than eight thousand miles for an error of forty-two feet, the width of the tunnel, to occur. Radio depends on essentially straight-line communication."

Bosley sank back, his chin quivering like an elaborate bridge party jello mould. "I—hadn't counted on *that*."

"Easy, sir, try to take it calmly like Mr. Smith and Miss Applewhite."

As the pilot drifted off, Bosley turned to the cowboy. "Yes, for God's sake, Smith, how can you take this so calmly? Why, you're not only going to die with the rest of us, but good lord, man, you're also losing a fortune!"

Smith studied Bosley calmly, as he has observed the whole situation. Finally, he spoke. One word.

"*Fools*," he said.

"Pardon?"

"Fools! All of you. Making a routine inner-planetary flight, were you? Well, I *knew* I was heading for my doom. Now who was right, Mr. Bosley, who was right?"

Bosley teethed his underlip like a ripe plumb. "But if you knew, why did you come?"

"Bosley, you just got through saying that I stood to lose a fortune if I didn't complete this trip."

"Yes," said Bosley. "Yes."

Smith settled back and regarded the girl beside him.

"Why are *you* so calm?" Smith asked. "I, at least, have the satisfaction of knowing I was right."

"Mr. Smith, because of my extensive training during the last five months in Zen and Yoga and related philosophies, I have completely mastered all negative emotions, such as fear. I could walk in front of a truck or off a cliff without batting an eye."

In spite of himself, Smith was impressed.

Bosley thinned his lips. "It works, does it? That philosophy stuff? It can make you calm at a moment like this?"

"Absolutely resigned," she assured him.

"You mean I won't run around like a chicken with its head off looking for a way out—some impossible means of escape?" Bosley demanded.

"That would be pretty undignified," Smith observed.

"You needn't worry about that. Just let me explain my philosophy and you'll sit there and die serenely."

"Confession," Bosley babbled. "Confession is good for the soul, and all that rot. You're trying to trick me. You're trying to make me confess!"

"Absolutely not," Sarah said. "You must *forget* worldly things. You don't want to remind yourself by talking about them."

To Smith, Bosley's face was beginning to look like a stewing tomato.

"Trying to trick me!" the businessman babbled on, as others in the craft began to regard him as distastefully as if he were fingering his nose. "Trick! Trying to make me admit I'm Smith's cousin, that I set a time relay switch to fire the retro-rockets prematurely so Smith would be late and he'd lose his inheritance—*to me*. I know what you're up to. But I won't say it—because I'm not really guilty. I didn't know about the rocket behind us. *I didn't know we would all be killed—I only thought we would be late!*"

Bosley stopped suddenly, aware of what he had said, and aware that everybody had been listening to his shouting.

"Trapped!" Bosley murmured. "Trapped down here with people doomed to die by my hand. Trapped with a bunch of snarling, howling wild animals who will tear me to shreds with their last breath. *Trapped* with the man I was trying to cheat and now whom I've murdered!"

Smith averted his tightly controlled eyes. "For God's sake, Bosley, stop making such a damned spectacle of yourself. Everybody is *staring* at us."

Bosley slumped in his seat. "Nevertheless, it's true, every word of it. I'm sorry, Smith. Cousin Amel. Genuinely sorry. Ha! Sorry I've sentenced you all to death. All of you—and all of me. But I didn't know, I didn't know. I thought we'd only be *late*, not that we'd be killed."

A handsome, gray-haired man placed a lean hand on Bosley's shoulder. "There now, we all make mistakes, my dear fellow. Cigaret?" he said.

Bosley started to accept, then shook his head. "I'm trying to cut down. Bad for my throat."

Suddenly, Bosley jerked up his head.

"Poison, is it? Hemlock in the tobacco, is it?" he cried. "No, my friend, you aren't going to dispose of me quite that easily. If you want to lynch me you'll have to do it with a rope. In null-gravity. Ha-ha. I'm guilty. I admit it. But I'll die with the rest of you. That's ironic, poetic justice, isn't it? What does it matter if I die a few moments sooner? You don't have the right to take the law into your own hands. I've committed a crime, but I deserve a fair trial."

Releasing his seat-belt, Bosley kicked free and hung defiantly in mid-air. "I'll defend myself," he warned. "I'll kill the first man who lays a hand on me."

Reluctantly, Smith released his belt and floated up towards his unknown cousin.

"Bosley," Smith said, "you're as hysterical as the next rider up after a Brahma-goring. I'm going to have to knock some sense back into you, and frankly, I'm going to enjoy it, I really don't much care for being cheated out of a fortune or planted in a death trap."

Smith launched himself at Bosley, but the fat man moved as gracefully as a balloon and kicked the cowboy in the stomach.

But Smith knew how to take a fall as well as Poe's Usher. He jack-knifed and landed on his feet in the middle of nothing, glaring at Bosley who now hung upside down to him.

Spurring himself on, Smith drove his knotted fist in the huge dimple that was Bosley's navel. It drove the angry pain out through the fat man's rounded mouth. Smith flattened the kiss-shaped lips with his other fist, as Bosley, remembering the carefree days of his boyhood, jerked a knee towards Smith's groin.

The rodeo rider caught the pudgy knee on his thigh as he would the ridged back of a bucking horse. He grabbed the crook of the knee and yanked upward, causing Bosley to crack the back of his neck against a bulkhead and to get his beefy shoulders caught in an air vent.

Smith anchored himself to a hand-hold rail used when the craft carried tourist class passengers with an angle of his leg, and used both fists to punish Bosley's distorted, bloated face. The knuckles rang against bone and bridgework, and Bosley's nose and lips puffed and bloomed out in blood.

Something was bothering Smith. Finally, he realized it was the driver who was separating him from Bosley before he killed him.

He allowed himself to be returned to his own seat and strapped down. There he sat staring at his bloodied hands.

"Terrible, isn't it?" Sarah Applewhite said. "The blood of your fellow man on your hand."

Smith turned his hands over and examined them, intrigued by the suppleness of his wrists. "Yes," he said. "There's blood on my hands. Yet I'm not afraid of it, or repulsed by it. But in the arena the merest of gored loins or a mangled foot or just the trace of crimson on a sharp hoof freezes me. I can't understand why I'm all right now. Unless—"

"Go on," the girl urged him.

"In the arena, if blood is spilled—particularly *my* blood—it means I've *failed*. But here it means I *succeeded*. I successfully beat Bosley. I don't think I'll ever be afraid of blood again."

"But you didn't really succeed, you know," Sarah said helpfully. "You gave in to your animal instincts, instead of conquering them. You shook this whole craft with your brute force."

Yes, he thought, it had seemed as if the world had shook with the thunder of his blows. It had been invigorating, satisfying. But there was something else here, his mind told him. He felt alive, and he wanted to live.

"Driver," he called. "*Driver!*"

A dozen helpful hands held Smith down as the driver was fetched and Bosley cowered back in his seat.

"Now what is this all about, Mr. Smith?" the driver asked with strained patience.

"Driver, I've got a way to save all of our lives," Smith said.

"May I remind you, Mr. Smith, that is my job, not yours."

"But *I* can actually do it!"

"Smith, I'm only human. How much backtalk do you expect me to take from you?"

"Listen to me, will you?" Smith pleaded. "Didn't you notice how the craft rocked while I was fighting Bosley? That's just what we need to save us."

"Oh? You want to have another round with Bosley, do you?"

"*No.* I mean that even though we don't have weight, we have mass and inertia," Smith said. "What happens when an automobile stalls off a powered road? You *push*. True, you generally get *out* and push, but we can all push *from inside*, by throwing our mass against the backs of the seats and developing enough inertia to move us."

"We can hardly 'push' this craft four thousand miles," the pilot said hesitantly.

"We won't have to," Smith went on. "If we push the craft it will begin moving. Left to itself it will only go so high and then fall back to the center, but with the rocket coming behind us, we will be helped by the shock wave of air that precedes it. If we are motionless that shock wave will not be able to overcome our inertia and we will crash. If we are already moving, then some of the inertia will already have been overcome and the shock wave will move us along a little faster. The air between will serve as an effective cushion and the second rocket will approach more and more slowly as we move along faster and faster. It will push us four thousand miles."

"The drive nodded. "Yes, I recall reading something like that in THE INTELLIGENT MAN'S GUIDE TO SCIENCE years ago. But there are many variables. If we don't manage enough speed, if the ship comes to peak height with our pushing and begins to fall back as the next rocket comes along—"

"Then we are dead, but no deader than we would be if we did nothing"

"It's worth trying," the driver said. "This will probably cost me my job if it does work—even my Individual Initiative index is dangerously high as it is, but damn it, I'd rather be unemployed than dead."

They tried it.

Two hundred and three human beings threw themselves against the solid backs of the contour seats in front of them, until with each lunge, the ship inched forward, lunge by inch, inch by lunge.

Bosley added his pennyweight to the effort by beating against the back of the chair in front of him with both fists, and screaming, "Let me out, let me out! I'll be *good*. I won't do it *again*."

And the craft was moving smoothly, falling upward with its speed squaring by the second.

Smith leaned back confidently. He looked at Sarah. He was feeling so invigorated that he decided her nose was not really too small after all.

"You'll lose your inheritance," she said comfortingly.

"I'm not so sure. I think we will be within the city limits of Capetown by midnight, and I will have a lot of witnesses to prove it. But if I do, I'm sure now that I can bear up under the loss."

"You have achieved self-mastery," Sarah said. "Now no matter how hungry, cold, starved and miserable you are, you will always be happy."

"Yes," he said casually.

"You see, you were wrong about something terrible happening to you if you descended into the depths. It is only thinking that makes a thing so."

"Yes," Smith said. "Will you step into the alcove with me? I have something to tell you."

They left their seats and enjoyed the luxury of walking.

Smith and Sarah walked into the privacy alcove between the restrooms where many a young man took a girl to steal a kiss or a bracelet.

"Sarah," he intoned deeply, "you don't know what a *satisfying* experience that was for me back there, how it let me conquer all my fears and anxieties about my work, my life, even this trip."

"You have achieved self-mastery," Sarah said, her breath sweet on his cheeks. "Now no matter how hungry, cold, starved and miserable you are, you will always be happy."

"Yes," he said. "I do have that to look forward to."

"And," she went on, "Now you recognize blood to be the stream of life that it is, and never again need you fear the spilling of it."

Smith gazed at the gentle beauty of Sarah's profile, a schematic diagram of youth and innocence.

"Miss Applewhite—Sarah," he said with deep feeling, "Will you marry me?"

AFTERWORD

It seemed easy for me to sell to H.L. Gold but I found it hard to sell to *Fantasy and Science Fiction*. Finally, they accepted my story, "The Depths" and even ran it as the lead story for the issue. But I had help.

The editor turned it over to their science expect, Isaac Asimov, to pass on my pseudo-science. Asimov replaced my Impervium metal with force-field projectors. I'm not sure that moved the story into conventional science. He also made a few other little changes, altering perhaps five per cent of the story.

Despite the differences in our age, education, success and no doubt I.Q. points, Ike Asimov and I had become good friends at the many SF conventions we both attended.

BAKER'S DOZENS

"Mr. Street, you are the foremost xenologist on Earth," the director of Extraterrestrial Investigations said to the tall man.

"I know," Street said.

"What do you know about the infamous criminal, Baker, the so-called 'Robin Hood' who is actually a scarlet fiend?"

"Everything."

"Surely not how he died."

"Everything but that."

The director put his briefcase on his knees. "Mr. Street, my agency received numerous accounts of his death, or deaths, on various worlds. Can you tell me which, if any, of these stories is true by studying our intelligence reports?"

"Easily," Street said.

"We have had Baker under observation many times by our planted Qrwells—our peepbugs—but you must understand that we need absolute *proof* on him since he has supporters even on Earth, and in waiting for that proof, we lost contact often at vital moments."

"I understand perfectly," Street assured him.

I

"Are there really space pirates?" Mrs. Fuljohn inquired of him, giggling furiously.

"Yes, Virginia, there really are space pirates," Baker assured her.

135

Mrs. Fuljohn lowered very long lashes over formidable eyes. "My first name is Christine. Will they come at us out of the void with all guns blasting?"

"I doubt it. They would want to rob the liner, not disintegrate it."

Baker excused himself and strolled toward the afterdeck of "A" class.

He had lied to the lady. (The hyper-Orwell focused directly on him picked up the tiny whisper of his subvocalizations.) He was a pirate, but there was one part of the cargo he did want to destroy, not steal—the first-grade readers for the Mission Houses for Alien Natives on Ignatz XI. Men called him a traitor to the human race, but he seethed at the corruptive propaganda being fed to the swinoid youngsters of the planet.

This little piggy went to market, this little piggy stayed home . . . This little piggy had roast beef, this little piggy had none . . .

It was insidious, evil. It said in effect that races who shared a common ancestor with the pig had better trade with Earthmen on their terms—on *any* terms—if they hoped to go on being allowed to eat.

Double-dealing Earthmen with their devious schemes were daily robbing literal-minded extraterrestrials like the Ignatz swinoids blind. Sometimes it made him ashamed to be an Earthman. Let some call him a renegade! He was going to help these sentient beings.

He had a plan, even if he lacked the armed battle cruiser that the pirates had in the teletapes. There was a small corvet waiting for him on Ignatz XI. It lacked the restricted official light-drive of military and police craft, having only a civilian planetary-field booster, but if all went well, it would be sufficient for his escape.

Baker glanced at the dial of his watch—it showed no telltale color of listening devices within his area. (The detector had been sold to him by an ETI agent and, of course, it lied.) Confident, he stepped over the chain separating him from the stairs to "B" Deck.

Wurmong was waiting for him as planned.

"*Si,*" the fat swarthy man said, "my brother, my nephews, my cousins—we will bring our extra luggage to the cargo hold tonight."

"I'll predispose the guards. Come right into Hold 7. Understand?"

"*Da,*" Wurmong assured him.

The man on watch collapsed soundlessly at a beam of nerve pressure on the neck, and Baker slipped inside, immediately beginning to eject the first-grade readers through the escape hatch by the gross.

The mercenary, Wurmong, and his army of family arrived with experienced stealth and began dumping the new books from their privileged luggage.

Baker replaced the contents of the opened crates with the variant readers. These volumes might be the tiny counterbalance needed to free a world of swinoids from domination by Earth. Who knew the full extent of the psychological effect of *The Three Little Pigs* on young, formative minds?

His work done, Baker sadly regarded the precious jewels and the negotiable bonds from the registered mail. There was no way around it. This had to look like a robbery. It was necessary that he take them. Quickly, he stuffed everything into his synthetic appendix . . .

Baker was allowed to disembark on Ignatz XI so that he might be traced to his alien fellow-conspirators.

The heavy-jowled biped who greeted him at the smoky tavern was joyous. "You have done the next best thing for us to enabling us to tell your busybody missionaries to go home. We look upon you as one of our own and are hungry for the sight of you. May you remain with us long."

"Too much work," Baker said, gagging over the native beer. "But I must ask you a favor. You implied you'd give me your right arm."

"Anything we have is yours. But would not a cadaver's limb suit you as well as mine?"

"I must escape from this world. You can give a private citizen like me something only a sovereign government can. I want the speed of light."

"Not that!"

"YES! I've earned it, haven't I?"

The swinoid nodded wearily. "You have. The device will be put in your spacer. Use it only in deep space."

He was now in orbit. That was far enough out. Earth patrols could still pick him up easily. The ETI spy pickup observed him as he reached out and put a finger to the button of the device given him by the Swinoids as Earth ships closed rapidly. He pressed the button.

In a crisping flash of flame, he lit with incredible speed.

II

"Naturally, we lost contact after the ship went up in flames. If that man was the true Baker, he was undoubtedly destroyed. Of course, we have a report from our spies on Klondike II of events running just about concurrently."

"If you'll allow one interruption," Street interjected. "As a competent xenological ethologist, I can assure you that Baker was, at least, not completely destroyed by the fire. His somewhat roasted remains would have been appropriated by the swinoids."

"How so?"

"These people are as similar to pigs as we are to apes. When one of their own wishes to die, as they thought Baker did, in their typical alien literal-mindedness, they dispose of his body in a special way. Remember how they said they thought of Baker as one of their own and were hungry even for the sight of him?"

III

Baker had been walking for two weeks across the primitive surface of the mining planet, Klondike II, to reach the shack in the gray shadow of the granite mountain. It wasn't gold he was after but escape. Unlike others seeking it, he had headed away the saloons. But the peepbug's lens of air had followed him.

Minutes later, he was knocking on the door. He *had* to have a means of transportation at least as good as government ships to do his work of helping the aliens, and make his escapes. At least as good and preferably better.

The door was cracked open by a kind-looking old man. "You got five seconds to get, before thirty thousand volts of electricity go through those floorboards you're standing on," the old man said kindly.

"Professor Gentle," Baker said hastily, "I have many friends. One of them has told me you have established a major breakthrough in electronics, that you have in fact invented a machine to transmit matter as radio and television transmit sound and sight."

"Some loose-lipped electronics jobber found that out, did he? Step right in.

"Do you suppose *I* might be teleported?" Baker asked tentatively.

"Of course you can, my boy. But first perhaps you'd like to take a look at some of the things I have teleported so far."

Baker looked at the animals—they were animals?—in the cages lining the laboratory. He had been hungry a minute before. Now he had trouble just swallowing.

"Like making the original adjustments on a video set," the old man explained. "Hard to get your focus, your horizontal and vertical interlineation just right. There's some distortion sometimes. Sort of—messy."

"On soul-searching consideration—" Baker began.

"Don't take another step toward that door. I've got the floor checkerboarded with electric grids where I can turn on the juice wherever you set your foot. Control's in my upper plate. Step in that coffin, boy. Just my little pet name for it; don't worry."

With some degree of reluctance, Baker stepped into the left of twin vertical boxes. The lid closed in his face and locked.

Before he could have time to begin worrying about his air supply, the cover sprang open, and he stepped out. "Test over?" There was an echo.

A man stood in front of the second coffin. Baker had entered the one on the left and he was still in front of the left box.

But he was also now in front of the cabinet on the right. He had been completely duplicated.

"That damned feedback again," Gentle grumbled.

In the first shock of this duplication and therefore seeming negation of his individual ego, Baker almost went mad.

"You did this to me!" said Baker and Baker to Gentle, each drawing a concealed weapon and shooting the old man in the heart.

"You two fellers drop your guns and stand still," a voice behind them said. "The professor was always saying I was the most simple-minded assistant he ever had, but I've got brains enough to pull this trigger on this old shotgun if you move."

(The ETI chief explained: "The rest is hearsay. Those miners spyproof their towns.")

The trial was short with Jeb, the assistant's, testimony, but the jury deliberation was unaccountably long on the primitive world where justice ran fast for a blind woman.

"We waited long enough," Jeb said to the other men in the saloon. "Let's break them out of the cellar and hang 'em.

The miners didn't let the jury set a precedent. They hoisted a few inside the bar and went out of Lone Splyg Hill and hoisted two more.

"What have you idiots done?" the sheriff yelled as they trooped back into Klondike City.

"Anticipated the verdict a mite," Jeb admitted.

"That's just it," the sheriff groaned. "It was ruled justifiable homicide.

Temporary insanity. At the time of the crime, each of the defendants was beside himself!"

IV

"Obviously," Street said, "this is no more than a folk legend."

"Are you sure?" the director of the ETI asked, fingering the report.

"It can't be anything else. Granted that all the other events were true, I would know Baker was still alive—only one, because neither could stand the threat of the other to his ego. You see, the case would never have come to trial. It would have been immediately dismissed."

"Why?"

"My dear fellow, both Bakers could not have been put on trial for the same murder, as any student of law would know. This would have violated the basic protection of double jeopardy."

V

A fast spaceship to put him well ahead of the law, and a place to hide out until things simmered down, that was all Baker wanted and it was what he had. He was too hot for more. ("This is how we reconstruct it from our informant's version," the ETI chief said.)

For the hundredth time, he located Wister VI on the star map. It had been discovered by the Gordon-Poul expedition half a century before. Few people ever knew about it, and most of those had forgotten it. He would never have known about it himself if it hadn't been on the credentials of that bank official.

With those papers he was set to spend several profitable years in the Great National Bank. He would be an alien, but somehow aliens always seemed to have more money than natives on any given planet.

As blastdown time approached, he read the characteristics of Wister IV and found his greatest inconvenience would be the intense sunlight from the double suns, not bright enough to burn but brilliant enough to dazzle. He searched the ship for sunglasses, but all he could find were snow goggles—a visor of black plastic with twin slits to look through. He put them on, resolving never to steal an improperly equipped spaceship again . . .

"Howdy, pardner." The humanoid at the spaceport was bald and green. He wore a wide-brimmed hat, chaps, and a large gun. Nothing else at all.

"Forgive my informal dress. Forgot my kerchief, boots and spurs this morning. Who might you be?"

Baker gave the title of his position at the bank, explaining it would be his job to help arrange for loans to the local ranchers

"You'll find this a friendly place. Tumbleweed is an *adult* Western town—We know the banker ain't always the head of the gang of rustlers."

As the weeks passed, Baker learned to live with the aliens' strange obsession with the things and persons of the Old West. They were even more fanatic than terrestrial Frenchmen over the American Frontier. It was not exaggerating to say that they regarded the men in the old films they got from Earth as gods.

They had appropriated appropriate Western given and surnames, but while there were plenty of Wills and Davys, and Rogerses and Crocketts, it was always Will Crockett and Davy Rogers. Anything other than that would be sacrilege.

Baker's biggest problem was getting a good mixed martini. Everybody on Wister Vl drank their rotgut straight. But by becoming friendly with the bartender, Gene Gibson, at the Golden Slipper, he managed to get his mixed drinks.

"Which do you think was faster on the draw, Matt Dillon or William S. Hart?" Tom asked Baker early one evening.

"I don't give a hoot, Gibson," Baker snarled, reaching for his martini.

Shocked faces along the bar turned toward him, and hands moved toward loaded guns.

"I meant pictures." Baker said hastily. "I wouldn't give one of my pictures of Hoot Gibson for two each of Ken Maynard and Tim McCoy."

"Everybody to his own taste," Gibson said agreeably.

Baker exhaled and gulped his drink. It had been a close one.

But as time wore on, the habits of the West-loving aliens grated more and more on Baker's soul. He was particularly irritated by the weekly ritual every male had of riding into the sunset. Since there were two sunsets in opposite directions, it was a long and involved and thoroughly annoying process.

Tom Wayne had kept Baker waiting an hour at the Golden Slipper to discuss his loan. Baker was exasperated and dry. Local custom regarded it as friendly to not begin your drinking before your companion arrived.

Gibson laid out the ingredients of the martini on the bar. "You going to wait any longer for Tom to finish riding into the sunset before I start mixing?"

Baker whirled angrily. "Nuts to Tom! Mix!"

Before the blasphemous words died on his lips, Baker saw death in the rising barrels of the vengeful six-shooters.

VI

"I doubt this story very much," Street said to the director.

"The planet and its conditions have been verified," the director replied.

"Even better reason to doubt that Baker died there. He probably was worshipped as one of the gods."

"Why do you think that?" the director asked the xenologist.

"Think it out for yourself. Imagine the reception that would be given to a man who stepped out of a spaceship, wearing what would appear to be a black mask, and who told these people he was the loan arranger."

VII

Baker jammed the accelerator of the groundcar down until his thumbnail turned white. The eye of the ETI peepbug observed the police car of the native authorities behind Baker's vehicle, closing fast.

This is how it happens, he subvocalized. A great career in interplanetary crime ends with an arrest by hick cops for selling dirty books. Why had he ever sunk so low? That was easy—it took a stake to do anything big and he had to get a pile by selling books, after *that* had happened to him on Wellington I.

The *Decameron, Forever Amber, Pierre Louys,* all the old classics like that still went over with some of the humanoid and biped races. (He had none of the newer stuff, only titles in the public domain—he couldn't force himself to fall to the level of a *literary* pirate.) But here on Lintz III he was slaying braces of fowl with a single stone. Lintzians were highly stimulated by intricate philosophy and mathematics. This allowed him to sell banned copies of Korzybski at outrageous prices, while at the same time introducing the native intellectuals to human semantics, a definite aid to the natives in throwing off the verbal domination by Earthmen.

The Humans First Lobby in the Galactic Legislature was willing to live with the difficulties caused by the absolute literal-mindedness of most extraterrestrials, so long as they could continue to make them believe in lifetime guarantees and unbreakable toys for inventive youngsters.

True, many a human traveler had lived to regret a chance remark to the effect he could eat a horse, and nobody likes to think of what happened to people who exclaimed a preference for being damned within range of obliging natives, but all in all, those were minor liabilities in the path of the infernal machine of progress. The ETI was working double-shifts to find human renegades who were teaching the semantic variations in words of human speech to aliens. On a world where philosophy and higher math were themselves proscribed because of the limiting factor of narcotic colloidal reaction, he also had to reckon with native cops.

He wasn't going to be able to outrun this squadcar. Baker let it pull alongside and dialed himself regretfully toward the embankment. Then as the police matched his maneuver, he switched on emergency power and sideswiped them with an ear-jarring crash. Thrown from the counterbalance of its gravitic suspension system, the squadcar sailed off as helplessly as a balloon . . . .

"Ryshid!" Baker yelled on entering his quarters. "Get my smoking jacket! Isn't dinner prepared yet?"

The turbaned, green-skinned native did what might have been called a *salaam* if he had been a Moslem instead of a Hindu. "Everything is in readiness, *Sahib*."

Baker was sorry he had spoken so shortly, but somehow he always did. Ryshid understood. Baker was under a terrible strain, not knowing when the ETI might descend on him. There was also the matter of Malissa, his wife, whom he missed very much. But as a Hinduphile, a true convert, Ryshid was of a gentle and forgiving nature.

As Baker settled back in his easy chair, someone started smashing in the back door.

By the time the police of Lintz reached the living room, Baker was gone.

"Alas," the sergeant-major intoned, "if only the sinner had repented his purchase of the forbidden book before instead of after he finished reading it."

As soon as he lifted the curtain of his own modest dwelling in the native quarter, Ryshid knew there was someone in the darkness, waiting for him.

"I hope you don't mind, old boy," Baker said. "Didn't know where else to go to escape being hunted down."

"I am overjoyed to find you well, *Sahib*. How did you escape?"

Baker told him about his escape, but somehow his talk kept coming back to Malissa, his wife. "I tell you it would take Kathleen Windsor to describe her. She's—but I'm a bore, Ryshid."

Ryshid drew the gun with a graceful movement. "As you say, *Sahib*. I have read of our traditional life in India, and as a Hindu I know what I must do when I find my home has been invaded by a hunted boar."

Ryshid squeezed the trigger.

VIII

"The shot," the chief said to Street, "unfortunately destroyed our peepbug."

"You were taken there," Street replied. "There is only one way to describe verbally Baker's attitude toward his man, proving this was all an act. A good Hindu would never harm Baker. His wife was a regular cow."

IX

Thorsen checked his gun inside his cummerbund. That was about the only place a man or woman had to hide a weapon in these times of relatively tight fashions on Earth. The gun was still there, safety off, as he firmly expected.

He settled back in his chair and glanced across the restaurant at Hastings, the traitor. An infamous outlaw such as Baker could count on few friends—one less than even he expected. The reward on the criminal had grown sizable. Not that Thorsen was going to get any of it. All he had to do was kill the poor devil on sight. It would be foolish to say that he didn't like killing; it was his job in the ETI, but sometimes he wearied of his work.

What did Baker look like?

It was a good question and it would give him something to think about while he waited. On the face of the existing evidence, it was obvious that Baker had somewhere discovered some means of superlative disguise. He could so change himself with stretching, shrinking, fattening, and slenderizing that if a man knew *he* wasn't Baker, he had to doubt everybody and anybody else.

Orders were to kill the first man who came up to Hastings at his table. He would have to shoot if it were his own father, or the director of the ETI, and there wasn't too much difference, he reflected.

He was seated where he could see both the entrance and the door to the men's room. Other agents were covering the back way. Baker would have to come from the tiered front.

Would Thorsen be able to kill Baker? If he got off the first shot, he would. Evening fashions were too tight for meteor shields. If he were wearing an electronic cuirass, he could tell it immediately by the twin spheres that gave that football-shoulder effect. Moreover, had anyone entered wearing such obvious armor, it would have been flashed to him. In that case, a hand bomb would have to be used, which would be unfortunate for Hastings, and possibly Thorsen.

Hastings wasn't showing his fear—he had been doped to hide that—but he was growing more alert. Baker must be coming!

Thorsen forced himself not to give things away by reaching for his weapon yet. He fastened his attention on the two doors into the café.

The shot blew most of Thorsen's lungs away, but the electronic wiring in his muscles kept the shock from killing him outright. He turned and managed to get off one shot before death started climbing up his arms from his fingers, and the weapon fell.

He should have kept in mind that no one had ever seen Baker and lived to tell it. Now he had seen Baker and he was not going to live either. But then Baker was dead even now, in spite of Thorsen's mistake.

Before he died, Thorsen took one last look at the figure with the long golden hair lying on the threshold of the ladies' room.

X

"This story is absolutely authentic," the director said. "Several ETI agents saw the whole thing. But somehow in the confusion somebody stole Baker's body."

"Really, Director!" Street said. "You don't actually believe Baker was a woman?"

"Are you suggesting a disguise?"

"It had to be. Baker's body disappeared by getting up and walking away. The only way it could do that was for it to be armored. The only way Baker could get into that building was for his armor to be hidden. There was only one way he could hide the two spheres of electronic equipment necessary to project the cuirass field, and he couldn't do it if he *really* had been a woman."

XI

The director leveled his gun at Street.

"I am at last convinced that there is only one way in which you could be so certain that Baker is not dead. You know he is alive, and you know it because you are Baker."

"You are correct," Street said. "I am the celebrated Robin Hood of space. It is too great an honor to deny."

"I will go into confinement for many years because of what I am about to do, but I must see the Galaxy rid of you."

The director fired the lethal charge at point-blank range and the tall man tumbled to the floor.

"I had to do it," the director said over the body. "It was well enough to frame you for Baker's crimes due to your suspicious knowledge of him, but I didn't know you were going to fail to protest, that you were going to go along with the lie. I couldn't stand another man living to take the honor for being Baker. There can be no living Baker but *me*."

XII

The tall man rolled over on the floor and sat up. "Then you admit that you are Baker? No, never mind firing again. I am wearing meteor armor under my clothes. It's sufficient to stop a gun blast."

"You are a clever devil," the director snarled.

"A man has to be clever to be Baker."

"You are NOT Baker!" the director shrieked. "I am!"

"Are you?" the tall man said superciliously. "Think why you came here. You've been working too hard, Director. You received too many stories about Baker. You began envying him his freedom of movement. Soon you began thinking you *were* Baker. Your analyst sent you to me, to make you see through this legend of Baker. It was to my advantage to do so."

The director wavered. "If I'm not Baker, who is?"

"I told you," the tall man said, drawing a gun and shooting the director in the head.

146

"I am."

He smiled down at the body.

"You weren't wearing armor, were you?"

Street reversed the dial on his gun and shot the director a second time. Quickly, he stirred from his paralysis.

"Sorry I had to do that, Director," Street said, "but I could see you were about to strangle me with naked hands. The important thing was to fix the idea firmly in your mind that I was Baker. If you thought I was, you would have to realize that you couldn't be."

"I do," the director said miserably as he climbed to his feet and dusted off his breeches. "But if I'm not Baker and you're not Baker, who is Baker?"

"Director, just as telling your stories and hearing my answers to them cured you of believing you were Baker, the events of this story are designed to make someone remember the true identity of Baker—that very person who now believes in a different personality of his own."

"Who is this person who is really Baker?" the director asked.

"The person who is now reading this story," Street said.

XIII

"I'm afraid it won't do, Mr. Street," the editor of *Man's True Space* said across his desk. "It's fiction. There can be only one Baker and tens of thousands would read the story in my magazine."

"You are missing the point, Mr. Trent," Street said. "There is only one manuscript and it is in your hands. *You* are Baker."

"No," Trent said. "No."

"Yes," Street said relentlessly. "Just as the director realized that *he* was *not* Baker, you must realize *you* are.

Trent lay back in his swivel, gasping. "All right, all right, I admit it. I am Baker."

"But you aren't really, Mr. Trent," Street said calmly. "I know you thought at one time you were Baker and then repressed the idea. But I knew at some future time the delusion might return and you would begin claiming to be Baker once more. As you said, there can only be one Baker. *I* am Baker."

"You lie," Trent snarled. "I know the truth now. I am Baker, and there *can* only be one."

The editor jerked the gun up from his desk drawer. The shots crashed at the same instant. Trent ran the letter spindle through his chest as he fell across the desk. Street settled back into his chair comfortably, death in his lungs from the gas bullet that had exploded against his armor.

XIV

The Director of Extraterrestrial Investigations opened the closet door and stepped into the office. "The fools," Baker said to himself.

He had no doubt that *he* was the true, the original Baker. He remembered clearly that he had stepped out of the left cabinet of Gentle's transmatter, the one which he had first entered. (He did remember that, didn't he? Yes! Doubting himself was the first stride down the road these two had taken.) His act to shock "Street" into realizing they were *both* Baker had been elaborate, but "Street" had gone schizoid.

He was no copy, but there were copies of Baker, dozens of them, all helping the downtrodden aliens from terrestrial exploitation and making fortunes for themselves. There were fat ones, thin ones, tall ones, short ones, all kinds of Bakers, thanks to the refinement of Gentle's distortion factors in matter-duplicating to an exact science, a desired result, not an accident like the duplication itself. Unfortunately, in a few, physical distortion meant mental disorientation. These no longer had to merely pretend to be other people than Baker.

It was too bad about them—and about all the other Bakers who had died. He really had died in all those ways on all those worlds in all those bodies, despite "Street's" clever excuses. Still it wasn't a bad life—helping the helpless and himself to all they could get.

Yes, Baker decided, dying was a good way to make a living.

AFTERWORD

Horace L. Gold, one of the great science fiction editors, often rewrote the stories of his authors, sometimes up to fifty per cent. He never rewrote any of my stories to that extent, but he did change a line here and there, and I generally could see that it helped the story.

On this one effort, "Baker's Dozens," I attempted to string together a long series of short-shorts, inspired by the wonderful Fredric Brown. In this one entry, Gold for some reason changed lines of mine killing the punch-line of the tale. Granted, these little stories were not masterpieces never to be touched, but the changes made segments totally pointless. For this printing, I have changed Gold back to common Harmon.

BY THE FRIGHT OF THE MOON

The only way to kill a vampire is with science, Dr. Altshuler thought to himself.

The lean, bearded scientist, a man in his late middle years, sat on the rug of the tent of his host, Achmid Bay. Altshuler was eating the dates and figs provided to him by Bay, always being sure to use only his right hand.

Bay ate nothing, but encouraged his guest to eat his fill.

It was natural for Bay not to eat, since Altshuler knew the man was a vampire.

On this expedition too many had died or disappeared. One would have to believe in an Egyptian curse on tomb seekers to explain it. Altshuler's studies had convinced him that it was Bay who was responsible, because it was he who had taken the blood of the luckless ones.

"Our conversation has been so interesting that we have talked the night away," Altshuler said. "It is almost morning."

"The blood is the life," Bay said.

"I believe I have heard that line before," said Altshuler.

"Tales travel. Men travel. A very long-lived man might have been born in Egypt but lived in central Europe for a time, a long time, and moved back to his remote Egypt to escape attention, to escape those who hounded him."

"Not quite morning," Bay replied. "We still have a little time before sunrise."

But not much. Altshuler had carefully checked the time of the sunrise in his almanac. When that hour came, Bay would be exposed. The sunlight might not destroy him, although the doctor thought that it might. But it would certainly send him fleeing from its exposure, and exposure would be what it was for this night-dwelling creature.

"I am interested in your theory as to why we have lost so many men on this search for tombs," Altshuler said.

"This is an old land, full of old superstitions," Bay said, fingering his beard.

"Our workmen are not scientists. They believe the old tales too easily."

"Old legends die hard," Dr. Altshuler commented. "Some stories persist in every land. In Egypt, there are tales of creatures who suck men's souls. In Europe, stories tell of the undead who suck men's blood. But both speak of stealing the life force."

Altshuler checked his watch. "I can believe that, Bay. I can ever believe that of you, Bay."

Bay rose to his feet. "You can believe much for a man who has not yet lived a single lifetime," he said.

"And who is not likely to reach the normal span of that lifetime."

The time was not quite right yet. But Altshuler had a diversion.

"Years of studying the vampire have taught me what one can not stand. Such as this."

The doctor drew from his inside pocket something of gleaming metal, a crucifix.

Bay laughed. "What do I care for the trappings of your infidel religion?"

The Arab made a gesture.

Altshuler became aware that the metal in his hand was growing warm. In fact, hot. In fact—burning! He dropped the cross.

"Now my dear doctor, we will become better acquainted. Intimately so for a brief moment . . . "

The doctor stepped back and threw open the tent flap.

To reveal only the star-studded night sky. Altshuler checked his watch again. It was time for the sunrise. As in some Arabian Nights tale, he had kept Bay enthralled all night until the sunrise. Except . . . He had not taken into account modern daylight savings time. It was still night.

Bay moistened his lips came nearer without seeming to take a step. But the Arab's eyes were fixed on something beyond Altshuler, something in the night sky. The doctor glanced behind him and saw the crescent moon on the horizon.

Bay's lips moved. "The holy crescent! It shames me! I can not stand its light on my unworthiness."

Bay lifted a hem of his robes, and the robes fluttered to the carpeted floor of the tent. Empty. Destroyed or merely fled? Dr. Altshuler did not know. But he did know now there were other powerful religions besides those of the West.

AFTERWORD

The above short-short story evolved from a story conference with Robert Bloch of some forty years ago.

I brought up the subject of how a vampire of another religion other than Christian would not be scared off by the sign of the cross. For instance, a Muslim vampire could not stand the crescent moon, with its sacred symbol (to him) shining down on him. Bob thought it was a good idea for a story, and made a few suggestions.

I wrote up the short-short and showed it to him. I think he penciled in a few words. Should we submit it under a joint by-line? (I certainly would have been happy to share a by-line with such a respected writer.) He said no, the story was basically mine.

I wrote it up and submitted it to the top market, then *Playboy*. It was returned with a friendly note.

All other available markets would only pay about five dollars for the story. The actual manuscript Bob looked at has been misplaced, and I wrote this new version in 2002, involving the same basic idea. I certainly wish Bob Bloch were around to change a few words and improve it. I also had uncredited collaborations with Isaac Asimov and Theodore Sturgeon, and one credited to Thomas Scortia and myself.

It was with the help of authors like this, and to non-professional but brilliant Redd Boggs that I owe my limited success as a writer. I hope readers might enjoy this glimpse into an evening shared by two SF writers many years ago.

STEELMASK MEETS THE ZOMBIE MASTER

From the shadows of Grainger Avenue came a faint metallic glint, a glimmer of reflected light that would have told a knowing passerby that in that gloom lurked the trench-coated figure who wore beneath his wide-brimmed hat the symbol of his name, a name known throughout the teeming multi-racial underworld of Los Angeles—the name of *Steelmask.*

The agent of the night was following a man who was just coming into the circle of light thrown by the corner streetlamp. In his strange career, Steelmask had shadowed many who sought to evade the clutches of law and order, but this man he followed this night was different from all the others. The man Steelmask followed in the lurking darkness was a *corpse,* a walking dead man!

In the illumination of the streetlamp the fact that he was dead was inescapable. Death was in his eyes, written on his face with patterns of decay. Yet he walked on with the animation, and the lifelessness of a robot.

From his watching place, Steelmask nodded to himself. He had seen this work before, in Haiti, in the Central American jungles. Even orthodox science had come to admit the existence of such men as these, created through the use of forbidden drugs. Yes, Steelmask knew he followed one of the living dead, a *zombie.*

Even as the master of midnight watched, the zombie entered an apparently abandoned building that had been once part of a minor movie studio, long since closed.

Steelmask glided to the side of the building with the remarkable athletic agility he had developed in simple necessity for staying alive. The silent avenger climbed the Spanish-influence decorations that ran up the wall.

At the top, he gingerly tested a tiny balcony meant only for ornament, and decided that while it gave a little under his weight, it would hold him for a time. Peering through a window crusted with the dirt of many years, Steelmask followed a strange scene below. Through the use of his keen senses and his ability to read lips, Night's Agent was a silent, unseen partner in the conversation that went on thirty feet below him in the midst of a deserted auditorium.

"Give it over to me!" snapped a stooped, glowering figure at the approaching man with the face of death.

Silently, the zombie brought an oilskin packet from his jacket, handed it to the hunchback, then fell.

The man with the crewcut glanced from the fallen zombie to the hunchback. "What's wrong with *him*?"

"Dead," explained the hunchback, tearing open the pack. "Really dead. He served his function. He delivered the drug." The little man rubbed a pinch of yellow-white powder between his fingers, and smiled.

"That's enough of the stuff to turn everybody in Los Angeles into zombies?" Crewcut demanded.

The little man nodded briskly. "Yes, yes. Interjected into the city's water supply, everybody who drinks it will become a mindless automaton—a zombie if you will. The word need have no superstitious connotations. Zombies are merely ones who have had the higher reasoning faculties burned from their brains by this rare Central American herb just now fetched me from my off-shore launch by our late friend."

Crewcut ran a palm over his bristles. "Knocking out everybody in L.A. with the stuff sounds like a good idea—if it works."

"It will," the little man said confidently. "You will have your loot—and I will have my revenge!"

"Sure, Doc, sure," Crewcut said soothingly, "you deserve it."

"I was going to be the greatest actor and make-up technician in motion picture history. I—Doctor Proteus—but my career was cut short by that falling Kleig light that left me *actually* deformed. I couldn't play a hunchback in every picture, they said. But—" Proteus chuckled—"I am about to be the star of the greatest horror story ever told—turning an entire city into millions of mindless zombies. Nothing can stop me! Nobody!"

Nobody except Steelmask, thought the shadowy avenger high above. He had come to a difficult decision. For the first time in his career, Steelmask was going to kill a man in cold blood. Too much was at stake—millions of lives. Proteus had to die, the secret of his drug dying with him. Securing his nylon climbing rope to the rail of the tiny balcony, Steelmask kicked open the small window and went through like a surging billow of black smoke. Expertly, Steelmask slid down the rope as it played out, dropping down towards the figures of Proteus and Crewcut who stood over the dead victim of zombyism.

As they saw the figure coming down at them, both the gangster and the deranged scientist set up calls for help, and instantly Steelmask saw that he had made what might well be a fatal mistake. These two were not alone!

Doors opened on either side of the huge room. Through one door poured a hoard of professional criminals, all heavily armed to guard this meeting place with revolvers, automatics, shotguns and submachine guns. And through the other door came a troop of dead men, the mindless slave victims of Proteus' evil discovery.

This was no time for the mercy blasts of his gas gun, Steelmask knew. As he struck the floor, still determined to destroy this evil, even at the cost of his own life, twin Colt automatics were in his fists, spurting orange flame in the semi-darkness. In answer to the thunder of Steelmask's big guns came the piping whine of the ineffectual .32's and .38's the gangsters carried, while one of the mob blazed away with a stream of sub-machine gun slugs.

Even as Steelmask's singing bullets took their toll among the killers, he triumphed in the knowledge that he would not have to destroy his own code of honor, that now if Proteus was to die, he would die in honest battle, as Steelmask fought in self-defense for his own life against overwhelming odds.

Besides summoning his hoard of marching zombies, Proteus took a more personal hand as he drew a scalpel-thin knife and launched himself at the metal-masked manhunter.

Turning swiftly, Steelmask took Proteus' blade, caught it as the stiletto slid down the barrel of his gun.

Twisting his gun sharply, Steelmask jerked the blade from the maniac's grasp and sent it flying from the barrel of the automatic.

A smashing elbow sent the scientist reeling backwards.

Now, the marching platoon of zombies was drawing near, their hands clutching for Steelmask. The avenger's guns spoke, but without effect against the walking dead. But as one crook gathered up the

submachine gun fallen from limp hands of another, Steelmask knew his only chance was to get these two hoards caught in their own cross attacks. Diving forward, Steelmask was aware of the ruthless thug following him with the barrel of the machine gun, heedless of the mindless mass behind the manhunter.

Steelmask dropped to the floor, a burst of machine gun fire slicing over his head, ripping through the marching zombies, literally cutting them down. One well-placed shot from Steel-mask's automatic put the machine gunner out of commission, but he quickly saw a new menace. Crewcut, the mob leader, had opened a compartment in the floor, opened a black bag and removed a small bottle.

"Okay, Ironhead," he called tauntingly at Steelmask, "see how you like drinking *nitro!*"

As the bottle came towards him, Steelmask threw himself forward as if to meet it in an apparently suicidal lunge.

The bottle struck the floor, and the tremendous explosion that followed registered as another California earthquake.

When the fumes cleared, Steelmask climbed to his feet, his clothing not even harmed. For in going to meet the point of the explosion, Steelmask had followed a fact of any physics textbook, a fact used by movie stunt-men and circus performers to stay alive—namely that the lines of force in an explosion go *outward*. At the center where Steelmask was, there was little explosive force.

But another figure rose from the debris and fallen bodies. Proteus stood unsteadily, training a gun on Steelmask.

"Before I die," the mad man said, "and before you do, I intend to see behind your celebrated steel mask, Enemy of Old."

Without hesitation, Steelmask removed the metal shield from his features. Doctor Proteus took one look at what lay behind the Steelmask itself, and his heart stopped. It stayed stopped. He fell dead. The shock was enough to finish the work of the explosion. Steelmask refastened the metal symbol of justice.

Yes, he thought, to look upon the face of Steelmask was enough to strike the fear of death into the unjust. For while Proteus had let his deformity drive him into bitter destructiveness, the man who had become Steelmask had reacted to his disfiguration in a war against international gangsters by burying his identity and devoting himself to the cause of humanity. And, unlike the reasons of others, Steelmask wore *his* mask not to conceal his face but to conceal the fact that he had *no* face.

AFTERWORD

This story must have something. It ran in *Fantastic Monsters*, a magazine devoted to movie monsters like Frankenstein, Dracula, the Wolf Man. Yet when a poll of the most popular features to run in the magazine the first year was conducted, this story came in No. 1. The story featured no movie monster. It was the story of no film. The poll was on the up and up. I was also the Associate Editor while my friend, Ron Haydock, was the editor. We counted the letters. There were approximately seventy letters voting for "Steelmask." The runner-up with about fifty letters was an article on how Jack Pierce created the make-up for Karloff's Frankenstein creature.

A decade later, I was the editor of another movie magazine, *Monsters of the Movies*, and Ron Haydock was my associate. Maybe we should have tried another Steelmask story there. As it was, our second monster magazine lasted no more issues than the first, while our inspiration, Forrest J. Ackerman's *Famous Monsters*, rolled on for many years.

THE LEGEND AT SUNSET

The time was a sunny October morning of a year in the early 1930s.

The place was the nineteenth floor of one of the great towers of the city, housing the editorial offices of the metropolis' great newspaper.

The tall man came out of the express elevator alone. He wore a long, dark overcoat of an expensive cut, a snap-brimmed gray Stetson of a moderately wide Southwestern style, and dark, smoked glasses, now often called sun glasses. He went to the outer door of the executive offices and walked in.

The secretarial trainee was working as a receptionist. She saw the fine looking man come in and was impressed with his magnetic persona. His presence seemed to fill the room. He was a man of undetermined years, although most people took him for late middle age.

"Good morning. I'm here to see the publisher," he said in one of the most magnificent speaking voices she had ever heard. "Please give him my card."

"Yes, sir."

The publisher had told her that he did not wish to be disturbed, but she made up her own mind. She was sure that order did not include this man.

As she got up from behind her desk, the pretty teenager glanced to the sun slanting through the windows to the caller's dark glasses.

"Should I close the drapes while you wait?" she asked.

"I'm fine," he said. He touched his dark glasses. "These protect my health."

As she walked to the door of the inner office, she read the visitor's card.

MR. SILVER
Precision Delivery Systems
"Fast as a Bullet We Come to Your Aid"

There was an embossed silver bullet on the calling card as well.

The publisher was deep in conversation on the telephone, but she approached quietly and put the calling card on the desk blotter in front of him. "A man to see you, sir," she whispered, reducing it to almost a mouthing of the words.

He glanced at the card, then stared. "Admit him at once!" The publisher turned back to the phone. "Forgive me, Governor. I must go."

The man entered them room, and the publisher sprang from his chair, with an energy that belied his graying hair. The two men embraced heartily, strong arms about each other in the Mexican style common along the Texas border.

The newspaperman stood back and examined the visitor. "Sir, it's wonderful to see you. It's been years! Too bad my boy is off at college. Given the restrictions, I was never able to quite explain to him who that fine looking man was who showed up at some of his birthdays."

"I'm sorry that it was impossible for me to be at his mother's funeral," the man said.

"I understand." Little needed to be said among these two. "How is our Faithful Friend?" the publisher said in Indian dialect common along the border of forty years before.

The visitor chuckled. "He's the same as ever. He'll be the same at one hundred. I sometimes feel selfish keeping him with me in my work. If he had returned to his people and assumed his natural leadership position, he might be a senator or governor by now."

The publisher, smiled. "I'd vote for him—or you—for President."

"He's back at our hotel. You'll see him later. Shall we sit?"

The tall man took the visitor chair and the publisher sat on the edge of his worn desk, his eyes intent on the older man. The visitor removed his hat, revealing hair that was still mostly black, but shot through with —appropriately—silver.

"Have you seen any of our old friends lately?"

"I visited Wyatt Earp out on the coast a few years ago. Saw him just months before the end. One of our old foes, Al Jennings, is still working as a production manager in the film business. I think he's making more money at that then he ever did robbing banks."

"Of course he never was a very good bank robber. You know the paper has been running a series of pieces on figures of the Old West—Earp . . . Buffalo Bill . . . lone riders, and vigilantes. Tall tales of the old timers, similar to those about Paul Bunyon."

The visitor smiled. "People like to tell stories. I understand a local radio station is running a series of programs about one of those mystery figures. They will soon run through those legends. Certain people in Washington have the facts, if they need to be known."

"Does that hot shot, Elliot Ness, have much work for you?" the publisher asked.

The other man laughed. "Strange you should ask about that. President Hoover didn't seem to have anything for me to do. I don't think he approves of me. But young treasury agent Ness occasionally has little jobs for me. I think he likes it that I don't seek public credit—more for him. As a matter of fact, it is a job for him that brings me to the city."

He grew more serious. "The case doesn't look all that dangerous. but one never knows. I want to renew our agreement. If they follow the instructions I carry on me, and you are contacted, you will see that my body is returned to lay beside your father and our comrades." He paused. "The Big Fellow sleeps nearby."

Tears welled in the other man's eyes. "I haven't asked about him in years. I didn't want to hear it. There were sightings of you on a white horse even into the twenties, but I was afraid it couldn't have been the same."

"Junior and Number Three were fine horses, but there was only one mount. No hooves ever beat the plains like his. He lived well into the Twentieth Century."

"Who can forget him? One of the most magnificent creatures who ever lived."

"He is with me always," the visitor said. He removed a keychain from his pocket, which included a miniature horse-shoe about two inches across. "Made from one of his last shoes. I like to think he is still helping me with his fine senses. I say, 'Big Fellow, which trail shall we take?' And I fancy he helps guide me. A whimsy."

"As you know, his line, and that of his son, once my mount, are carried on at our horse farm in Michigan," the newspaperman said. "There is one new stallion there that I think might be of use to you."

'I'd love to ride him," the man said with enthusiasm. "But not for 'business'. This is the automotive age. Crime has moved to the cities. I use a Cord—silver in color—a conceit. Our friend generally drives. I think he has become more at ease with the Twentieth Century than I have."

"I doubt that!" the publisher said. "There's nothing you can't master."

The man shrugged. "It gives him something useful to do. We'll be going out tonight, on Mr. Ness' business. If all goes well, we'll stop by the house at around midnight." The visitor judged the time of day, from the angle of the sun slating through the window, but checked his wristwatch. "I'm afraid I have to leave. I have preparations to make."

The two men stood up. The publisher said, "It is a pity you never married and gave the world a son to carry on."

The visitor stood, remembering. "Certain women have stirred me. Everything need not be put down on the page. But it was the example of the many dear old Padres I know in the West who showed me that my way was the path of duty."

The visitor placed his hand over the other man's on the desk. "Of course, you are my son, more than only my nephew. Your son carries on our line."

"Sir, could I ask you your present age?"

The tall man smiled. "I'm as old as my teeth. If I give age a number, that will make it real."

"One more thing. sir . . . Could you remove the dark glasses?"

The visitor removed the glasses.

It was the face he had first seen more than fifty years before, etched with even more character and determination, if that were possible.

"The world should have seen more of that face."

The visitor put the glasses back on. "No, the mask was better. Now I must go to get ready for my next meeting."

"I hope it will be as pleasant as this one has been for me."

"I think not. A meeting with a traitor is very seldom pleasant." He gave a chest-high Indian salute, and turned to leave the room.

The publisher thought, there goes the greatest man I have ever known in two different centuries.

The shiny new Cord stood in front of a skyscraper framework of steel under construction, reaching into the night sky. At the wheel sat a dark man in a dark suit, no longer young, but ramrod straight. He was waiting for someone inside the new construction. Somewhere a dog howled. Or was it a wolf? It was said wolves still prowled the hills above the city.

Inside the structure, two men talked in the half light of a small bulb next to an elevator. One was a tall aristocratic man, in a gray European-cut suit. He had a small mustache and a scar on his left cheek. The other was shorter. His round face and his clothes seemed too tight for his round body.

The red-face man spoke. "Count, you will find in this roll of papers the complete plans for the new pursuit plane the Army is going to have built. I want nothing for myself, but the work of the bund must go on."

"Ve already agreed to the twenty thousand pounds—that is, dollars." The mustached man slapped a wallet of thin, fine leather against the palm of his free hand. "Chust hand offer the plans."

Red Face eagerly pushed the roll of papers forward. The receiver started to give up the wallet, but hesitated, and tucked it under his arm. He spread open the roll, slanting it towards the only source of light. "Vat you say seems to be here. Gut, gut . . . Good. Very good. I'm sure my friend in Washington will be very glad to have these back."

Red Face seemed to go white. "Your voice! Washington?" He snatched from the crease in his back a Luger.

A .45 Army Colt automatic appeared in the hand of the man who had been called "Count." The gun spoke once. Red Face shrieked.

"Your fingers sting from the shock of my bullet," the man who had earlier visited the publisher said, "But I fired at and hit your gun. I must say you wouldn't have lived very long with a draw like that back where I come from." He put his automatic in its shoulder holster.

Thirty feet away, on the uncompleted floor, a silver bullet caught a gleam of light, flattened like a coin on the railroad tracks.

"You were a fool to holster your gun," Red Face screamed. "I am strong as a bull!"

Fingers like sausages closed about the supposed "Count's" throat, but fingers like steel bands grabbed wrists above the sausage fingers and broke the traitorous American's grip like a child's. Arms were twisted behind the round man's back and he was fastened to the nearest upright girder with a pair of handcuffs. The man doing the fastening remembered when he would have used rawhide strips.

The supposed "Count" turned his back, and using an old bandanna, wiped away the makeup scar and mustache. He replaced his smoked glasses which were engineered so that he could see perfectly well at night. In the distance, he heard the wail of a police car. "That will be Mr. Ness' agents coming for you, accompanied by the local police." He tucked one of his "Mr. Silver" calling cards into the round man's shirt pocket.

The sweating traitor glared at the man. In the uncertain light, he could see only that the upper part of his face was blacked out. The greasy one squealed, "Who are you, you masked meddler?"

There was a laugh from the other side. "I've been called many names ... Certainly not that one for the first time."

The police siren was very near as he ran to the silver Cord. The driver said, "Hear sound of your gun only."

"Right. No need for you to come." He tossed the stolen plans and wallet of supposed payoff into the back, placed a hand on the door frame, and vaulted into the passenger seat. "Let's travel."

The power of the great car surged through his thighs. The wind rushed by his cheeks. He could believe he was once again riding a white stallion, fine as light. The dark spectacled masked man now in his seventy-eighth year, lifted his voice to call to the spirit of the horse that seemed to race beside them with a cry ending in the horse's name, to echo among the high rise of buildings that marched along a trail he first blazed in another century, another world.

AFTERWORD

The editor told me that my book was running a few pages short and they needed something to fill out *Radio and TV Premiums*. It certainly is not usual to put a fiction story into any non-fiction book, but the publisher seemed really needful of anything to fill the gap. I tried this story of something that had been in the back of my mind for sometime.

Al Jennings was a real-life Western bandit who robbed trains in Oklahoma. After serving a prison term he got a job in the movies, and worked as a production manager in films for many years. Around 1940, he heard himself dramatized as one of the villains on *The Lone Ranger* radio show, for his exploits around the turn of the century. At this time, he was only in his sixties. He complained, threatened to sue, but nothing came of it. But it occurred to me if one of the villains from that era could live on into the Twentieth Century, then so could some of the heroes.

This story is about one such hero.

When the almost legendary SF fan, Redd Boggs, my friend for fifty years, since I was a boy, read the story he was offended that my beloved hero could be depicted as working on assignment for J. Edgar Hoover, a man for which Redd had little regard. I changed it to having him working for Elliot Ness.

The rest is the way I wrote it.

I know something of such heroes. Curley Bradley, the last man to play Tom Mix on the radio was my friend for ten years, and I'm told considered me his adopted son. The man who played the Lone Ranger on radio for the longest period, Brace Beemer, was my cousin.

NO SUBSTITUTIONS

Putting people painlessly to sleep is really a depressing job. It keeps me awake at night thinking of all those bodies I have sent to the vaults, and it interferes to a marked extent with my digestion. I thought before Councilman Coleman came to see me that there wasn't much that could bother me worse.

Coleman came in the morning before I was really ready to face the day. My nerves were fairly well shot from the kind of work I did as superintendent of Dreamland. I chewed up my pill to calm me down, the one to pep me up, the capsule to strengthen my qualities as a relentless perfectionist. I washed them down with gin and orange juice and sat back, building up my fortitude to do business over the polished deck of my desk.

But instead of the usual morning run of hysterical relatives and masochistic mystics, I had to face one of my superiors from the Committee itself.

Councilman Coleman was an impressive figure in a tailored black tunic. His olive features were set off by bristling black eyes and a mobile mustache. He probably scared most people, but not me. Authority doesn't frighten me any more. I've put to sleep too many megalomaniacs, dictators, and civil servants.

"Warden Walker, I've been following your career with considerable interest," Coleman said.

"My career hasn't been very long, sir," I said modestly. I didn't mention that nobody could last that long in my job. At least, none had yet.

"I've followed it from the first. I know every step you've made."

I didn't know whether to be flattered or apprehensive. "That's fine," I said. It didn't sound right.

"Tell me," Coleman said, crossing his legs, "what do you think of Dreamland in principle?"

"Why, it's the logical step forward in penal servitude. Man has been heading toward this since he first started civilizing himself. After all, some criminals can't be helped psychiatrically. We can't execute them or turn them free; we have to imprison them."

I waited for Coleman's reaction. He merely nodded.

"Of course, it's barbaric to think of a prison as a place of punishment," I continued. "A prison is a place to keep a criminal away from society for a specific time so he can't harm that society for that time. Punishment, rehabilitation, all of it, is secondary to that. The purpose of confinement is confinement."

The councilman edged forward an inch. "And you really think Dreamland is the most humane confinement possible?"

"Well," I hedged, "it's the most humane we've found yet. I suppose living through a—uh —movie with full sensory participation for year after year can get boring."

"I should think so," Coleman said emphatically. "Warden, don't you sometimes feel the old system where the Prisoners had the diversions of riots, solitary confinement, television, and jailbreaks may have made time easier to serve? Do these men ever think they are actually living these vicarious adventures?"

That was a question that made all of us in the Dreamland service uneasy. "No, Councilman, they don't. They know they aren't really Alexander of Macedonia, Tarzan, Casanova, or Buffalo Bill. They are conscious of all the time that is being spent out of their real lives; they know they have relatives and friends outside the dream. They know, unless—"

Coleman lifted a dark eyebrow above a black iris. "Unless?"

I cleared my throat "Unless they go mad and really believe the dream they are living. But as you know, sir, the rate of madness among Dreamland inmates is only slightly above the norm for the population as a whole."

"How do prisoners like that adjust to reality?"

Was he deliberately trying to ask tough questions? "They don't. They think they are having some kind of delusion. Many of them become schizoid and pretend to go along with reality while secretly 'knowing' it to be a lie."

Coleman removed a pocket secretary and broke it open. "About these new free-choice models—do you think they genuinely are an improvement over the old fixed-image machines?"

"Yes, sir," I replied. "By letting the prisoner project his own imagination onto the sense tapes and giving him a limited amount of alternatives to a situation, we can observe whether he is conforming to society to a larger extent."

"I'm glad you said that, Walker," Councilman Coleman told me warmly. "As I said, I've been following your career closely, and if you, get through the next twenty-four-hour period as you have through the foregoing part of your Dream, you will be awakened at this time tomorrow. Congratulations!"

I sat there and took it.

He was telling me, the superintendent of Dreamland, that my own life here was only a Dream such as I fed to my own prisoners. It was unbelievably absurd, a queasy little joke of some kind. But I didn't deny it.

If it were true, if I had forgotten that everything that happened was only a Dream, and if I admitted it, the councilman would know I was mad. It couldn't be true. Yet—Hadn't I thought about it ever since I had been appointed warden and transferred from my personnel job at the plant?

Whenever I had come upon two people talking, and it seemed as if I had come upon those same two people talking the same talk before, hadn't I wondered for an instant if it couldn't be a Dream, not reality at all?

Once I had experienced a Dream for five or ten minutes. I was driving a ground car down a spidery road made into a dismal tunnel by weeping trees, a dank, lavender maze. I had known at the time it was a Dream, but still, as the moments passed, I became more intent on the difficult road before me, my, blocky hands on the steering wheel, thick fingers typing out the pattern of motion on the drive buttons. I could remember that. Maybe I couldn't remember being shoved into the prison vault for so many years for such and such a crime. I didn't really believe this, not then, but I couldn't afford to make a mistake, even if it were only some sort of intemperate test—as I was confident it was, with a sweet, throbbing fury against the man who would employ such a jagged broadsword for prying in his bureaucratic majesty.

"I've always thought," I said, "that it would be a good idea to show a prisoner what the modern penal system was all about by giving him a

Dream in which he dreamed about Dreamland itself."

"Yes, indeed," Coleman concurred. Just that and no more.

I leaned intimately across my beautiful oak desk. "I've thought that projecting officials into the Dream and letting them talk with the prisoners might be a more effective form of investigation than mere observation."

"I should say so," Coleman remarked, and got up.

I had to get more out of him,. some proof, some clue beyond the preposterous announcement he had made.

"I'll see you tomorrow at this time then, Walker." The councilman nodded curtly and turned to leave my office.

I held onto the sides of my desk to keep from diving over and teaching him to change his concept of humor.

The day was starting. If I got through it, giving a good show, I would be released from my Dream, he had said smugly.

But if this was a dream, did I want probation to reality?

Horbit was a twitchy little man whose business tunic was the same rodent color as his hair. He had a pronounced tic in his left cheek. "I have to get back," he told me with compelling earnestness.

"Mr. Horbit—Eddie —" I said, glancing at his file projected on my desk pad, "I can't put you back into a Dream. You served your full time for your crime. The maximum."

"But I haven't adjusted to society!"

"Eddie, I can shorten sentences, but I can't expand them beyond the limit set by the courts."

A tear of frustration spilled out of his left eye with the next twitch. "But Warden, sir, my psychiatrist said that I was unable to cope with reality. Come on now, Warden, you don't want a guy who can't cope with reality running around loose." He paused, puzzled. "Hell, I don't know why I can't express myself like I used to."

He could express himself much better in his Dream. He had been Abraham Lincoln in his Dream, I saw. He had lived the life right up to the night when he was taking in *An American Cousin* at the Ford Theater. Horbit couldn't accept history that he had no more life to live. He only knew that if in his delirium he could gain Dreamland once more, he could get back to the hard realities of dealing with the problems of Reconstruction.

"*Please*," he begged.

I looked up from the file. "I'm sorry, Eddie."

His eyes narrowed, both of them, on the next twitch. "Warden, I can always go out and commit another anti-social act."

"I'm afraid not, Eddie. The file shows you are capable of only one crime. And you don't have a wife any more, and she doesn't have a lover."

Horbit laughed. "Your files aren't infallible, Warden."

With one gesture, he ripped open his tunic and tore into his own flesh. No, not his own flesh. Pseudo-flesh. He took out the gun that was underneath.

"The beamer is made of X-ray-transparent plastic, Warden, but it works as well as one made of steel and lead."

"Now that you've got it in here," I said in time with the pulse in my throat, "what are you going to do with it?"

"I'm going to make you go down to the vaults and put me back to sleep, Warden."

I nodded. "I suppose you can do that. But what's to prevent me from waking you up as soon as I've taken away your gun?"

"This!" He tossed a sheet of paper onto my desk.

"What's this?" I asked unnecessarily. I could read it.

"A confession that you accepted a bribe to put me back to sleep," Horbit said, his tic beating out a feverish tempo. "As soon as you've signed it, I'll use your phone to have it telefaxed to the Registrar of Private Documents."

I had to admire the thought behind the idea. Horbit was convinced that I was only a figment of his unfocused imagination, but he was playing the game with uncompromising logic, trusting that even madness had hard and tight rules behind it.

There was also something else I admired about the plan.

It could work.

Once he fed that document to the archives, I would be obligated to help him even without the gun. My word would probably be taken that I had been forced to do it at gunpoint, but there would always be doubts; enough to wreck my career when it came time for promotion.

Nothing like this had ever happened in my years as warden.

Suddenly, Coleman's words hit me in the back of the neck. If I got through the next twenty-four hours. This had to be some kind of test. But a test for what?

Had I been deliberately told that I was living only a Dream to see if my ethics would hold up even when I thought I wasn't dealing with reality?

Or if this was only a Dream, was it a test to see if I was morally ready to return to the real, the earnest world?

But if it was a test to see if I was ready for reality, did I want to pass it? My life was nerve-racking and mind-wrecking, but I liked the challenge—it was the only life I knew or could believe in.

What was I going to do?

The only thing I knew was that I couldn't tune in tomorrow and find out.

The time was now.

Horbit motioned the gun to my desk set. "Sign that paper."

I reached out and took hold of his wrist. I squeezed.

Horbit's screams brought in the guards.

I picked up the gun from where he had dropped it and handed it to Captain Keller, my head guard, a tough, old bird who wore his uniform like armor.

"Trying to force his way back to the sleep tanks," I told Keller.

He nodded. "Happened before. Back when old man Preston lost his grip."

Preston had been my predecessor. He had lost his hold on reality like all the others before him who had served long as warden of Dreamland. A few had quit while they were still ahead and spent the rest of their lives recuperating. Our society didn't produce individuals tough enough to stand the strain of putting their fellow human beings to sleep for long.

One of Keller's men had stabbed Horbit's arm with a hypospray to blanket the pain from his broken wrist, and the man was quieter.

"I couldn't have done it, Warden," Horbit mumbled drowsily. "I couldn't kill anybody. Unless it was like that other time."

"Of course, Eddie," I said.

I had banked on that, hadn't I, when I made my move?

Or did I?

Wasn't it perhaps a matter of knowing that all of it wasn't real and that the safety cutoffs in even a free-choice model of a Dream Machine couldn't let me come to any real harm? I had been suspiciously brave, disarming a dedicated maniac. With only an hour to spare for gym a day, I could barely press 350 pounds. I was hardly in shape for personal combat.

On the other hand, maybe I actually wanted something to go wrong so my sleep sentence would be extended. Or was it that, in some sane part of my mind, I wanted release from unreality badly enough to take any risk to prove that I was morally capable of returning to the real world?

It was a carousel and I couldn't catch the brass ring no matter how many turns I went spinning through.

I hardly heard Horbit when he half-shouted at me as my men led him from the room. Glancing up sharply, I saw him straining purposefully against the bonds of muscle and narcotic that held him.

"You have to send me back now, Warden," he was shrilling. "You have to! I tried to coerce you with a gun. That's a crime, Warden—you know that's a crime! I have to be put to sleep!"

Keller flicked his mustache with a thick thumbnail. "How about that? You won't let a guy back into the sleepy-bye pads, so he pulls a gun on you to make you, and that makes him eligible. He couldn't lose, Warden. No, sir, he had it made."

My answer to Keller was forming, building up in my jaw muscles, but I took a pill and it went away.

"Hold him in the detention quarters," I said finally. "I'm going to make a study of this."

Keller winked knowingly and sauntered out of the office, his left hand swinging the blackjack the Committee had taken away from him a decade before.

The problem of what to do with Keller wasn't particularly atypical of the ones I had to solve daily and I wasn't going to let that worry me. Much.

I pressed my button to let Mrs. Engle know I was ready for the next interview.

They came. There were the hysterical relatives, the wives and mothers and brothers who demanded that their kin be Awakened because they were special cases, not really guilty, or needed at home, or possessed of such awesome talents and qualities as to be exempt from the laws of lesser men.

Once in a while I granted a parole for a prisoner to see a dying mother or if some important project was falling apart without his help, but most of the time I just sat with my eyes propped open, letting a sea of vindictive screeching and beseeching wailings wash around me.

The relatives and legal talent were spaced with hungry-eyed mystics who were convinced they could contemplate God and their navels both conscientiously as an incarnation of Gautama. To risk sounding religiously intolerant, I usually kicked these out pretty swiftly.

The onetime inmate who wanted back in after a reprieve was fairly rare. Few of them ever got that crazy.

But it was my luck to get another the same day, the day for me, as Horbit.

Paulson was a tall, lean man with sad eyes. The clock above his sharp shoulder bone said five till noon. I didn't expect him to take much out of my lunch hour.

"Warden," Paulson said, "I've decided to give myself up. I murdered a blind beggar the other night."

"For his pencils?" I asked.

Paulson shifted uneasily. "No, sir. For his money. I needed some extra cash and I was stronger than he was, so why shouldn't I take it?"

I examined the projection of his file. He was an embezzler, not a violent man. He had served his time and been released. Conceivably he might embezzle again, but the Committee saw to it that temptation was never again placed in his path. He would not commit a crime of violence.

"Look, Paulson," I said, a trifle testily, "if you have so little conscience as to kill a blind old man for a few dollars, where do you suddenly get enough guilt feelings to cause you to give yourself up?"

Paulson tried his insufficient best to smile evilly. "It wasn't conscience, Warden. I never lie awake a minute whenever I kill anybody. It's just—well, Dreaming isn't so bad. Last time I was Allen Pinkerton, the detective. It was exciting. A lot more exciting than the kind of life I lead."

I nodded solemnly. "Yes, no doubt strangling old men in the streets can be pretty dull for a red-blooded man of action."

"Yes," Paulson said earnestly, "it does get to be a humdrum routine. I've been experimenting with all sorts of murders, but I just don't seem to get much of a kick out of them now. I'd like to try it from the other end as Pinkerton again. Of course, if you can't arrange it, I guess I'll have to go out and see what I can do with, say, an ax." His eye glittered almost convincingly.

"Paulson, you know I could have you watched night and day if I thought you really were a murderer. But I can't send you back to the sleep vaults without proof and conviction for a crime."

"That doesn't sound very reasonable," Paulson objected. "Turning loose a homicidal maniac who is offering to go back to the vaults of his own free will just because you lack a little trifling proof of his guilt."

"Sure," I told him, "but I don't want to share the same noose with you. My job is to keep the innocent out and the convicted in. And I do my job, Paulson."

"But you have to! If you don't, I'll have to go out and establish my guilt with another crime. Do you want a crime on your hands, Warden?"

I studied his record. There was a chance, just a chance . . .

"Do you want to wait voluntarily in the detention quarters?" I asked him.

He agreed readily enough.

I watched him out of the office and rang for lunch.

The news on the wall video was dull as usual. A man got tired of hearing peace, safety, prosperity and brotherly love all the time. I dug into my strained spinach, raw hamburger, and chewed up my white pill, my red pill, my ebony pill, and my second white pill. The gin and tomato juice took the taste away.

I was ready for the afternoon session.

Matrons were finishing the messy job of dragging a hysterical woman out of the office when Keller came back. He had a stubborn look on his flattened, red face.

"New prisoner asking to see you personally," Keller reported. "Told him no. Okay?"

"No," I said. "He can see me. That's the law and you know it. He isn't violent, is he?" I asked in some concern. The room was still in disarray.

"Naw, he ain't violent, Warden. He just thinks he's somebody important."

"Sounds like a case for therapy, not Dreamland. Who does he think he is?"

"One of the Committee—Councilman Coleman."

"Mm-hmm. And who is he really, Captain?"

"Councilman Coleman."

I whistled. "What did they nail him on?"

"Misuse of authority."

"And he didn't get suspended for that?"

"Wasn't his first offense. Still want to see him?"

I gave a lateral wave of my hand. "Of course."

My pattern of living—call it my office routine—had been reestablished through the day. I hadn't had a chance to brood much over the bombshell Coleman had tossed in my lap in the morning, but now I could think.

Coleman entered wearing the same black tunic, the same superior attitude. His black eyes fastened on me. "Sit down, Councilman," I directed.

He deigned to comply. I studied the files flashed before me. Several times before, Coleman had been guilty of slight misuses of his authority:

helping his friends, harming his enemies. Not enough to make him be impeached from the Committee. His job was so hypersensitive that if every transgression earned dismissal, no one could hold the position more than a day. Even with the best intentions, mistakes can be taken for deliberate errors. Not to mention the converse. For his earlier errors, Coleman had first received a suspended sentence, then two terminal sentences to be fixed by the warden. My predecessors had given him first a few weeks, then a few months of sleep in Dreamland.

Coleman's eyes didn't frighten me; I focused right on the pupils. "That was a pretty foul trick, Councilman. Did you hope to somehow frighten me out of executing this sentence by what you told me this morning?"

I couldn't follow his reasoning. Just how making me think my life was only a Dream such as I imposed on my own prisoners could help him, I couldn't see.

"Warden Walker," Coleman intoned in his magnificent voice, "I'm shocked. I am not personally monitoring your Dream. The Committee as a whole will decide whether you are capable of returning to the real world. Moreover, please don't get carried away. I'm not concerned with what you do to this sensory projection of myself, beyond how it helps to establish your moral capabilities."

"I suppose," I said heavily, "that I could best establish my high moral character by excusing you from this penal sentence?"

"Not at all," Councilman Coleman asserted. "According to the facts as you know them, I am 'guilty' and must be confined."

I was stymied for an instant. I had expected him to say that I must know that he was incapable of committing such an error and I must pardon him despite the misguided rulings of the courts. Then I thought of something else.

"You show symptoms of being a habitual criminal, Coleman. I think you deserve life."

Coleman cocked his head thoughtfully, concerned. "That seems rather extreme, Warden."

"You would suggest a shorter sentence?"

"If it were my place to choose, yes. A few years, perhaps. But life, no, I think not."

I threw up my hands. You don't often see somebody do that, but I did. I couldn't figure him. Coleman had wealth and power as a councilman in the real world, but I had thought somehow he wanted to escape to a Dream world. Yet he didn't want to be in for life, the way Paulson and Horbit did.

There seemed to be no point or profit in what he had told me that morning, nothing in it for him.

Unless—Unless what he said was literally true.

I stood up. My knees wanted to quit halfway up, but I made it.

"This," I said, "is a difficult decision for me, sir. Would you make yourself comfortable here for a time, Councilman?"

Coleman smiled benignly. "Certainly, Warden."

I walked out of my office, slowly and carefully.

Horbit was sitting in his detention quarters idly flicking through a book tape on the Civil War when I found him. The tic in his cheek marked time with every new page.

"President Lincoln," I said reverently.

Horbit looked up, his eyes set in a clever new way. "You call me that. Does it mean I am recovering? You don't mean now that I'm getting back my right senses?"

"Mr. President, the situation you find yourself in now is something stranger and more evil than any madness. I am not a phantom of your mind—I am a real man. This wild distorted place is a real place."

"Do you think you can pull the wool over my eyes, you scamp? Mine eyes have seen the glory."

"Yes, sir." I sat down beside him and looked earnestly into his twitching face. "But I know you have always believed in the occult."

He nodded slowly. "I have often suspected this was hell."

"Not quite, sir. The occult has its own rigid laws. It is perfectly scientific. This world is in another dimension—one that is not length, breadth or thickness—but a real one nevertheless."

"An interesting theory. Go ahead."

"This world is more scientifically advanced than the one you come from—and this advanced science has fallen into the hands of a well-meaning despot."

Horbit nodded again. "The Jeff Davis type."

He didn't understand Lincoln's beliefs very well, but I pretended to go along with him. "Yes, sir. He is our leader—doubts your abilities as President. He is not above meddling in the affairs of an alien world if he believes he is doing good. He has convicted you to this world in that belief."

He chuckled. "Many of my countrymen share his convictions."

"Maybe," I said. "But many here do not. I don't. I know you must return to guide the Reconstruction. But first you must convince our leader of your worth."

"How am I going to accomplish that?" Horbit asked worriedly.

"You are going to have a companion from now on, an agent of the leader, who will pretend to be something he isn't. You must pretend to believe in what he claims to be, and convince him of your high intelligence, moral responsibilities, and qualities of leadership."

"Yes," Horbit said thoughtfully, "yes. I must try to curb my tendency for telling off-color jokes. My wife is always nagging me about that."

Paulson was only a few doors away from Horbit. I found him with his long, thin legs stretched out in front of him, staring dismally into the gloom of the room. No wonder he found reality so boring and depressing with so downbeat a mood cycle. I wondered why they hadn't been able to do something about adjusting his metabolism.

"Paulson," I said gently, "I want to speak with you."

He bolted upright in his chair. "You're going to put me back to sleep."

"I came to talk to you about that," I admitted.

I pulled up a seat and adjusted the lighting so only his face and mine seemed to float bodiless in a sea of night, two moons of flesh.

"Paulson—or should I call you Pinkerton?—this will come as a shock, a shock I know only a fine analytical mind like yours could stand. You think your life as the great detective was only a Dream induced by some miraculous machine. But, sir, believe me: that life was real."

Paulson's eyes rolled slightly back into his head and changed their luster. "Then this is the Dream. I've thought—"

"No!" I snapped. "This world is also real."

I went through the same Fourth Dimension waltz as I had auditioned for Horbit. At the end of it, Paulson was nodding just as eagerly.

"I could be destroyed for telling you this, but our leader is planning the most gigantic conquest known to any intelligent race in the Universe. He is going to conquer Earth in all its possible futures and all its possible pasts. After that, there are other planets."

"He must be stopped!" Paulson shouted.

I laid my palm on his arm. "Armies can't stop him, nor can fantastic secret weapons. Only one thing can stop him: the greatest detective who ever lived. Pinkerton!"

"Yes,"' Paulson said. "I suppose I could."

"He knows that. But he's a fiend. He wants a battle of wits with you, his only possible foe, for the satisfaction of making a fool of you."

"Easier said than done, my friend," Paulson said crisply.

"True," I agreed, "but he is devious, the devil! He plans to convince you that he also has been removed to this world from his own, even as you have. He will claim to be Abraham Lincoln."

"No!"

"Yes, and he will pretend to find you accidentally and get you to help him find a way back to his own world, glorying in making a fool of you. But you can use every moment to learn his every weakness."

"But wait. I know President Lincoln well. I guarded him on his first inauguration trip. How could this leader of yours fool me? Does he look like the President?"

"Not at all. But remember, the dimensional shift changes physical appearance. You've noticed that in yourself."

"Yes, of course," Paulson muttered. "But he couldn't hoax me. My keen powers of deduction would have seen through him in an instant!"

I saw Horbit and Paulson happily off in each other's company. Paulson was no longer bored by a reality in which he was matching wits —with the first master criminal of the paratime universe, and Horbit was no longer hopeless in his quest to gain another reality because he knew he was not merely insane now.

It was a pair of fantastic stories that no man in his right mind would believe—but that didn't make them invalid to a brace of ex-Sleepers. They wanted to believe them. The stories gave them what they were after—without me having to break the law and put them to sleep for crimes they hadn't committed.

They would find out some day that I had lied to them, but maybe by that time they would have realized this world wasn't so bad.

Fortunately, I was confident from their psych records that they were both incapable of ending their little game by homicide, no matter how justified they might think it was.

"Hey, Warden," Captain Keller bellowed as I approached my office door, "when are you going to let me throw that stiff Coleman into the sleepy-bye vaults? He's still sitting in there on your furniture as smug as you please."

"You don't sound as if you like our distinguished visitor very well," I remarked.

"It's not that. I just don't think he deserves any special privileges. Besides, it was guys like him that took away our nightsticks. My boys didn't like that. Look at me—I'm defenseless!"

I looked at his square figure. "Not quite, Captain, not quite."

Now was the time.

I stretched out my wet palm toward the door.

Was or was not Coleman telling the truth when he said this life of mine was itself only a Dream? If it was, did I want to finish my last day with the right decision so I could return to some alien reality? Or did I deliberately want to make a mistake so I could continue living the opiate of my Dream?

Then, as I touched the door, I knew the only decision that could have any meaning for me.

Councilman Coleman didn't look as if he had moved since I had left him. He was unwrinkled, unperspiring, his eyes and mustache crisp as ever. He smiled at me briefly in supreme confidence.

I changed my decision then, in that moment. And, in the next, changed it back to my original choice.

"Coleman," I said, "you can get out of here. As warden, I'm granting you a five-year probation."

The councilman stood up swiftly, his eyes catching little sparks of yellow light. "I don't approve of your decision, Warden. Not at all. Unless you alter it, I'll be forced to convince the rest of the Committee that your decisions are becoming faulty, that you are losing your grip just as all your predecessors did."

My muscles relaxed in a spasm and it took the fresh flow of adrenalin to get me to the chair behind my desk. I took a pill. I took two pills.

"Tell me, Councilman, what happened to the offer to release me from this phony Dream? Now you are talking as if this world was the real one."

Coleman parted his lips, but then the planes of his face shifted into another pattern. "You never believed me."

"Almost, but not quite. You knew I was on the narrow edge in this kind of job, but I'm not as far out as you seemed to have thought."

"I can still wreck your career, you know."

"I don't think so. That would constitute a misuse of authority, and the next time you turn up before me, I'm going to give you life in Dreamland."

Coleman sat back down suddenly.

"You don't want life as a Sleeper, do you?" I pursued. "You did want a relatively short sentence of a few months or a few years. I can think of two reasons why. The answer is probably a combination of both. In the first place, you are a joy-popper with Dreams—you don't want to live out your life in one, but you like a brief Dream every few years like an occasional dose of a narcotic. In the second place, you probably have political reasons for wanting to hide out somewhere in safety for the next few years. The world isn't as placid as the newscasts sometimes make it seem."

He didn't say anything. I didn't think he had to.

"You wanted to make sure I made a painfully scrupulous decision in your case," I went on.

"You didn't want me to pardon you completely because of your high position, but at the same time you didn't want too long a sentence. But I'm doing you no favors. You get no time from me, Coleman."

"How did you decide to do this?" he asked. "Don't tell me you never doubted. We've all doubted since we found out about the machines: which was real and which was the Dream? How did you decide to risk this?"

"I acted the only way I could act," I said. "I decided I had to act as if my life was real and that you were lying. I decided that because, if all this were false, if I could have no more confidence in my own mind and my own senses than that, I didn't give a damn if it were all a Dream."

Coleman stood up and walked out of my office.

The clock told me it was after five. I began clearing my desk.

Captain Keller stuck his head in, unannounced. "Hey, Warden, there's an active one out here. He claims that Dreamland compromises His plan for the Free Will of the Universe."

"Well, escort him inside, Captain," I said.

I put away my pills. Solving simple problems such as the new visitor presented always helped me to relax.

AFTERWORD

I am happy to say I have had no personal experiences with incarceration. But I think everyone has considered what it would be like to be locked up for years, decades, forever. What if I was falsely identified as an ax murderer and convicted and sent to prison? What would it be like? How would I handle it? Of course, how could honest, law-abiding people like us ever be convicted? Maybe easier than we think. My late, dear friend, Bob Greenberg, a robust man with all his limbs present, was detained by the Chicago police as a suspect in a robbery—even though the robber was described as only having one arm. Thankfully, even in Chicago, this discrepancy was noticed after only six hours.

Being a science fiction writer I would naturally consider alternate forms of incarceration as I do in this story. The subject of the penal system seems to be as much a topic of conversation today as when this was written. Perhaps beneath the frothy concept, the story does have something to say.

MINDSNAKE

"Witch! Witch!" The cry was among the walkers, but he didn't bother to track it down. It was no longer a fighting word to Hammen. He wore it like a badge of honor. It tasted of brass, but it gleamed on him.

A puzzled growl came from the Familiar at his heels. The dog could never understand how people could hate Hammen. Lad, the dog, often asked Hammen how anyone could possibly hate Hammen, and Hammen always told him to shut up; he couldn't understand—he was only a dog.

The walk ramp was crowded this afternoon with people fresh from the transmatter stations, eager to tell themselves they were walking on a strange planet. Hammen passed among the nudists, the cavaliers, the zip-suiters, the zoot-suiters, the Ivy-coated, the Moss-covered, walking not for novelty or exercise but because he preferred to go everywhere under his own power. Even to the stars.

Hale and Lora saluted him a few paces away from the entrance to the station. They were a beautiful blond couple, with brightly polished faces. Hammen didn't much like them, but he didn't feel sufficiently pressed to be rude enough to let them become aware of it.

"How goes it, kids?" he asked them.

"Couldn't be better," Hale said.

"Of course not," Lora added.

Hammen's slate eyes moved from the man to the woman. "Are you troubled?"

"This isn't the time to talk about it, not before you and Lad transmit yourself," the girl said quickly.

It wasn't, Hammen admitted to himself. Only now that they had let it slip, he would rest better knowing the whole truth of it.

"Come on," Hammen urged. "It's not as if I wasn't interested."

Hale looked at his wife. "Lora doesn't like Wagner any more."

"Perdition!" said Hammen. "I *never* liked Wagner. She's growing up."

Lora put a half-closed fist to her lips, and didn't look at either of the men, or at the dog who stood with freshly pointed ears.

"No," she said softly. "I lost something on the last one. Gee, I wonder if the Mindsnake likes Wagner now? Still, it's not as if I had stopped liking music altogether, or books. Not this time."

Hale grabbed her arm roughly. "You're sure doing a great job of getting Hammen ready for the jump."

Lora's eyes clouded. "I'm sorry, Ham." She looked up, smiled warmly, kissed her fingertips and placed them on Hammen's lips. "Companion's Code, huh?"

He took her hand and for the moment liked her. "Okay, honey. I guess even a Witch squeezes in under the wire for that."

The young team was abruptly embarrassed "Oh, well, Witch," Hale said deprecatingly, "what does cargo know, anyway?"

Hammen laughed and scratched Lad's ears. "They know I'm a Witch. But it has its advantages—I don't have to worry about Lad losing his taste for Wagner. A dog does not have that much to lose. If it comes to that, he's just gone."

Lora shuddered delicately, the way of a watered flower. "How could you stand to lose a Companion with so little feeling?"

"I've lost three Companions, and got myself and my cargo into port. They were only dogs."

Hale looked at him sharply. "But you were Companioning with them. It must have been," he selected a word, "difficult for you."

"Don't absorb the cargo's superstitions about Witches and their Familiars. They have fogged, even dirty, ideas. They were just dogs to me. Like Lad."

"A dog, that's all he is," Gordus said in a manner designed to explain the thing patiently to Hammen.

"Lad is a dog."

"Why do you emphasize the point now?" Hammen demanded.

The Companion sat on a seat formed from a single S-shaped plastic surface. Hammen studied the bulk of Gordus, Coordinator of

Transmatters, who sat hulked in his utility chair in the bubble office over-hanging the City of the Sea, on the world of Lanol . Hammen was comfortable, cooled, relaxed, amused by a light play of sensory electron music, and aggressively unhappy.

Gordus sat in his great chair patting the hair on the back of his left hand with his right palm, as if the fist were a sleeping kitten. At Hammen's feet, Lad's neck muscles quivered uneasily.

"Your record, Hammen," Gordus said at last, "is a good one."

"How could it be better? I've never lost one member of a cargo."

"But you have lost three Companions."

"Familiars. Dogs."

"But it shows weakness." Hammen's face heated. "I never show weakness."

"Not your weakness, my dear, dear boy," Gordus said in exaggeration. "The weakness of the Witch-Familiar relationship, the weakness of Witches as Companions at all. Don't take it personally."

Hammen leaped to his feet. Lad's muzzle gleamed white.

"Not take it personally?" Hammen cried. "How else can I take it? You are questioning the worthiness of my profession, of my way of life. You question the honor of many of my friends—my associates. Witchery is an ancient profession. My grandmother and uncle were Witches before me. Witches have an unparalleled record of service to Transmatters and to the human race. How dare you, sir!"

Gordus waved a fat hand in front of him, laughing up and down the scale. "No, no, no. Peace, please. You have no need to plead so strongly for the cause of Witches. You don't have to be a Witch, you know, Hammen. You're good enough to be a regular, full-fledged Companion. The reason you get so many of your cargo through is that you in the most literal sense Companion them all. It would be possible for you to use a fellow Companion on your jumps instead of a Familiar."

Hammen sat down, no longer angry, or energetic. "No. No, it wouldn't be possible for me to do that. I can take people on an occasional jump, for high pay. But I couldn't stand the same kind of contact, day in, day out, with another human being. Pay doesn't come that high."

Gordus gave another laugh, and killed it sharply. "And there you were a few moments ago bragging about all the service Witches had been to the human race, and when we get down to it, it turns out you hate the human race."

Hammen tasted the inside of his dry mouth and longed for a way out. "I don't hate it; I just can't stand it. There's a difference."

"If you say so. But tell me, do you like your fellow Companions, or even your fellow Witches, any better than you do your cargo?"

"No," Hammen admitted.

"Good. Then we can stop this foolish talk about the Witches' service to mankind, since you don't give a damn about either Witches or mankind. You care only about one Witch; your interests are entirely self interests. Correct?"

"Yes."

"Good. Better. Now I suppose you are not entirely satisfied with the benefits you now receive as a Witch? You would like more money, pleasure, power, prestige? You have ambition, greed, hunger, desire?"

"Yes."

"Fine, I didn't think you had altogether ceased to be human. Then I can tell you that the Transmitter Service has to perform its most important mission, and you are thought to be the best man for it."

"Most important mission?" said Hammen. "Best man?"

Gordus became happy. "Those are questions? But I can't tell you the answers. Not yet. First, you must promise us the added protection of taking a human Companion for this assignment."

"Why should I want to do that, Gordus?"

"Because I have promised that you would, and I never fail."

Hammen stood for the second time. "Sorry. Not a good enough reason for me."

Gordus' face splintered into confusion. "But as your superior, as your coordinator, I order you to take a human Companion for this assignment."

"Gordus," Hammen said, "you were once a Companion yourself."

"When I was younger, while my wife was alive."

"Then rescind your order or I'll kill you—under the Code, in a duel."

Gordus sneered. "I have never been beaten."

"Obviously," Hammen said. He didn't point out anything about his own status.

It was a final thing.

"Are you armed at this instant?"

The coordinator shook his heavy head.

"Then I plead grievance and choose weapons. Appeal?"

The other shrugged. "Choose."

Hammen was breathing deeply and regularly, in preparation. "Before this is closed, I want to remind you that the Law and the Code both state that no one can interfere in the relationship between a Team."

"Doesn't apply," Gordus said. "The act of '9'7 recognized the Companionship of Witches, but it did not extend the privilege to Familiars. Naturally not. You are a Companion and I could not separate you from a human Companion, but I can order you to break from Lad."

"That isn't just."

"I know. But we're talking about law, not justice."

"Do you wish aid from your fellow Companion?" Hammen asked.

"In later years, I have often wished for it, but my formal reply: No."

"Then," Hammen said, "I name our weapon as the body. The time, this instant. I can kill you easily with my bare hands, and Lad will help with his teeth."

An eyebrow-hedged ridge of fat above Gordus' left eye angled. "Use the dog and you'll get in trouble."

"Not before a Companions' Court. But if you so state your preference, I'll only use my own body."

"Hammen, about this matter," the coordinator said. "I'll think about it."

"An hour," Hammen said, and turned on his heel.

"Hammen," Gordus called out. Hammen looked back to face a leveled destruction gun.

"You know the Code," Gordus explained. "The Challenge wasn't withdrawn. You struck the field. A coward may be killed by any weapon."

"You are too modest," Hammen told him.

Gordus smiled and fed the gun to a compartment of his utility chair. "I only wanted to prove a point. I can kill you anytime, anywhere. No one can beat me. Can they? Can they, Hammen?"

The sweat stung Hammen's palms so hard he could almost taste the salt in it with his fingers.

"I'll do it."

"Gratitude is a part of honor. Yes. The Code. You do believe in that. But you haven't asked me yet who your human Companion on the Jump will be."

"Who?" Hammen asked.

"As you yourself pointed, I still come under the Code myself."

"I agreed to take a human Companion but I did not agree to take Gordus himself," Hammen explained to his wristphone in the alcove outside the coordinator's office.

"I think it's a terrible thing," Lora said. "But why won't you jump with him—Gordus, I mean?"

"I hate him," Hammen explained.

"Oh, sure. I guess I do too. I'd never thought of being a Companion with him. Ugh! Oh, Hale's swimming in now."

Aside: "Over here, darling. Ham's calling."

From afar: "Who?"

Aside: "Hammen. The Witch."

"Why didn't you say so?" Into the phone: "Hi, fellow. What can we do to you?"

"You can do a lot for me."

"For you, huh? That comes high, you know. What'll it be?"

Hammen retold his story, and finished with, "That's why I called you two. I need a human Companion, anybody other than Gordus."

A slithering of voice, then faint, but distinct, from Lora: "I couldn't do it and I can't let you do it. Afterward, whichever of us, it would be as if that one was no better than a dog."

Hammen stared ahead of him at the alcove wall.

"Ham" Hale said, "why did you come to us with this?"

"You were friends of mine," Hammen said.

"No."

"No?"

"We aren't friends of yours, Ham," Hale said patiently. "We're just acquaintances of yours. We'd like to help you out, but not enough to split our team for you. Surely you've got some real friends, people you took better to than us . . . Hell, man, don't you know what a friend is?"

Hammen thought of it. "I suppose not."

"But there must be someone," Hale said in embarrassment, "a woman."

"I know a woman Witch on another world. We make love together sometimes. But I know her only well enough to know better than to ask favors of her."

"There are lots of Witches," Hale said in nervous exasperation. "One of them is bound to Companion with you on a thing like this."

Ham touched his fingers to his wrist. "I think not. No other Witch is going to help me set a precedent to put them out of the trade."

"But the Code!" Hale said furiously. "Surely you can count on your fellow Witches under the Code."

"Why? I couldn't count on my fellow Companions under the Code," said Hammen, and pressed his wristphone into silence.

Hammen stepped from the alcove back into Gordus' office to find a lovely golden woman groveling at the coordinator's feet. The coordinator was smiling at the pleasure of the thing.

"What's this?" Hammen demanded.

"Cargo," Gordus said.

"Is she ill?"

"Mad."

"Then she can't be transmitted. No one could hold together a disintegrating personality in transmission," Hammen said.

"It will be difficult. Unprecedentedly difficult. That is why it will take the two of us acting as Companions to bring her safely to Earth."

"Why is it so important that she get to Earth?"

"Ask her," Gordus suggested.

Hammen glanced down and saw Lad nosing pointedly at the woman. Often he forgot that the dog was constantly at his side. His eyes lifted up to the woman.

She had fine features, impressive blonde hair, and she was wrapped in a frazzled blanket, indigo rubbed away to white threads here and there.

"What's your name, woman?" Hammen asked.

"I know what it is."

"Of course you do," he said sharply, "but I don't."

"I know you don't."

"There isn't much that you don't know, is there?"

"I know everything," she confessed humbly, honey eyes down.

Hammen whirled to Gordus. "What do they want with her on Earth?"

The coordinator gestured eloquently. "She knows everything. Do you think they know everything on Earth? Don't believe propaganda. There are things she can tell them."

Hammen looked again to the creature huddled on the floor. "What could she tell anyone?"

"There are words buried in any conglomeration of letters. Confusion is the basis of all codes." 'There is always a cipher for any code."

Hammen exhaled. "Never mind. What do I care what they want with her? All right, I'll try to take her through. You don't want me to use the dog?"

"No. It won't do."

"Then let me take her alone. I could do it this once."

"Negative. Besides, need I remind you that you have already graciously agreed to take a human Companion?"

"And," Hammen said ponderously, "I can't get any Companion other than you to go with me."

"You can't? Sad. But why wouldn't I be acceptable?"

"I hate your soul."

"No doubt," Gordus sighed. "But I believe you said you hated all people."

"I can't stand people, only some people especially do I hate."

"I see. But surely it is only a small difference in degree, not kind, between the contempt and aversion you hold for humanity at large and that which you hold for me. Surely that difference is too small to cause you to break your word, given under the Code."

"I suppose it is." The words tasted bad in his mouth. "Very well. I'll transmit with you."

"Of course you will," the coordinator said smoothly.

" Are you ready to transmit now?"

"Of course we are."

Hammen stood within the platform diagram with Gordus and the woman. Beyond the boundaries stood the technicians, one at the control mosaic, the other holding to the neck of Lad, who suffered it under orders.

"Wiggle away from the Mindsnake, citizens," a technician called.

A native, Hammen thought. He had never been in transmission himself. No one who had ever joked about the Mindsnake, or rarely even spoke of him.

Hammen looked around him, slate eyes chalking the outline of the diagram in which they stood. It was only a rectangle, but shouldn't it be rather a pentagram?

From the time of Aristotle, the populace equated science with magic. Wasn't the diagram only a sign to conjure the demon, Spatium, to do the boon of transporting his servants across the void without decay of time?

No. Instantaneous transmission of matter wasn't magic. It had always been a part of folklore as teleportation, but just as machines had been made to duplicate the legendary feats of human extrasensory perception, machines made to let men speak over great distances to duplicate the strange voices of mystics, and machines made that would indeed show strange visions over vast expanses, science had made the Transmatter for null-time object displacement.

Transmatters were a logical, progressive theoretical implementation. If electrical impulses could recreate patterns first in sound, then in light, it followed relentlessly that someday some form of impulses would be found to recreate matter. Energy and matter were only different forms of one unity.

Fortunately, matter duplication had come before matter transmission. As the researches of Phillips established, an exact duplicate is not the original.

A duplication of a man is only a duplicate, not the original, unless the elan vital, the spirit, the soul, is transmitted, for it cannot be duplicated. A duplicated man is a perfect robot, capable of memory and learning, and developing into a human being in time. But it is not a human being immediately, and it can never become the original of the duplicate. Every human viewpoint is unique and irreplaceable.

Duplication of matter was uneconomical. The power outlay was too great, the equipment too costly to build and operate. So transportation by transmission was investigated. Again, it was too expensive except for very great distances, trips of light-years to worlds established over the generations by the spaceships which had reached virtual light-sped and could not go beyond it.

Personalities of transmittees got lost among the Stars.

Transmitted poets arrived with a dim itch for a brutal fight, due to some residue of glandular acid from a parting insult affecting their birth trauma on the new world.

Great conductors solidified, hating music.

Competent engineers were imported with an infantile urge toward lyric verse.

And the Companions came into being as a profession.

Men with will power, psionic abilities, strength of character. You could call it what you liked, depending on your profession, your politics, your religion. At any rate, men and women who could hold human personalities together on the long, instantaneous voyage through null-space.

But still some personalities drifted away.

Or, some darkly superstitious people suggested, were they sucked away?

They were.

Personalities in transmission were being captured by an intelligent entity, unimaginably vast in size, which some believed used the movements of galaxies as the synapse responses of its brain.

It was a vast entity, but not a very intelligent one, due to the square of signal decay and noise over light-years. Moreover, it was psychopathic. From contact with human minds, it had decided it was, or would become (it was obviously confused on the point) the god of the humans.

It proposed to do this by eventually incorporating all intelligence into itself. But, seemingly, only intelligences in transmission were soft enough for the Mindsnake to get a hold on.

The Companions were harder-shelled.

But the Mindsnake grew stronger.

And Companions began traveling with other Companions, as teams, to resist the Mindsnake.

And there came a class of Companions who did not need the help of any other man or woman, but only a touchstone of reality, something familiar of Earth—the mind of a dog or a cat or some other animal. Familiars. So was born the Corps of Witches.

And here, Hammen wondered, was this where the Witches came to an end?

He looked at the bulging head of Gordus. He couldn't see inside it. Maybe there would ultimately be men who could, but he could only contact other minds when they were taken off the level of matter and energy, and placed in null-space. Where there is no space, there can be no barriers.

There was nothing but confusion in the woman's mind if he could touch it. Nothing but boredom and routine in the minds of the technicians.

Hammen's eyes moved to the dog. He suddenly decided Lad looked sad. But dogs have no human facial muscles, and it would be impossible between a man and a dog for one to look into the other's mind, while they weren't in transmission.

Uselessly, he permitted himself to wish Lad was going with him . . . .

The heavy shoulder muscles of the dog ripped him free from the technician's grasp and Lad threw himself across the diagram line as the coordinates of the transmatter phased.

Transmission. No time. No space. Hammen felt an overblown wave of force.

"How's that for power?" Gordus demanded.

It came as words to him, a communication between people had come to him all of his life. Deaf-mute Companions had told him communication in transmission came to them as hands and fingers feeling of words.

"You've never had a real Companion before, have you?" Gordus asked. "You've never felt real Power like this before?"

"Power? I've heard members of the cargo scream as loud from terror and horror. We don't scream in transmission, Coordinator. Let the Snake sleep."

"Power," the coordinator repeated. "I always held my cargo together with power."

"When you were a Companion, the Snake wasn't as strong as it is now. Quiet, please."

Hammen felt out for his Familiar. A tail wagged somewhere. A head cocked to one side in puzzlement, concern. What wasn't a hand petted that which wasn't a head.

"Just us—just the two of us—to see after the woman," Gordus said with a leer in his voice.

Didn't he know about Lad crossing the diagram? Hadn't he seen?

"You sound as if you were about to suggest we team up and rape her. It's hardly practicable here."

"But that's it, Hammen! That's it! I want to rape her mind!"

"Go away, Gordus. I don't believe in you. Nobody really makes a career out of being that swinish."

"My profession is power, Hammen. I find your attitude unprofessional."

Hammen reached out for the girl. "What do you want from her?"

"She knows everything, Hammen. Don't you want to know everything?"

"No," Hammen said. "I'd never be able to remember it."

The girl was retreating from them. Had she been snagged by the Mindsnake? No. Only drift. Hammen threw an anchor into her, braced himself against his Familiar, and pulled. She came apart at the seams and flew off in all directions, gibbering.

He raced after all the pieces of the woman at a practiced steady trot and gathered them all in. He made a rough boundary and compartmentalized her.

For an instant, he looked through the Jumble that was her mind. Sensuality, sloth, greed, hate, envy, pride, hunger, death wish—it was the usual human pattern well enough, but they were letters that spelled out no words. It would be impossible to find any information in that psychic junk heap.

Deftly, Hammen turned Gordus back on.

" … must know. You'll have to help me, Hammen."

"Why must I?"

"Simplicity. You must. We stay here until you do. You can't close the transmission without me, and I will not do it until you help me pick the woman's mind. We can wait forever until you decide to do as I order. There is no time here."

Gordus was a blind old man stumbling in the dark. He hadn't seen Lad join them inside the diagram. He probably wasn't even aware that Hammen had the woman under tow.

"Listen to me, Gordus. That about there being 'no time' here is a mathematical abstraction. Practically, it has its limitations. There is some flow of some kind of duration here, otherwise our questions and answers would come at the same time."

"What are you trying to teach me?" Gordus demanded. "I was a Companion before you were born."

"But then the Mindsnake wasn't so active or so powerful. If the 'duration' of our transmission is too long, he'll get a clear fix on us—and that will be that."

"I'll risk that. Will you?"

"No," Hammen said. "You're a fool out here in transmission. You don't know what you're doing. What do you expect of me?"

"Link with me, Companion, as you should. Help me gain her knowledge."

Hammen knew that he was being asked to help gain access to information intended for the Federation authorities on Earth. But he rarely thought of himself as a Federal, and he knew very few worlds would allow extradition of him on a Federal charge. At the moment, he was mainly concerned with saving himself and his cargo from the Mindsnake. As distasteful as it was, Gordus was a part of his cargo, and a man had to have a few ideals. Gordus was not qualified to be a Companion after the generations of growth of the Mindsnake. He was only a pitiful fool now. (How long before the Snake gets so big I will not be qualified? How long before no one is qualified? How long before the Snake comes out of null-space and stalks the planets?)

Hammen shrugged and joined Gordus.

They struck for the mind of the woman.

Her name, they learned, Isodel.

They found that out, and incredibly, more.

In some way Gordus' mind paralleled the girl's. There was much of a kind about them, and Gordus could piece together the fragments of her identity. But then he was reaching down for something, and he prestidigitated it up and out of sight.

Hammen realized that Gordus had succeeded in getting what he wanted and in keeping it from him. He was less of a doddering old fool than he appeared.

"What was that?" Hammen demanded. "What did you take?"

He tried to shake it loose from the coordinator.

"Let go of me!" Gordus cried out in immaterial indignity.

Hammen released him.

Completely.

Gordus screamed soundlessly as he retreated toward infinity.

"Shall I catch you?" Hammen asked.

The scream changed in pitch.

The Witch brought him back.

"You stayed," Gordus said. "Somehow you stayed. That dog. Somehow you've got your damned Familiar with you, haven't you, Witch?"

"No," Hammen lied fluently. "Only feeble minds like yours require a contact. Shall I tell you something about Witches? The Familiars are a deception. We don't need them at all. We are lone wolves."

"Wolves are you? So now I know what your grandmother before you was."

Hammen laughed.

And sobered.

"What did you take, Gordus?" he demanded.

"What do you know about her?" asked Gordus.

"Her name is Isodel."

"Isodel Van Der Lies."

"I've heard of her. Somewhere," Hammen said hesitantly.

"A great theoretian," the coordinator explained sullenly. "Probably the first authentic female genius of the race of man. On a par with Plato, Shakespeare, Newton, Einstein."

"What theory of hers were you after?" Hammen pursued.

"A method of destroying the Mindsnake."

"You want to take the credit from her."

"I want only to take the theory from her, Hammen."

"You mean you don't want the Mindsnake to be destroyed. You are afraid its destruction would mean the end of the Companion Corps which you head."

"Not at all. I only want the theory so I can reverse it. Once you know how to destroy the Mindsnake you also know how to create one. You see, I intend to become another Mindsnake, one who knows too much of destruction to ever be destroyed"

"Listen carefully, Gordus," Hammen said with infinite care. "You're ill. You don't know what you're talking about. It can't be done."

"The ultimate dream . . . . ultimate Power."

"That's pure psychosis, Gordus!"

"Is it? Watch how easily I begin to grow. I have the woman's mind now."

It was true.

The poor, mad genius woman was gone.

"Stop it, Coordinator. You don't know what you're doing!"

Hammen tried to reach him.

"That's it, that's it. Come ahead, my boy. I'm becoming a Mindsnake. Now I am a Mindsnake. Come ahead. Let me swallow you next."

"You fool," Hammen broadcast. "You are the Mindsnake now. Don't you think anyone's ever wanted power before? Won't you let yourself remember how it was when you were a Companion? This is how it always happens. You've let yourself be swallowed by the Snake. You ran right into its jaws."

"No." Gordus thought furiously. "I—"

And the Snake digested the tiny egg in its gullet and "I" blurred and was washed over by "All."

Hammen struck at it in anger and humiliation and terror and it retreated with frictionless speed.

The Snake took something with it.

It took Gordus, and it left that part of the woman, Isodel, that he had been able to capture. But the part of Isodel matched by Gordus' mind was jerked free.

She was freed of hate, anger, lust . . .

She was left an impossibly ideal woman—all Mother, Sister, Lover . . .

Against his will, by immutable laws of nature, Hammen fell monstrously in love with her.

Hammen was among the first of Companions or Witches to join the Suicide Squadron.

He did it to protect Isodel and her descendants for all time to come, and he did it in impotent fury at his reason for doing it. The Companions transmitted in droves to abolish their profession. They transmitted against the Mindsnake.

The Federation on Earth had made use of Isodel's theories. They were only a formal mathematical statement of what had always been known—destruction reaches a critical mass and destroys itself by turning against itself. Hammen had refused to join one human mind, he joined countless ones in a huge drive against the Snake.

They became one with each other and they became one with the Snake, and the Snake turned on itself and destroyed itself and them, and they turned on themselves—and stopped.

They hung together for an unmeasurable time—and broke apart.

They were a super-entity like the Snake. But where the Snake had been mad, they were sane.

They drifted through the haze of twilight and broke apart, their hands gliding away into the shadows.

Hammen was gloriously happy. He had never been happy before and he was not at all sure he liked it.

"Jobs are so hard to find these days," Isodel said, her lovely face brightly sane. "What will you take up, darling?"

"There's still need for Companions—and Witches," he explained. "There seems more of a tendency for members of the cargo to drift away than ever. The Mindsnake at least gave them something to resist, a foothold of friction. Now there is nothing—nothing to do but drift, drift, drift. People in transmission will need Companions for a long time to come."

"I need a Companion," lovely Isodel said.

His heart leaped ridiculously.

"But not a Witch," said gorgeous Isodel.

Pain, very great physical pain.

"I love you," priceless Isodel went on. "How could I help it? I am a woman and I love the father image. You are my father—symbolically, fortunately, not biologically. You held the sane part of me while Gordus dragged off the unsane part. You gave me—this me—birth. I love you. But I don't love your dog."

"My dog?" said Hammen.

"No woman can marry a man and his dog."

"I see," said Hammen, seeing it all, and living.

You could see everything—about yourself and live. It wasn't easy, but you could do it. Especially if you had the training and experience of being a Companion. Or a Witch.

"It would kill Lad to separate him from me for long, you know," Hammen said.

Isodel's beautiful eyes misted. And she said in all her infuriating gentleness, "Then it is impossible for us, if we have to destroy a living—"

"He's just a dog," he pointed out. "I would wring his neck cheerfully if it would do any good. But it wouldn't."

Isodel looked sad, and brave, and wonderful.

"Don't you see, Isodel? It's impossible for me to do the right thing. If it wasn't Lad, it would be another dog, and if it wasn't a Familiar to make me a Witch, it would be something else to make me different, because I am different. I have to live with that. Among the right people, I am the left man."

So he left her, and walked out of the Floating Gardens onto the walkway and Lad fell in at his side, and he listened without anger to the hushings and keenings of the crowd.

"Witch! Witch!"

AFTERWORD

This story gave me a thrill as a beginning writer. It was my first story to be solo featured on the cover of a science fiction magazine; in this case, *IF*. There it was in bold letters: "Mindsnake by Jim Harmon". The full color illustration showed two space suited men fighting each other against the backdrop of the cosmos, a somewhat symbolic representation of this story.

I tried to incorporate a number of concepts in this one entry, influenced by the great A.E. Van Vogt. It seemed to appeal to a number of readers and I received a number of forwarded fan letters about it. For awhile I considered expanding it into a novel, but somehow never did. In those days of limited publishing, it was very difficult for a new writer to place a novel. Novels were all done by the established leading figures of the genre. At the present, I believe any professional writer who writes a good SF novel can find a place for it. Depending on the reception of this volume, I might follow my own judgment.